I0742491

WAR MACHINES

AYAN PRATAP

ISBN-13:

978-1-7336806-0-8

ISBN:10:

1-7336806-0-8

For my family, always!

CONTENTS

A NEW WORLD

The two birds sliced through the mist with dogged urgency. They weren't supposed to be in a rush, but then again, unlike humans, machines don't procrastinate. The wind slapped their titanium bodies side to side as every gust tested their resolve. Whenever the elements tried to sway them from their path, Recon, the navigator bot, adjusted his thrusters and muscled his way back on course. Scout, the smaller of the two, didn't have to do much as he sat mounted on top of Recon.

Beads of moisture raced down the conjoined brothers' matted black bodies as they penetrated the ocean of fog and approached the island of Chisil. Out of the white emerged a flock of tufted puffins charging towards the machines at fifty miles an hour. Recon found his five-foot-wide circular body too rigid to maneuver on a dime, but the puffins were young and agile. In a split second, the puffins twisted, turned and ducked, avoiding any collision. With their elaborate face masks and receding calls, the puffins mocked the machines as the last one of their kind flew past. The bots continued on course towards their mission, deeper into the endless milky white that surrounded Chisil.

. . .

Resting somewhere in the middle of Russia and Alaska, the island of Chisil is among the most remote places on Earth. Unpredictable weather and frequent storms also make it one of the most hostile. But the most remarkable feature of the island is the volcano, *Chisil*. Chisil: to scatter – that's what the native Alaskan Aleuts had named it after witnessing the power of the devastation it was capable of unleashing. Once roaring, the volcano would *chisil* its spew far and wide. For now, all six thousand feet of it was silent as Recon banked around it towards the mission's predetermined coordinates.

He initiated descent some three miles east of the volcano as the faint glimpse of a fern-cloaked hill came into Recon's view. He hovered over a spot and double-checked the position. His onboard cameras scanned the rocky surface below as he zeroed in. With the coordinates confirmed, a small surveillance camera ejected from a side hatch and flew away. Recon shook as a metal arm unfolded from his underside, the end of which expanded, exposing an array of high-intensity lasers mounted along a disc. The arm inched closer to the surface while the bots maintained their position in the air. The lasers fired in three second bursts, rotating every now and then, hunting for adjacent virgin spots. A dozen bursts later, the disc collapsed into its original fitting, and the arm retracted.

He flew higher and once at the right height Recon opened a hatch and aimed down at the center of the area around which the lasers had cut. He shot a projectile and gained even more altitude. The bots waited as the moments stretched.

Suddenly, it exploded.

Their bodies rattled as the canister that Recon detonated flung debris in all directions. He stabilized himself as his sensors recovered. With the soft breeze scattering the dust, the bots set their sights at the new opening they had just created into the world below.

With a single command, Scout came to life and separated himself from Recon's back. He circled around and scanned the area as he tried to get his own bearings. He took his sweet time staring at the opening before descending.

As Scout approached the darkness, he turned around and looked up. He could still make out Recon's silhouette through the fog much higher up in the sky. The two machines peered deep into each other's eyes as the gentle breeze let them converse in silence. If there was any lack of resolve in Scout's commitment towards his creators' mission, he didn't show. He just wanted to extend the moment, as he knew he would never see Recon again.

Soon, it was time. Scout knew he had to go.

His creators had given him everything. They gave him a life, made him alive. It was because of them he was more than just the sum of his components. Now, it was his turn to do his part, to make their effort worthwhile. He knew he had to pay back his debt of life. To do something for those who had done something for him. To do something for those who had done *everything* for him, no matter the personal sacrifice.

Scout turned towards the opening and powered up his energy-hungry lights. They illuminated the edge of darkness and sent a shaft deep into the unknown world below. He began his final descent, gently.

Just a few inches from darkness, he once again turned around and looked up. Recon still watched over him. The limited depth and nuance of circuitry and code couldn't prevent him from feeling as he did. One of those uneasy feelings one gets when coming face to face with the unknown. He wondered if Recon would miss him? He knew he wasn't looking for any sympathy. It was futile. He knew

Recon loved him but was as much bound by duty as he was. Both followers of the same code but bearers of different destinies. Scout understood Recon's coldness. How feelings would dull his resolve. But for Scout himself, emotions were what drove him.

They exchanged a few more precious thoughts, for the very last time.

The motors whirred as Scout turned. His lights illuminated the darkness as he passed through into the unknown world below.

A GLIMPSE

Myra squinted her big brown eyes and leaned towards the computer screen in front of her. Scanning detail in every inch of the dark, fast-moving images had started to strain her, but she knew she didn't want to miss it. Even at full brightness, there were instances where she barely made out anything. Only an occasional static interruption reminded her to correct the slouched posture that kept creeping in, uninvited. She didn't keep herself fit with all that forced cardio over the years only to end up bent.

The chair next to her creaked as Eustace shifted his weight and continued staring at the same screen as her, trying to pick up anything Myra may have missed. Both wore black V-neck t-shirts with 'X-corp' printed on them. A third chair lay empty nearby in front of another screen showing the same dim images.

There was almost a sense of friendly competition as both wanted to be the first to spot it, if *it* were to ever happen. An eerie silence lingered in the small makeshift control room except for the sounds of their breaths inter-mixed with those of computer fans and hums. Occasionally, the whole room rattled and reminded them where they were, but most things were already secured. They weren't moving anywhere.

The transmission interrupted again as Scout ventured deeper into the cave system and beamed more of the hidden world live. At roughly the size and shape of an office printer, Scout packed an impressive array of instruments within his rigid body. But more than half of his weight was batteries. It had to be. It was crucial that he lasted for as long as possible into his mission. The smart energy-saving design enabled him to first land, observe and scan, and *then* fly forward, as opposed to being continuously airborne.

"Toggle thermal," Eustace pressed the talk switch and spoke into the mic next to the keyboard.

Scout obeyed and beamed thermal images as he turned and scanned the large opening in the cave that he sat in.

Eustace studied the almost mono-color heat map that was now up on Myra's monitor. "Nothing... Switch to IR and investigate port side."

Scout retracted the landing pod and made his way towards a passageway deeper into the cave system. As he squeezed through a narrow gap, a larger opening was revealed in the images.

The *lava tube*, as Eustace liked to call these underground caves, extended for what seemed like an eternity in front of Scout. The tunnels were adorned with ancient jagged lava formations and the IR images accented each peak and crevice, making them more pronounced.

Eustace leaned in to take a closer look at the different layers of deposits on the cave walls that the IR images now made visible. "That's how high the previous lavas must have flowed," he explained.

Something caught Myra's attention. "What are those?" She pointed at the screen.

Scout pivoted to inspect the formations hanging from

the ceiling that she had mentioned. Myra leaned in as she studied a cluster that transfixed her.

Eustace began explaining, "shark tooth stalactites... Over time as lava dripped from the ceiling and the flow rose from the bottom, it formed those... Quite magical, right?"

More like teeth waiting for their next meal... You're brave, Scout. I could never go down there. Myra thought as she continued nodding and studying the stalactites.

"Check starboard side," Eustace spoke into the mic.

Scout pivoted and began scanning to his right.

"Toggle cameras."

Scout toggled between IR, thermal and night vision one by one. He then cycled back to default color mode and turned on his lights. The beams penetrated deep into the darkness of the lava tube.

"Turn 'em off!" Eustace said as something caught his attention.

Scout obeyed, reverting back to IR and awaited further instructions.

Myra pulled her chair away as she noticed Eustace leaning even closer. He was now mere inches from her screen. She stared at his salt-and-pepper hair while his head blocked her view. "What is it?"

Eustace leaned towards the mic. "Check that puddle straight ahead."

Scout flew over promptly and stared down at a puddle of water in a small opening on one of the cave walls.

"A puddle?" Myra asked.

"Most likely dripping rainwater or moisture from above. There could be many more of these. Even passageways to the ocean... Take a temperature reading," Eustace spoke into the mic without looking back at Myra.

Scout shot a laser beam into the pool and instantly got the reading of 115 degrees Fahrenheit.

"Hot!"

Eustace just nodded. "Zoom in."

Scout zoomed in, but all that the images revealed was calm, still water.

"Perform a sample analysis."

A small door on Scout's underside slid open and a tubular arm extended out, at the end of which were two pincher-like attachments. The bottom had a mini collection disc and the top a powerful analyzer camera. Scout extracted a sample, blasted his lights and let the camera see. Eustace centered himself in front of the monitor as the image gradually came into focus.

Myra scooted over and went to the second monitor. She leaned in close as the image adjusted one more time and then, she saw *them*. *Unbelievable*, she thought as her eyes widened ever so slightly and she took in the whole picture that had filled her screen.

Unaware of being observed, a swarm of tiny tadpole-like critters swam frantically in the puddle. Twisting, turning and rolling, they did what they were supposed to be doing at their age.

Magical... indeed, Myra thought.

Eustace's lips parted ever so slightly as he stayed trans-fixed on the motion of the shoal. Once again, complete silence lingered in the room except for the fans and hums. He looked at Myra. There was a sparkle in her eye. She put her hand over his and let out an awkward smile as she turned away. *I'm not gonna cry.*

She looked back at Eustace and thought she saw a tear rolling down his cheek. She moved over and hugged him, tight. None of them spoke. They just remained embraced.

Suddenly, Eustace broke free and got up, "Tag this hole and tell him to continue searching. Frank!" he yelled on his walkie as he exited the control room.

"Yes, father," Myra said to the empty door. She turned around and stared at the charged up little swimmers.

So full of life... alive. I'm happy when you're happy, Dad!

She began reaching for the talk switch when suddenly she yanked her hand back and sprung up like a spooked cat. Her heart raced, and eyes scanned the already familiar room as if she had never been there before.

"Dad!... Dad!" Her words traveled beyond the control room, but she didn't hear anything back. She unclipped the walkie from her waist and pressed the switch. "Barry, come in."

"Myra!"

"Barry! can you come to the control room?"

"Yes, but not right now. I'm calibrating the printers."

"Forget the printers, can you come here right now? Please."

"You guys found something?"

"Barry! There's a huge spider on my keyboard."

"Oh come on. It's just a spider. Just move it."

"Can you come, please?"

"I gotta take care of this calibration. It's a mess. I can-."

"Fine!"

"Myra!... Myra," Barry continued. She didn't reply and clipped the walkie to her waist.

She inched back towards the door all the while keeping her gaze transfixed at the dark and slender body of the four-inch-long spider. Its far-reaching legs clutched few of the keys as it rested on the keyboard, next to the mic.

Myra looked up briefly at the screen and saw the same image of the tiny critters, floating around with youthful zeal. She knew Scout was awaiting further instructions.

She looked back down. The spider was still there, motionless as a rock. Myra felt a sudden wave of energy rushing through her as she noticed goosebumps all along her body. Still, she couldn't resist staring at the arachnid's fine pointy legs and black sacks. However many eyes the long legs must have had, Myra knew a few of them were watching her. The thought made her breathing heavier and labored when suddenly, the whole place rattled.

The monster began crawling.

Myra sprung out of the control room and slid the door shut with a loud clank.

INCOMING

The *Polar Explorer* cruised comfortably at ten knots as it cut its way through the chilly waters of the north Pacific. Its 250-foot-long body, with the hull painted blue and the rest white, blended seamlessly with the frigid melting landscape that surrounded it. A few arctic gulls circled above the decks waiting for any discarded scraps of food.

At the bridge, the young Officer of the Watch kept one hand on the wheel and other close to the throttle as the lookout next to him scanned far into the distance for rogue floating masses of ice. Their periodic adjustment kept the behemoth on course.

In a side room, the second mate perused the navigation charts and weather reports that lay in front of him. A buzzing caught his attention and moments later the printer spat out a new document. He finished his task then attended to it.

His gaze deepened as he studied every detail. The paper and the information both were still warm to the touch. He referenced it regularly as he verified a few websites on his computer.

"Captain Emerson, come in," he spoke into his walkie, then waited. His eyes still fixated on the paper.

"Captain, come in."

He rolled his chair out of the small office and peeked into the bridge.

"Where's the captain?" he asked the Officer of the Watch.

The Officer shrugged.

"Maybe the helipad," the lookout said.

The second mate got up and felt all four pounds of the bright red jacket he pulled from the side closet. He put it on, tucked the paper in, zipped it up and stormed out the bridge.

He hugged the rusty old railing as he navigated his way out onto the deck. The metal may have been showing its age, but he knew it was there should he needed it. The frigid wind forced his hood on as he wondered when they would finally be through the corridor of ice. He couldn't wait to get to warmer waters. The icy corridor now stretched to only a fraction of the size compared to what it had been when he first joined the fleet of the *Polar Explorer*. With the unpredictable climate pattern altering the natural weather cycles of many parts of the planet, he knew that warmer waters wouldn't be more than a few hundred miles away. He ducked as he climbed up and down through a network of side stairs, all taking him closer to the stern.

As he reached the final small set of frozen metal stairs, he looked up once again at the towering hangar that rose in front of him. Painted dark under its shadow, the second mate just stood there and gazed for a few moments. No matter how many times he had seen it, the hangar's sight always left him in awe. In his seven years of work onboard the *Polar Explorer*, he had never seen anything this great being commissioned or carried onboard the vessel on its numerous voyages around the globe. A few meters ahead, he caught the silhouette of a few men in the distance, their red jackets barely visible through the haze.

If Captain Emerson hadn't inserted the gel height risers in his boots that day, the second mate could have easily missed him, but his salt-and-pepper crew cut confirmed the identity. The Captain stood alongside his first mate and searched for something in the sky through his binoculars. It was an almost futile exercise as the mist kept forcing them to play visibility games.

The second mate finally reached the stern. "Captain, you gotta see this," he blubbered as he unzipped his jacket and handed over the document.

Captain Emerson's gaze deepened as he studied the paper. He looked up at the second mate, who was almost out of breath and then at his first mate. Before he could say anything, a loud engine sound from behind commanded their attention.

Recon slowed down as he approached the *Polar Explorer* and with the finesse of an expertly orchestrated ballet, he made a gentle, effortless, graceful landing on the sign with a big yellow H and a circle around it.

THE BRIEFING

Myra watched Eustace as he plugged the projector cable to his laptop. He worked back and forth between the computer and the screen behind him, shaking the wire, unplugging then replugging.

"Did you check the screen share settings?"

"Ah! Of course."

The chairs in the hall were starting to fill as Eustace continued tinkering. The area was compact but could still comfortably seat a dozen people. Eustace didn't need room for that many. His team only had nine. The small folding chairs were lined in a U-shaped pattern around the edges with a couple in the middle. Myra glanced over the settings as the picture still wasn't up.

On Eustace's side sat an attentive man with a big round face, straight posture, an immaculately clean crew cut, and equally neat X-corp T-shirt and military-style cargo pants. Younger than Eustace but older than most X-corp engineers, Frank prided himself for being in better shape than most around him. The days he didn't work out were the days he hated life, and he didn't enjoy hating life for too long. Frank took in the energy as murmurs began filling the hall. A bottle of Krug stood firmly near his foot.

The hall had a few oval windows but late evening provided zero visibility outside to the sea. The warm lights reflected off the dark wood and made everyone feel welcome. Finally, Eustace managed to get the picture to the screen. Someone in the room started cheering, others joined in.

"Is that everybody?" Eustace asked.

"Where's Barry?" someone said.

Eustace looked around, "Yeah, we're missing Barry." He yanked the walkie from his belt. "Barry, report to the dungeon, immediately. I repeat, report to the dungeon!"

Everyone chuckled, except Hunter, who sat motionless, making people next to him aware of his short, loud breaths.

Many members of Eustace's team still couldn't get used to the humor-filled style that he ran X-corp with. But they all appreciated whenever it provided some relief from their almost always serious nature of the work.

Working for X-corp was a paradox. On one hand, the employees were doing the most ambitious, challenging and potentially dangerous work of their lives and on the other, they were having a field day out in the open world, having fun soaking up the beauty of nature. Most of them loved it, most of the time.

Suddenly, the small wooden hall door slid open, and Barry walked in. He was instantly met with friendly stares. He scanned the room without holding eye contact for too long, then nudged the door shut behind him.

"Sorry guys, I was working the printers. There's a—"

"Do it after you see this." Eustace interrupted him.

Barry remained by the door, looking for a chair. He spotted one in the middle of the group, decided to stay put.

Before starting the video, Eustace took off his glasses

and looked at the whole team sitting in front of him. They started cheering, he returned a generous smile back.

"Thank you... thank you."

The team cheered and applauded even more.

"I just want to thank each and every one of you for your invaluable contribution to our mission. Today, we implemented Phase One, and I'm astonished how lucky we were."

"The video!" someone said.

"Yes, yes, in a second... I want to take a moment and acknowledge the fact that this journey has been difficult for all of us. To reach even here has taken years of hard work and sacrifice. All of you have paid a high price for this mission. You've been away from your families and accepted the dangers that our mission brings."

Every pause he took allowed the dead silence to spread across the hall. All eyes were glued on him as his tone drew them closer, almost magically, to his words. Perhaps this was the same quality that had inspired many of them to have agreed to be a part of the Chisil mission.

"Oftentimes the first breakthrough is the hardest to achieve, and it seems we are headed in the right direction. I know you guys are excited, but just remember the complexity of our mission, and that it gets harder from here on out. It'll require us to be on our best game all the time. Chisil is a remote and hostile place, and we don't want to be spending any extra time there than necessary. Not with such a large setup and under our particular situation with the government. So, I trust all of you will utilize each and every moment that we'll be allowed. I know our stay is not welcome, but this mission is important for all of us, and we must continue forward with the full resolve in our beliefs and why we chose this project in the first place." He took a brief pause as his thoughts drifted. He restrained his emotions then continued. "Finding those amphibians is the only way to save Chisil. The world will not come together to protect what it doesn't know exists. It'll be an honor to discover a new species. We found the babies, and if anything Phase One has taught us is that there is hope that we'll find the adults. I know they are down there... they have to be... It's an opportunity of a lifetime."

They know about all this, Dad! Please don't get emotional. They just want the video! Myra thought as she tapped her foot. She took a deep breath in. "Dad, I think everyone is waiting for the video."

Eustace gave her a smile then hit play, and some of the video that Scout had beamed earlier appeared on the screen. The team cheered and watched intently as Eustace explained different features of the cave and various types of lava formations.

Suddenly, silence spread across the hall once again. Everyone had their undivided attention towards the screen. It was as if the whole team had fallen into a deep trance. There was no need for words. The fact that they were watching never-before-seen living things gave them goose-bumps. Someone broke the trance as others followed with applause and cheering. Some couldn't control their emotions. Being so far away from home had an amplified effect on each peak and valley their mission brought. Each victory or setback in this remote environment was more pronounced, and a few of them actually relished the height-ened doze. Myra looked around as some let their emotions show while others exercised restraint. She looked up at Eustace, who was still mesmerized by the critters on the screen. He turned around towards the team.

"Let's give a round of applause for Frank. Without his precise planning and logistics, we would still be tightening bolts and screws in LA."

The team burst into applause.

"Not to forget Barry... our analog computer! Always on top of *all* of the software. The Bug Man!"

Myra shook her head. *Again? Why do you always pick on Barry, Dad?*

Eustace's style at times bordered towards what some would call unprofessional, but the whole crew had gotten accustomed and smoothly transitioned to a more casual work culture once they joined X-corp.

"Hunter! I'm still not sure how you taught the bots to communicate so well. You're like their mother." A few chuckled as more applause followed. Everyone except Barry turned towards Hunter who nodded with a restrained smile. As big a smile as he could muster without aggravating his left shoulder which he had sprained in a recent fall. Each nod sent vibrations down his bulk, rattling the potbelly that he had worked so hard to earn.

"And finally, Myra. The AI should have been listening to Barry and Hunter more, but they all are in love with her. Without her emotional support, this mission wouldn't have been possible. She binds us all!" He took a deep breath as he stared at his daughter. "Her faith in me has driven us all to the far end of the world."

The team applauded once again, all focusing on Myra. *Come on, Dad! That's a little too much.* She returned a soft smile back to Eustace then looked away.

Eustace glanced at his wristwatch. "In thirty-six hours, we'll be landing. Myra, Frank, Barry and Hunter, I want you guys on the prep ASAP. We only have one chance at this. I want everyone to get plenty of rest now. As little as you need. I don't wanna see anyone half-awake washed aboard or dropped from the side of the *Explorer* while running around. And those of you who aren't coming with us, we'll miss you, but you guys will miss all the fun!... No, really, we'll miss yo—"

A sharp knock interrupted his speech. A few members of the team turned back towards the door. Barry took a moment then slid it open a foot.

"Captain!" Barry said as he opened the door more.

"I'm sorry to interrupt, but I'm afraid I have some urgent news," Captain Emerson said to Eustace. He handed Barry the paper and gestured to pass it around as he began talking. "The latest weather report indicates a strong north Pacific storm pushing towards us swiftly. I'm afraid we'd have to cut your stay on the *Explorer* short... You'll have to make the landing tomorrow, after sundown." The Captain looked around the room. "You'll lose twelve hours."

"Impossible! How can we get all the systems and AI ready by tomorrow? These are complex machines with huge data storage. To get all the systems ready, checked, rebooted and all the gear moved out by tomorrow is... is insane... it's impossible," Barry complained as Eustace studied the paper that was now in his hands.

"I'm sorry, but we don't have any other option. I won't have my crew or vessel get caught in the middle... I want them outta here before that storm hits."

"But how can we move all the gear in time while the systems are still being rebooted and scanned?" Barry asked.

Captain Emerson was about to say something when Eustace interjected. "We'll get it done, Captain."

Emerson took a moment before speaking. "Thank you, Mr. Oar!" He pressed his lips, looked around the room, nodded and stepped out into the corridor.

Whispers started filling the small briefing hall.

Myra glanced at Eustace and then at Barry who stared at the floor, gripped by some thought.

THE PREP

Myra slid her hand through the narrow opening and struggled to move the large hangar door. It barely budged. "I can't do it."

"Yes, you can. You just don't *wanna* do it," Barry said as he moved closer and slid his hand through the gap as well. "Hang on a second." He tightened the wrist brace that covered his right hand and half the forearm.

They both took a deep breath and pushed. The forty-foot-tall hangar door slid open a few feet.

"When are they gonna fix this?" Myra asked as she slipped through the opening.

"Doesn't matter now."

"Well, it'll matter tomorrow."

"If it's like this tomorrow, at least it'll buy us some time," Barry said as they shut the door behind them to its original position.

"I can't believe they're still working on it. I'm not sure we'll have enough time," Barry's voice echoed as he complained about the hangar door a little more and they moved towards the control station at the far end. Myra nodded in agreement as she glanced at the two engineers who were busy doing maintenance work on the *Whale*.

It was Barry himself who had started calling the X-corp helicopter *Whale* since the first time he had seen it. 75 feet long and 20 feet high, the machine dwarfed everything in its vicinity. Modeled after the concept of the US Army's *Osprey* military transport helicopter, the *Whale* boasted its own unique design: a long metal tube for the center hull with imposing wings on either end, each with its own set of rotors, a total of four compared to only two in the *Osprey*. The wings' innovative foldable design enabled the helicopter to be stored in relatively tight spaces like the hangar onboard the *Polar Explorer*. Someone had suggested *Quadprey* was a more appropriate name, but Barry had already named it *Whale* and Myra had loved it, too.

The big bird was not only innovative for its exterior design but also for its duel energy source. With its hybrid technology, 80% of the power was derived from the batteries that lined its underbelly, and the rest was reserved for the fuel-guzzling engines that powered the rotors. The smart power design ensured that the helicopter could be commissioned for remote long distance missions where fuel supply would be limited or non-existent while still being environmentally friendly. The fuel-powered engines generated the liftoff thrust while the batteries did most of the heavy lifting once airborne.

Myra waved at one of the engineers as she and Barry passed them. The other engineer had his nose buried too deep into the blades tilting assembly to be bothered. A soft smile appeared on Myra's face as she glanced at the utility and transport vehicles parked behind the *Whale*.

It's gonna be epic. Myra thought as she neared the vehicles.

The first transport was the six-wheel drive Amphibious Utility Vehicle, a custom truck designed explicitly for the

Chisil mission. Able to seat eight passengers, the AUV was capable of traversing uneven rocky surfaces with amphibious capabilities of crossing deep lakes and marshes.

The other was a smaller Jeep-style 4x4. The RUV was the workhorse of the X-corp vehicle family. Capable of fast maneuvers and light transport, it could quickly be outfitted for a variety of tasks. Thick metal armor that lined its body ensured plenty of rollover protection for its passengers.

"Everything's a fucking mess around here," Barry shouted as he kicked a pen that was on the hangar floor.

Myra laughed.

"What're you laughing at?"

"You!"

"You think it's funny? Well, *someone* has to do the work here. Please, let it be me. Me. Me." Barry said as he raised his right hand into the air.

Wish you could see your face when you're angry, Myra thought as Barry rambled on, powering up the control station.

"You can do it. It's just a little extra pressure. I'm sure it'll bring the best out of you," Myra said as Barry logged in.

He looked at Myra, and before he could reply, something behind her caught his attention. He stormed past Myra. "That bastard!"

Myra followed.

They crouched next to *Falkor.* Solid as a bull, tall as a stallion and loyal as a dog, the only quadruped bot X-corp ever manufactured lay silent now as Myra gazed into his dimmed eyes and braced to hear what Barry had to vent next.

"I can't believe it! How we suppose to exit early when people still haven't finished old jobs? That jumbo-ass bastard."

Myra just listened as she stroked Falkor's face.

"Hunter should be hunted," Barry said after a long pause.

Myra couldn't help but giggle. "Why do you hate him so much? Stop being so jealous."

"Jealous? That loser has nothing on me." Barry rushed back to the control station.

"Maybe, but he is competition. Stealer of your limelight?"

Barry grabbed the Master Key from the lanyard around his neck and plugged it into the USB port of the station, choosing not to reply. Myra smiled and slowly drifted away towards the five humanoid robots that hung in their individual bays, hooked up with cables.

She looked up and just stared at the bots. She could muster the same curiosity even when they were asleep as she did when she had first seen them come to life years ago. Their bond was inseparable. She had grown alongside these machines and bore witness to their learning and evolution.

"Initiating *Wake Up*," Barry's voice echoed in the hangar.

Myra took a few steps back, instinctively.

Barry looked at the one closest to him. "Zeus, Wake up."

Soon, the first of the humanoid robots sprang into action. His head tilted up as the onboard cameras and sensors scanned the area around him. As he stood erect, the hooks slid back and dropped him on the floor. The cables unhooked one by one and retracted to their bays. He turned around. "Myra! Barry!"

A faint satisfactory smile appeared on Myra and Barry's face. As tall as a grown man with an exoskeleton painted a blend of green and soft gray, Zeus was suited to blend into outdoor environments. His joints and movements uncannily mimicked human motion. X-corp engineers had taken special care in modeling the design to emulate human moves as closely as possible while enhancing other abilities such as strength, and ability to dial in touch sensitivity.

The robots had been sleeping for the last seven days as Barry tweaked their software and occasionally woke one or the other to test the results of his adjustments.

"Artemis, wake up," Barry said.

They waited for Artemis to come to life.

"Artemis! Wake up!" Barry's voice echoed once again.

Myra looked at Barry. "Maybe the mics aren't working."

"They were working yesterday."

"Artemis! Wake up... " Myra's voice lunged across the hangar.

"He's deaf," Barry said.

"And the rest?" Myra looked at the other bots still in their bays, "Mimi, Tori, Sam, wake up."

One after another the three bots leaped into action. Mimi and Tori were the sizes of an average human female while Sam was designed to be slightly shorter, which made him more suited for missions that required being in tighter spaces.

The bots greeted each other with their individualistic rituals as Barry's fingers kneaded the control station keyboard. With the underlit glow bouncing off his pale skin and ginger hair, he looked like a severe version of Garfield, only much skinnier. The frown thickened as he plunged deeper into the software.

"Did you check the mic?" Myra asked.

"All systems look fine. Not sure why he's not listening."

The sound of the hangar door sliding echoed and pulled their attention away from the station. The chilled night wind forced its way in and along came Frank. His firm walk guided him straight towards Myra and Barry. He glanced at the robots as he came closer. "We're getting there."

"Not really, I dunno what's wrong with Art. He won't wake up," Barry said as he checked the software once again.

"Artemis, wake up," Frank's voice filled all the empty space that was in the hangar.

Artemis sprung into action, immediately. He detached from his station and walked over to Frank.

"But he didn't respond to us!" Myra said.

"There have been some changes. A few. From now on, Artemis will only respond to me. Unless I assign other commanders."

"But why?"

"You would have to talk to your father about that."

"Hunter! He helped you, didn't he?" Barry asked.

Frank just stood there. A faint, almost invisible grin on his face.

Barry let out a sigh.

"Artemis will help load the vehicles and gear. Lemme know if you guys need anything." Frank turned and walked away.

Myra watched him leave as he almost treaded the exact path that brought him in. "Why would Dad do that?"

"I knew it. This Hunter... We should just steal his Master Key," Barry said.

"Let's load in all the gear. Zeus, make sure everything fits and is secured. We don't wanna make multiple trips," Myra addressed the bots.

Barry and Myra watched as the bots got to work. Sam and Mimi jumped on the vehicles as others secured the large equipment cases and began dragging them into the belly of the *Whale*.

Myra noticed a much quieter Artemis focused on the loadout as the other bots tried to cheer him up.

Why.

She stormed out of the hangar.

A MOMENT

E ustace scanned the horizon outside the porthole from his cabin somewhere in the basement as the *Polar Explorer* glided effortlessly under the starry night. The table lamp illuminated the fog his heavy breaths deposited on the polycarbonate pane. His gaze wandered onto the featureless ocean, eyes forgetting to blink.

He brought his attention back into the cabin and tilted up the photo in his hand. A long, satisfying look later he took another sip of the whiskey that was in his other hand. He pulled the picture closer. His eyes wanted to, but he restrained. "You would've been so proud of her. She's doing so well for her age. I love her energy and enthusiasm. A true gem... I got lucky."

He finished the slow monologue and waited. Once he made up the words the photo would have said, he continued. "I feel alone, Cat... so very alone. Miss you!" He kissed the photo. He studied it a little more as each passing moment took him deeper into distant memories. "Wish you were here today. You would be proud."

He clenched his jaws, then let out a smile. His emotions rode an unpredictable roller coaster. A sudden knock on the door pulled him back to reality. He wasn't expecting anybody, let alone someone who would knock with such sharp staccato rhythm. He quickly collected himself, shoved the photo back in his wallet and slid the door open a little.

"Do you have a second?" Myra asked.

"Of course!"

She quickly stepped in and sat on the edge of his well-made bed.

Eustace slid the door shut. "What happened?"

"Dad, why is Art only responding to Frank's orders now?"

"Oh... I knew you would ask."

"Then tell me."

Eustace came around and sat next to her. He studied her face with the same attention as the photo. He smiled as he noticed her expression deepening. "It's a safety net. We can't trust the bots blindly, my dear."

"But we aren't! That's why we have Barry and your favorite Hunter with the keys who can literally make these bots do whatever they want."

"Well, not really... even with the keys."

"Dad, are you getting my point? I just don't like Frank being the only one able to control Art. It's scary. He can make Artemis do anything!"

"Trust me, there's a reason for it."

"And? What is it?"

Eustace stared at her. He always enjoyed such pleasure games. Holding off till the last moment to evoke a reaction from the other person. He made sure to delay answering just a few extra seconds with her. It was a delight for him to watch her reactions as she tried to figure things out. In moments like these, he got to see more flavors of her personality. "More than the bots, we have to keep an eye on Barry and Hunter. It's a good thing they both don't love each other."

"Barry can do no harm. I dunno about Hunter, but then

again, Frankie likes him."

Eustace just smiled as he studied her further.

Myra couldn't help but notice her father's face had become a shade redder from all the emotional swells he must have went through earlier. She looked over at the table by the window and saw the whiskey glass, almost empty. Her tone changed. "Aren't you excited?" She bounced as she angled towards Eustace.

He waited a second then smiled and nodded.

"Me too... It'll be the biggest adventure of my life!" She said with some restraint.

"Mine too!"

"Of course!"

She gave him a tight hug. "I should let you sleep."

Eustace kissed her forehead. She left the room and shut the door behind her.

Myra stood in the hall under the warm glow of the overhead lamp. The silence of the lower deck couldn't help clear her thoughts.

Artemis!

She entered the small cabin, unfolded on her bed and just stared at the ceiling. Except for her breathing, the only other sound was whatever the little plastic table fan made. She looked around. Clothes, books, electronics, everything needed to be packed. *I hate packing. How come we never made a bot for that.*

She went to a side table and gently picked up her bowgun, a rifle with an arrow chamber on top. She looked through the scope and aimed at the ceiling. Once the light bulb was in the crosshair, she made a *phish* sound and jerked back. She slung the bowgun strap over her shoulder and began stuffing clothes from the floor into her military-green duffel bag.

THE MEETING

As the sun peeked above the horizon, the light began warming up Captain Emerson's morning face. With the fog gone, the open sea ahead stood clear for anyone to conquer. It was still cold, but the coffee kept him warm. Many concerns occupied his mind that morning. Though externally he was much calm and composed, thoughts kept wrestling within. He wondered whether they would make *it* happen before the storm. He turned around and glanced back. The one he was expecting hadn't arrived yet.

The first mate frequented between the small side office and the bridge, double-checking reports and the plotted route.

"Captain!" a sharp voice emanated from the other end of the bridge.

Captain Emerson turned and found Frank standing in the distance. Dressed in the same military-style X-corp uniform, Frank appeared ready for anything the day was going to throw at him.

Captain Emerson looked down at the small envelope Frank carried.

"Enjoying the view?" Frank asked.

"Please give us a moment," Emerson said. The first mate quietly exited the bridge and shut the door behind him.

Frank walked up. "Stunning," he said as he took in the view outside the bridge windows.

"Let's hope it stays this way."

Frank motioned the envelope towards Emerson, "It will."

Emerson ignored the gesture, turned around and headed towards the small side office. Frank watched him go, then followed.

"The cameras," Emerson said as they both entered the office.

Frank grinned and passed him the envelope again.

Emerson immediately felt its weight. He lifted the flap and took a peek.

Suddenly, the whole office shook as the *Polar Explorer* crossed over an unexpected swell.

EXIT

The evening sun waited outside for the hangar door to start moving. It began opening with a *thud*. Inch by inch the rays found their way in and painted the *Whale* warm. The ship's crew had finally gotten around to fixing the long-ailing hangar door. They had to. It was time.

The two ropes struggled as the pulleys cranked harder from the far end of the stern. Like a giant snail being dragged from its slumber, the lines forced the *Whale* out. Gusty Pacific winds deposited salt against its military green body as they blew the propeller covers off.

There was a new urgency. The stern was busy. The crew, the deckhands, everyone toiled with a single goal in mind. A flurry of activities all geared towards getting X-corp off the *Polar Explorer*. Captain Emerson had strict orders to make the time for the exit, and his personal supervision ensured they were carried out as planned. A man who relished doing as many things by himself as possible, he supervised the organized chaos from the upper deck.

The two X-corp engineers flanked either side of the *Whale*, periodically checking the clearance between the helicopter and the side walls.

At the starboard stern, a few deckhands prepped the two dinghies as others began maneuvering the crane in position. The inflatable boats were hefty, and their heavy construction made them unstable as the wind rocked them from side to side. Each slap swung the dinghies like a pendulum's needle suspended from the crane.

Trapped at the dark side of the hangar, Hunter waited as he watched the *Whale* being towed out in front of him. With his patience running out, he squeezed through the narrow gap between the machine and the side wall, his extra bulk nearly pinned one of the engineers. As he made his way across the helipad and to the far end of the stern, Hunter joined Myra, Frank and Artemis as they stood in silence, watching the slow pull. He looked to his right at Artemis, Frank and then Myra. Nobody looked back. He pulled out the half-eaten energy bar from his cargo pants and took a big bite. Dressed in their outdoors military grade X-corp camo uniforms and shiny aviators, the team looked sharp and prepared, except for Hunter, who still wore the same baggy clothes he had put on some two days ago.

Zeus, Mimi, Tori and Sam began pouring out of the hangar once the *Whale* was fully out. Frank watched the bots as they gathered near Myra. A small chatter filled her side of the formation. "I'm excited," Mimi yelled as she stared at the nose of the *Whale* in front of her.

Myra stood in silence as the wind shook her, occasionally. She saw Barry dashing out the hangar, several papers in hand and struggling under the weight of his massive backpack. Barry tried to rush, but the load wanted to keep him put. Myra waved at him. *Poor Barry, you're gonna die!*

Barry tried but couldn't wave back. He boarded the *Whale* through a side door as the two X-corp engineers entered the cockpit.

Hunter looked at Artemis and Frank, still ignored. He followed behind the engineers and entered the *Whale* too.

Myra started towards Eustace as he climbed up onto the stern from one of the lower decks.

Eustace looked up and froze as he took in the view in front of him, the full size of the *Whale* as its propeller blades began folding out.

"Almost there," Captain Emerson said as he walked down from the upper deck towards Eustace.

"Captain, thank you! We couldn't have done this without you," Eustace yelled over the Pacific winds.

"I didn't do anything special – you paid me, and I did what you paid me for... I wish you guys luck!" Emerson extended his hand. Their knuckles whitened as Eustace returned the handshake.

Myra rushed and hugged Eustace. The lashing wind masked their conversation from bystanders.

The four propellers started tilting into their vertical position as the blades finished fanning out. With its wings now spread, the *Whale* dwarfed everything.

Frank began walking towards Zeus and others. "There's a new loadout scheme," he shouted over the wind.

"New scheme?" Zeus asked.

"The chopper is too heavy. All that load will drain the batteries fast. We won't be able to optimize energy efficiency. I had the team not load the printers. I want you and Sam to bring the printers in those dinghies."

The bots looked at the small boats as the crane lifted the first one higher above the *Explorer*.

"The chopper is too heavy? But, there was still space. I'm affirmative we can manage the printers and the machines," Zeus said.

"It's not about fitting in. It's just too much weight. I won't risk a crash because of uneven poundage, and that storm isn't gonna spare us any turbulence."

Mimi, Tori and Sam looked at Zeus.

"Will you send the *Whale* back for us? I have a negative feeling about bringing the printers in the dinghies. They are too large." Zeus's voice became fainter as the blades churned harder.

"I don't have time to discuss. It's been decided, just bring those damn printers in the dinghies. You'll have the sat phones if you need anything. Mimi and Tori, you both are with me," Frank looked at Zeus, then continued, "They are light."

Mimi and Tori looked at Zeus, confused. On one end they wanted to be safe and secure with the rest of the team, but on the other, they didn't want to leave Zeus and Sam behind.

"Come on, girls," Frank said to Mimi and Tori as the sound of the props tore through the air and he moved away.

"I don't understand," Mimi said as she watched Artemis follow behind Frank.

"We don't have to understand everything. We just follow. There's no time," Tori said then marched behind Artemis.

Mimi spent a few more moments with Zeus and Sam, then left.

The draft stirred by the four propellers pushed every unsecured object to the outer edges. Captain Emerson and the deckhands hung on to their railings.

Myra stood close to the rear hatch of the *Whale* and waved at Zeus and Sam, calling them to board. The bots stood in the distance, motionless.

The wind threw Myra's dark hair all over her face, "What're they doing there?" she asked as Frank neared the rear hatch.

"Oh, we got some gear they forgot to load. I'm leaving the boys in charge of its safety until we turn the chopper back around."

"Huh?"

"Don't worry, we'll send the chopper back ASAP. Or, they can take the dinghies."

"Dinghies?! No way! We're sending the *Whale* back."

"Yes, of course," Frank said as he stepped inside.

Myra stood there on the rear hatch ramp, still staring at Zeus and Sam. *You guys are gonna be alright! We'll come and get you soon.* She shouted, "Don't worry, we're sending the *Whale* back!" The wind masked her words as Sam waved at her.

Zeus and Sam watched as the rear hatch closed shut, almost as if in slow motion. Time appeared to have slowed down for them as thoughts entered and exited their minds and the developing swells rocked the *Explorer* up and down.

One after another, all four props pushed harder, and the deafening sound sent shivers up the spine of those who dared not maintain their distance. Somewhere in the middle of tussling the mighty Pacific winds, the *Whale* began generating lift. The deckhands turned away and ducked to evade the frigid slaps. The *Whale* swayed left and right as the combination of lift and wind wobbled it. If there was a time, it was now. It could not hover too long and let the *Explorer* pass under it.

The blades cut through the air harder as the engines whined and delivered more power. The seventy-five-foot machine began ascending higher in the sky.

It was airborne.

Zeus looked up at the fast receding bird. For a moment he thought he saw Myra in one of the windows.

As the *Whale* rose higher in the sky, the props tilted down and began thrusting it forward and away as the *Explorer* shrunk under it. Minutes later, the bird made a U-turn and did a flyby over the ship at 85mph.

Zeus and Sam stood at the stern, watching their hope vanish into the rapidly darkening Pacific sky.

9

CHOPPY

Zeus looked up at the crane lowering Sam's boat as he steered his dinghy away from the *Polar Explorer*. The two large strapped cases behind him blocked the view as his boat danced up and down in the swells the mothership generated. He stood up and watched Sam as the crane lowered the second boat. It was hard for him to let Sam out of sight, even if that meant driving blindly ahead, looking backward and risking a collision with the *Explorer*.

The crane creaked as the load reached bottom and Sam's boat dangled just a few feet above, water thrashing its underside. With a loud *snap,* Sam's boat landed in churning waters and immediately began swelling up and down. Zeus watched Sam struggle to steer away from the mothership. *I'm not certain about this,* Zeus thought.

What the much larger case in the back robbed Sam in maneuverability was made up in speed. Sam gunned the throttle and carved out a path as he began putting some distance between him and the turbulence the *Polar Explorer* generated.

Leaning over the starboard side railing, Captain Emerson watched Sam's boat race away into the distance.

Zeus zoomed and locked onto the Captain's face. The dark sky and the crane light painted Emerson's face warm, but for Zeus, it was as cold as the water that splashed on him when Sam made a sharp turn and parked next to him.

"How many more miles?" Sam asked over the radio.

"Thirty," Zeus replied after checking his GPS.

"Can we go faster?"

"No, we're *maintaining* cruising speed. *Especially* you. I don't want you at any more than 20 knots."

As the *Explorer* was left behind, so were the swells. The stretch of the night ocean was surprisingly calm. No thunder stressing their audio sensors or brutal winds forcing them off-course.

"It's gonna take foreverrr!" Sam groaned.

"Just relax. We'll touch Chisil within an hour."

"That's too delayed."

Zeus scanned the featureless mass of cold water in front of him. No matter which direction he turned, he saw the same view lit by the high moon. If it weren't for the sounds of the two boats, it would have been eerily calm. Calm in the middle of the open ocean? If it wasn't tranquil, the soothing moonlight certainly made it appear so. *An hour is indeed too long.* The thought entered Zeus's mind as he soaked himself in the serene beauty of the north Pacific. *An hour is too long. Too long for something to happen.*

The sudden swaying of his boat yanked him out of his trance. He scanned the horizon, the water had a new stir in it. He stood up and peeked behind, over the cases. A faint wave approached him. He zoomed in, toggled the thermal and saw a large pod of White-Sided dolphins bouncing in and out of the water, racing towards them.

As the dolphins neared, they infused the water with newfound energy. Zeus watched members of the hundred-strong pod zoom past him. Most of them just passed, but a few curious ones continued swimming alongside the boats.

"Do you see this?!" Sam asked as he pointed at the ones next to his boat.

Zeus nodded then brought his attention back to the few near him. *Excellent swimmers. So graceful... like water sliding over silk.* He heard Sam's engine revving louder.

"Sam!"

Zeus pushed the throttle and thrust his boat forward. Sam had already gained some distance but his being the lighter boat, Zeus was soon closing the gap. As he raced ahead, the Dolphins matched his new speed. They jumped in and out every few seconds as the new pace demanded more oxygen. As he was closing the gap, Zeus couldn't help but notice Sam's excitement. He saw him yelling and waving at the dolphins who remained with him, no matter how fast he went as he tried to outrun nature. *I'm glad you're enjoying this.* Zeus thought as the lingering sensation of being left behind by the team finally faded and he joined this rare moment with Sam.

As Zeus closed in, he raised his fist in the air. Sam copied the motion with the same charged up enthusiasm. The two bots, with their newfound agile companions, continued blazing through the dark waters.

"A mile out. Almost on top of the coordinates," Zeus radioed Sam.

"I can see land," Sam said.

"Slow and steady. Just keep at my tail at all time."

The racy excitement of the dolphin run had been replaced with the slow and mindful approach as the boats entered the waters that hugged Chisil. Hundreds of years of volcanic eruptions had sent molten lava rushing towards the sea, resulting in an intricate network of unpredictable solidified molten structures under. The sharp edges showed little mercy. They didn't care who it was. They delivered the same fate to whoever dared venture too close.

A few meters in, the boats neared the entrance of the cove that was to lead them to the landing coordinates. The night vision and thermal cameras helped anticipate and look for potential lava deposits that were too close for comfort. Although the onboard sonar worked tirelessly as they snaked through the shallow waters, it was still best to be vigilant.

The cove was surrounded by towering mountains on either side with water running through the middle. Formidable road blocks that certainly made navigation challenging. It was unclear how much of the hills were made of the solidified lava, but, it did manage to cover large portions of them. Streaks of ancient deposits hung from their uneven sides and melted into the water.

Zeus focused on the left cove hill a few hundred feet in front. The hanging streaks of solidified lava commanded his attention. *Stunning! Myra must see these.* He began taking thermal and IR images. Wide shot, medium and zoomed in – for a few moments, he found himself lost. A sharp roaring sound suddenly yanked him out of his tender moment.

"Sam!" Zeus yelled as he watched the second boat overtake him and race towards the cove.

Sam pushed the throttle harder and left Zeus behind. He looked back, anticipating what Zeus would do. Soon, his boat was approaching the cove, and the gradual bend took him out of sight.

Zeus thought about speeding up but decided otherwise. "Sam! Slow down!"

"We're almost there!"

"I said slow down!"

Out of nowhere, a sharp tearing sound echoed through the hills. It didn't alarm or surprised Zeus. He slowed down as he navigated the bend and noticed Sam's boat some twenty feet ahead.

Sam stood on the starboard side watching as Zeus approached. "I didn't know they were so close."

"I told you to slow down!"

"I was doing OK. The boat didn't turn fast enough."

"That's what happens when you don't volunteer to haul an elephant onboard."

Zeus noticed the water that was rushing fast into Sam's lopsided boat. He extended his hand. "Move over."

Sam grabbed it quickly and crossed over. "The printer?"

Zeus remained silent as he moved over to the edge. He put one foot on Sam's boat and unbuckled the fasteners that secured the printer. Both dinghies wobbled as he tried to balance his weight.

"Give me a hand," Zeus said.

They both grabbed onto the side handle of the printer case and began sliding it over to Zeus's already-full boat. As the printer slid to the port side, it lifted Sam's dinghy up from the other end. When they pulled all two hundred pounds of the case all the way to the edge, Sam's boat dipped further into the water.

"Pull!" Zeus ordered.

With one strong pull, they slid the printer over, and it now rested between the two boats.

Each new tug let more air out of its punctured tubes as Sam's dinghy slid deeper. For a moment, the printer floated on water, but as Sam's boat went under, all two hundred pounds of the case began dragging the bots *in* with it.

"Let it go!" Zeus shouted.

"No!"

"Shut Up. I said let it go!"

Sam let go of the handle.

An explosion of bubbles rose up as the weight of the printer took itself and Sam's boat into the depths near the cove. The bots stared at the commotion in the water as Zeus's dinghy still wobbled from the stir the incident had created.

My humans! How am I gonna explain this? Zeus wondered.

10

BASECAMP

The thin strips of solar panels soared high up in the air, expending the last bit of energy stored deep in their flexible bodies as they struggled to break the cloud cover. On the other side waited the warmth of the morning sun and much-needed replenishment. The electromagnetic wave transmitters attached to their ends made them some-what lopsided, but the gyros kept all four strips in sync, effortlessly chasing the sun just as paper kites drift in the direction of the prevailing wind.

As their dark bodies absorbed every new ounce of the warmth, they began transmitting the juice some forty feet below to the receiver that rested on a small cliff. A few cables snaked downward and connected to a power bank the size of a small refrigerator. As long as the sun provided its warmth, the system was designed to maneuver autonomously. Adjusting for Earth's rotation and angling, the kites frequently pivoted for maximum absorption of energy. After sunset, the solar kites were programmed to descend automatically and sleep for the night in their protective cases.

On the opposite side of the cliff with the power bank,

eons of geological forces had carved out a channel, dozens and dozens of feet in width. Tall cliffs guarded its either sides and provided ample protection from the elements for the *Whale,* as it rested, secured in the middle. The channel was the perfect landing spot. Large enough to comfortably accommodate something the size of the *Whale*, but not so big as to stretch the operation too thin.

The custom designed projectors the team had mounted on the cliffs above the channel had started working. They beamed uncannily accurate holograms of geographical features that blended seamlessly with the surrounding land-scape, providing a camouflaged roof over a large chunk of the channel. Although, the military surveillance satellites passed several times a day over large parts of the Aleutian island chain, including Chisil, the projections made sure nothing stuck out worthy of investigation. Besides, the almost constant cloud cover mixed with fog and the absence of anything out of the ordinary ever happening in the Aleu-tians except for an occasional volcanic eruption kept the watchers of the satellites uninterested in the region, for the most part.

The flurry of activity kept the channel occupied. The team hustled as they set up basecamp. The engineers were busy performing maintenance checks on the *Whale* while Barry and Hunter tried to get along as they worked on the computer terminal. Some of the bots were busy setting up the gear. Tents, drilling machines, cables – all sorts of things had to be unloaded. The unload was to be executed in stages. In stage I, only the most critical gear was to be brought out, and once basecamp was set up for full opera-tion, depending on how much the mission grew, the camp would have also been expanded.

Myra honked twice as she began reversing the RUV. The sound amplified from inside the *Whale* and took Tori by surprise as she was crossing behind.

She jumped to the side and watched Myra pull out. "Don't run us over with your high horse!"

Myra smiled and winked at Tori as she backed the RUV and headed towards the west end of the channel. With the RUV's hybrid engine, the initial kick reminded her that it drove just like the electric cars in southern California. Unlike her electric back home in Pacific Palisades, in which Myra could cruise down the Malibu coast however fast she wanted to, she had to be conservative with the RUV. The supplies were limited and the terrain uneven.

Myra parked the RUV close to the six-wheel AUV that she had already driven out some twenty minutes ago and began walking back towards the rear of the *Whale*.

Both transport vehicles stood facing out at the west end of the channel. That side was more forgiving. Small clumps of grass poking out of relatively smoother rocks made for a more accessible path for the vehicles to be driven out compared to the east, which had taken much more beating from the past lava flows and geological events.

"Myra!" a familiar voice stopped her in her tracks. She paused, then continued walking.

"Myra, listen!"

Zeus came around and stood in front of her. She continued staring down. "Myra, you have to believe me."

She looked up. Even with the rigidity of a robot's face, the tiny changes in the way Zeus's lens iris flared, the way his head tilted, the way his hands moved and other minute details all told Myra something.

"I thought the Whale wasn't gonna come back."

How can you think that I wouldn't send it back for you guys? Myra thought as she stared Zeus in the eye.

"I tried calling Frank's sat phone and couldn't get hold of him, and Emerson kept pushing us to leave. What could I have done?"

Myra stood motionless, arms still folded around her chest.

"I don't know why Frank had us do this. We could have easily fit in on the first flight out."

Myra's eyes were about to get watery, and just before they turned into tears, she pulled them back. "What if something were to happen to you and Sam?"

"I know!... I know."

"No! You don't know. You should have stayed on the ship and waited. I would've made sure the chopper got back. You just didn't give me enough time and decided to take the boats."

"We never got a chance to speak with Frank once you guys left," Zeus took a moment. "I don't know why he told you that we wanted to take the boats?"

"I dunno either, Zeus."

"Nobody knows."

"I'll talk to Dad about it," Myra paused and looked around. "Good thing we don't need the printer right now. They might not even miss it, except Barry. I'll handle him. We need to focus on tomorrow. Help the team with what they need." Myra turned and began leaving.

"Myra!" Zeus walked up to her.

They both looked into each other's eyes again.

Zeus began to say something, but she interrupted.

"I don't want to lose you, Zeus."

He took her hand and began caressing it. His sensors felt every stroke as Myra's skin rubbed against his titanium. They kept staring into each other's eyes.

"You never will!"

11

DEEPER

"Continue with Infrared," Eustace leaned in and spoke into the mic placed in front of him on top of a black plastic case.

Much smaller than the control room onboard the *Polar Explorer*, the tent barely had enough room to hold two people with a single monitor and a jungle of cables connected to video backup recorders, external antennas, walkie chargers and other gadgets that rested in their bays, collecting juice.

The other man who sat transfixed on the static-filled images was Frank. Even looking over Eustace's shoulder, he was ready to spot anything that was more than just monotonous cave terrain.

The static increased by the minute as Scout ventured deeper into new areas of the underground cave system. Being the first ones to ever discover these caves, Eustace and his team had only mapped out the coordinates of the area from where Scout would descend. Whatever Scout was to actually discover once down there was as good as anybody's guess. All Eustace could do now was to keep following his hunch in guiding the ailing bot *right* and hoped they would see a glimpse of the amphibians that had brought them three thousand miles from home.

Scout felt the grind every meter he ventured deeper into the cave system. Continually switching between thermal and IR to avoid obstacles and Eustace's hunch was managing to keep him on what seemed to be the correct course. As the cave narrowed and began closing in, Eustace continued asking Scout to use thermal, even if it taxed his batteries.

Frank leaned in towards something on the screen. "Plants?"

"No... There can't be." Eustace squinted. "Jesus, are those vines? Switch to thermal."

Static filled the screen as Scout switched from IR to thermal and hovered looking straight ahead at the narrowing walls. The shark tooth stalactites were lined randomly across the ceiling. Some were as long as two feet, and others were small, all pointing their jagged ends down.

The static finally cleared and Scout beamed clear thermal images.

"Damn, those *do* look like vines," Eustace said.

Something caught Frank's attention. "Zoom in... Are those barbs?"

"Move in," Eustace spoke into the mic.

The narrowing walls ahead were not the first time Scout had had to squeeze his way through. The men in the tent couldn't see, but all along his body, there were numerous scrapes and dents, souvenirs that marked the struggle he had faced as he navigated this deep into the caves. If there was any hesitation, Scout didn't show and just like a tank, boldly thrust forward.

The silence, as the two men waited for Scout to get closer was only broken by the hums of fans and the constant dripping of water outside as droplets rolled off the tent fabric and landed on waterproof cases that were too big to fit inside.

"Keep on thermal," Eustace spoke when Scout had suddenly changed to IR. He couldn't get enough of the vivid imagery.

As Scout neared the walls, the screen filled with dozens of long rope-like objects glued to the walls, emanating a reddish-orange glow.

"What's that?" Frank asked.

"Definitely vines."

"No, the movement."

Eustace looked closer as the image stabilized when Scout came to a steady hover.

"Is that liquid inside? The vines are see-through?" Eustace asked.

The liquid inside the vines registered hot on the thermal scanner. It wasn't clear whether the vines were transparent, but Scout was able to get a faint glimpse of the hot moving liquid inside. When Scout took a reading, it spat out 107 Fahrenheit. None of them had seen anything like this before.

As Scout panned around the area, he beamed images of dense growth all over the walls. They were littered with vines. Some fat, others thin, all clutching the rocks tight.

"This end is thin. Looks like the vines are getting bigger as they go deeper," Eustace said, pointing at the screen as he explained.

"Extract a sample," Frank spoke into the mic.

Scout narrowed one vine and closed in.

"This is incredible," Eustace said.

Scout extended the sample extraction needle closer and jabbed the vine in a snap. As soon as the needle penetrated, a barb shot out and hit one of Scout's front-facing cameras.

The momentum threw him off balance, and his whole body spun. Scout wasn't sure how rigid the surface of the vine was and to ensure penetration, a fast jab was necessary. As he spun around, he realized maybe it wasn't such a good idea to jab it after all.

The cracked camera glass impaired his vision. He could no longer see like before. There were only two cameras onboard, and both faced forward, separated by only a few inches. The barb narrowly missed the second. Otherwise, that would have cut his life short, prematurely.

"The needle," Eustace said, watching the dissolved sample needle as Scout extended the arm and lifted it in front of the second camera.

"What!" Frank said.

"It dissolved?"

"Some sort of acid."

Some motion on the screen commanded Eustace's attention. "They're moving. The vines are moving!"

Frank leaned in.

The vines were indeed moving. They scraped up and down along the cave walls and appeared to be retracting towards the deep far end. It was as if something at the far end was pulling strings.

Eustace cranked up the volume and stuck his ear as close to the speaker as he could while keeping an eye on the images. "Sounds like slapping ropes."

The movement intensified, each stroke sent echoes through the cave system. The sounds that returned from the deep put Scout on high alert. He was never designed to handle such situations. His only mission was to beam images and video and take samples. Such a scenario was never anticipated. Especially one that involved an unusual plant-like system with acidic liquid coursing through its veins.

Out of nowhere, a sharp barb shot out and hit Scout on the side. He rotated frantically, scanning for the source. The barb left a deep dent in his metal body. He made frequent turns and circled around as he tried to plan his next move. The one working camera scanned every inch desperately as it hunted for any more threats.

It's always the unknown that's more frightening. Somehow, knowing what one was about to come face to face with has an almost calming effect, to a degree. If the threat can be figured out, something can be done about it. If Scout could never guess what was about to happen, he would never be able to devise any strategy or be able to give the computer time to cope with the situation. That was the problem with sentient machines. If they had been mere machines, it would be easy, but the thinking and feeling part kept the vulnerability portal always open.

"Fly back, retreat," Eustace yelled into the mic.

"No. Stay and document."

Frank covered the microphone and turned towards Eustace. "Sorry, but this is invaluable. We need to see this..." He turned towards the monitor. "Looks like it's not gonna be a walk in the park down there."

Frank's covering of the microphone was futile as Scout had lost his focus. It didn't matter what they said now. His sensors were going berserk. There was no way of knowing what he would encounter next. He tried plotting a few scenarios, including retreat but the confusion left him lost and spinning furiously, wasting the last bit of its dwindling energy reserve. Just as he was buried in a thinking trance, another barb shot out and hit his top, this time denting him even deeper.

The force was such that it pushed his whole body down by a foot. He felt every second of it. A moment later, another barb shot out and hit the small arm that held the needle. The momentum of the impact spun Scout in a full circle.

Just like a chain reaction, one after another, more barbs came out of nowhere. Out of everywhere. Too many to count, too many to defend against. There was nothing Scout could do but spin around and take the hits as they were served.

One barb, larger than others, zoomed out of its origin point and hit straight at the second camera, flinging Scout several feet into the air. Once the momentum was lost, he finally crashed on the rocky cave floor.

The men stared at the screen but only saw broken images severely interrupted by static, the frequency of which had increased by now as Scout struggled and his systems began shutting down.

The only reliable data the men still received from the scene were the sounds. Their ears were filled with more audio of banging and thrashing vines, along with the loud whirring sounds of Scout's motors as he tried to start, stop and restart them.

Scout continued trying to fire up his motors repeatedly in a desperate attempt to fly away. It was futile. He just lay on the cave floor, his body jerking back and forth from the motion but unable to do anything more. He couldn't see anything but could hear the sounds getting louder. More than hearing, he could *sense* the next few moments. In those moments, a strange calm descended upon him. It was almost as if he had forgotten about the present and the computer played images from the past, particularly the ones where he had turned back and looked up at Recon one last time just before entering the caves.

Still glued to the speaker, Eustace and Frank listened closely. The same lingering silence had returned, the hums and the dripping water. Eustace looked up at the static on the monitor. He took several seconds before speaking. "Zeus will go down in the cave tomorrow, not Sam."

Frank kept staring at Eustace as he found himself short of words while he processed what they had just witnessed.

Eustace turned and looked at Frank, "Also, let's arm him."

12

TWILIGHT

The moments that mark the transition from light to darkness always stir things up. The life forms that had been finishing their daily chores begin winding down. They find shelter and huddle with a different mindset. A volley of evening calls mark the beginning of this new phase, a phase where some creatures leave certainty behind and embrace whatever the darkness is to bring. The transition is routine but never easy. Perhaps the calls and company of their fellow beings aid in easing this feeling.

If it had been a little darker, the hanging half-moon would have backlit the smoke that rose high up in the air. There was still some time. As the smoke went out, so did some of the tension that had plagued Eustace since morning. The cigar was almost done. He continued his walk towards the distant calls of hundreds of puffins nestled in their burrows. A chance to witness their behavior would have beckoned fond memories, but he didn't want to venture out too far. He sat on a rock, cigar stub between his fingers, and stared into the distance as the birds continued their calls. The soft breeze and the chorus were enough to keep him distracted. There were very few things he loved more than the natural world.

A gentle touch on the shoulder broke his spell. He looked up, just to confirm. Myra smiled as she stared at her father.

The soft moonlight accented the valleys and peaks of Eustace's face. *You're one handsome father,* Myra thought. Even with a few extra pounds, to her, he was still handsome. A mature man with a round face and long gray hair who had lived a fierce life, following his passion and going boldly in the direction of his dreams. That handsome face didn't return a smile in exchange. Hers faded away fast, too. She came around and sat on the rock next to him. Myra absorbed the same sounds and sights her father did. *I knew I would find you here.* She could still hear some of the team members prepping for the next day in the channel behind them, but Eustace seemed to not care.

The wind rustled Myra's hair. She looked at Eustace and let out a sigh. "Will you tell me what's been bothering you? What happened?"

He took his time. "Nothing."

"Come on, Dad. I know it's *not* nothing."

She stared at him as he sat in silence.

"About tomorrow..."

Myra gave him all of her attention.

"It's a strange feeling... All these years, we've been working so hard for this. We had a great run. The hard work, the deadlines, the adrenaline rush..." He took another pause. "The mission was the fuel. But... but now I have this strange feeling." He looked into Myra's eyes. "I'm not sure if we should continue with this mission."

The look on Myra's face was a mix of surprise and curiosity. *Why are you saying this?* "Why not?"

"I just have this feeling... maybe it's just not a good idea."

She leaned closer. "This is all you ever wanted for the

last seven years Dad. We're already here. We made it. Chisil was your dream!"

"It's *still* my dream." He looked in the direction of the distant birds. "I still remember the day my father brought me here. All those old memories. It was a fantasy land... There was something pure about this place, something magical." He took a pause as one of the birds produced a loud call in the distance. "It's *still* magical."

Myra smiled, nodded.

Eustace took a short pause. "I'll be fine, I just need some time." Deep down he knew he wasn't going to be entirely comfortable. What happened to Scout still lingered in his mind. Although both Eustace and Frank were confident Scout had only encountered some sort of predator plants, which could easily be avoidable in future with proper planning, the incident still introduced the element of uncertainty in his mind.

"Think about what will happen if you stop," Myra said.

Eustace kept staring at the ground, playing with his cigar stub.

"You're the *only* chance Chisil has. If we stop now, it would mean giving carte Blanche to those mining companies. They'll tear this place up and dig till they can't anymore."

Eustace just listened. None of her words were news or new to him, but anything Myra said had always affected him. More than mere facts, it was the emotions behind her words that always shook his core.

"I can't wait until you discover the *bians* and show them off to the world." Her body shook a little. "It gives me goosebumps just thinking about it," she continued, looking at him.

Eustace took a deep breath and got up with one big push. He looked in the direction of the fading bird calls as he rubbed the cigar stub on the rock. His breathing had a new energy. He knew their mission had the potential of stopping the government from green-lighting the contract for the mining companies.

Myra's words once again rekindled his desire to be the first to bring the world's attention to these new species. He looked at her. "Let's find those bians!"

Myra smiled. *That's more like it. I'm so proud of you, Dad. You'll do it. Only you can do it!*

13

EXPLORATION

The RUV jostled back and forth as Zeus navigated it over the rocky patch in front of them. Far in the distance to their left, members of a rather large colony of migratory birds struggled to secure nests on the cliffside as others patrolled and glided to and fro from the open ocean. The breeding season was imminent and with it the arrival of an incomprehensible number of avian visitors who called Chisil home for the few short bountiful months.

A few miles out straight ahead stood the Chisil Volcano. Even from a distance, Myra and Zeus could feel the weight and power of this sleeping inferno. They drove in silence. It was one of those moments where words were not necessary as the ever-changing landscape and sights kept them captivated.

Zeus ducked to get a clearer view through the windshield. Now some hundred feet away, the volcano totally dwarfed them. No matter how low he went, he could not see the summit. "Massive."

"Of course!" Myra fired back.

"I think we are already too far away."

"Nah, not far enough yet. A little more," Myra said as she glided her fingers over the bowgun on her lap.

Zeus watched her fingers. "We should head back. You know it'll take the same amount of time to get back."

Myra laughed.

"I'm sure they are looking for us."

"Don't worry, Barry knows where we are. Nobody is panicking, except you." Myra glanced at her wristwatch. "There's still plenty of time before Sam starts. We'll be back before they begin prepping him."

Zeus stared at the distant birds. "I wonder how many birds nest on Chisil?"

"Some three hundred thousand, or more. You can count and see if that's correct" Myra looked at him.

"It must have been devastating last time Chisil exploded."

"Yup, fifteen-kilometer-high ash and plumes, lava burning everything in its path. At least the birds could fly. The ones who won't be able to fly..." She looked at him.

"Yes. Next time it explodes, some new animals certainly wouldn't be able to fly."

"Yeah..." Myra sighed. "I always wondered if the initiative was a good idea. I mean, it definitely saved polar bears from certain extinction, but Chisil might not have been the perfect place to relocate them and others. This volcano scares me. At least they kept them to the east. Let's hope they won't venture to this side," she said as they turned and admired the receding volcano behind them.

Myra aimed her bowgun and got ready. "Pull!"

Zeus hurled a thin, chipped stone disc they had collected back in the channel into the air. Myra lined up the sight and pulled the trigger. An arrow shot out at four hundred feet per second and tore the stone disc into a dozen small pieces.

"Fluke," Zeus said.

"Oh yeah, sure sure."

She cocked the bowgun, dropped another arrow on the rail and took a breath in.

"You won't get this one," Zeus said.

"Pull!"

Zeus hurled another one into the air, this time giving it a little spin. The disc continued gliding and turning in the sky before smashing onto the ground. She had missed.

"Told you, that was a fluke!"

I'll show you! Aim low, Myra, Aim low. She reloaded the bowgun, fixed her stance and locked her sight. "Pull."

Zeus took a second to spin around and threw this one with the power of an Olympic athlete. Myra shot the arrow in the direction, but the disc had already traveled far, fast.

"What the hell was that?" Her shoulders dropped.

"Come on. Hurry. Three more," Zeus said as he prepared another disc.

She missed another two.

It wasn't a fluke! You need a lot more practice, Myra! Why can't you aim low? You're never gonna be the one-shot wonder. "I'm tired. This thing's heavy," she complained, wasting the last arrow they had carried into the ground.

Zeus laughed.

"You gonna get the others?" Myra asked as she retrieved the arrow she had just shot.

"Of course!" Zeus mocked.

Myra stared at it continually as she crouched next to it. Her intense focus penetrated deeper into the darker layers of her heart and mind. Death had always been uneasy for her. Death had always stoked the fire of her emotions and made her extremely sensitive. Zeus stood nearby, looking around. He put a hand on her shoulder, but she didn't react. Her trance still consumed her.

In their quest for fetching the last arrow, they had stumbled upon the lake that was in front of them now. The small ripples glinted as the midday sun baked the water relentlessly. Something caught her attention. She lifted her head from the large body at her feet and looked at the water in front of her. It took her a second to make sense of what she saw. A fish, belly up. The visual pulled her back into the sullen mood. She scanned the water and noticed more dead fish, numerous bodies floating and bobbing as the wind caressed the water. Some she could see near, and others were far away, spread all across Lake Shadow.

Zeus bent down. "So, what do you think?"

He looked at the same dead fish that had caught her attention and then to the others around them. "The animals, all of the trees..." he added as they tried to make sense.

"Maybe something contaminated the water," Myra said.

"But that doesn't explain the charred trees."

He looked closer at the body that Myra sat next to. Something caught his attention. "Can you move over?" He moved in and tried to wiggle it to see what was underneath. The giant body barely budged. "It's massive."

Myra stood up and stepped back. Zeus shoved his hands underneath and anchored his feet into the ground. With one herculean pull, he lifted its side and turned it over. The massive antlers dug a few inches into the damp soil near the lake as all 1200 pounds of the dead albino moose turned over and exposed the underside. His tongue still hung out, and lifeless eyes communicated helplessness. Around the body were deep grooves in the soil, a remnant of the struggle he must have gone through as the life force had left his body.

Myra covered her nose as she squinted and a frown

appeared on her forehead. She watched the maggots that infested the gaping gash on the freshly exposed underside. The stench was unbearable. She pressed her hand harder.

Zeus crouched and perused the gash. He noticed a large object stuck inside it, wrapped in intestines. He pulled it out. A foot in length, the object was unlike they had ever seen before. The exterior was a hard metal reinforced with what seemed like a substance similar to carbon. Most of the colorful markings and outlines were burnt, but the overall size and weight were significant to have caused what it did.

"Looks like this broke off from something larger."

Myra stared at the object. "How can that be? There are no humans on Chisil."

"Maybe it fell from one of the satellites."

Myra studied the object then scanned the horizon past Lake Shadow, as far into the distance as she could see. "Maybe there are more pieces like this around? Maybe some in the grass over there, or in the tree line."

"Maybe," Zeus kept the piece with him as he stood up. He looked around for more. As he scanned the tree line, he did a slow double take. Something in the distance had caught his attention. He zoomed in.

"What is it?" Myra moved closer and stared in the same direction but couldn't see anything except the blanket of healthy and charred trees across the far side of the lake. "What is it? Tell me."

Zeus remained focused, scanning the area around what had caught his attention. He almost didn't hear her words.

Zeus navigated the RUV around the lake towards the thing that had caught his attention among the charred tree line.

The albino moose lay silent at Lake Shadow's bank. His eyes were now closed, and tongue no longer hung out of his lifeless mouth.

14

REMOTE CAMP

B arry paced back and forth as he waited for someone to answer from the other end. He tried again and then one more time. He wondered if Myra had turned off the sat phone or the call wasn't reaching her. *Maybe she's inside the RUV.* He thought. "Myra, come in," he tried the walkie. Was she out of range?

He stared at the sat phone then turned it over and removed the battery bay. Thirty seconds later, he reinstalled them and hoped for the best. He tried again but got the same disconnected call.

"Fuck." Barry dug into the phone menu. A minute later, he looked up at the cloud cover that hovered above him.

The remote camp had been set up close to the opening that Recon and Scout had created into the cave system. A few hours ago, Artemis and Mimi had blasted it wide enough to let a human pass through. A ladder now hung down, ready to take Sam underground.

Some of the team moved in and out of the two tents at the remote site as they occupied themselves with premission prep while the rest stayed back at the channel including the two engineers who had to perform maintenance on the *Whale* almost constantly. Hunter was busy performing last minute adjustments and checks. The power, software, memory, mechanics, communications, cameras, all systems had to be in line before Sam could go down.

"Where are they?" Eustace asked Barry. His tone had gotten more and more severe as time went by. Part of him was concerned for their safety and part of him was annoyed. Although, in this case, he was mostly annoyed. Safety wasn't as big a concern when Myra was with Zeus.

In the back of the six-wheel AUV, near one of the tents, Frank was busy perusing through the hard plastic black cases. They contained modular, custom weapons designed by X-corp. These killing machines could be modified based on the specific missions they would be deployed in. Although, they were only to be used in self-defense. He opened one of the cases and grabbed the base frame of one of their advanced handguns. He then proceeded by adding various modules to make it operational. The modules were part metal, part dense plastic. Such material combinations allowed the guns to be modified easily as new plastic parts could be printed remotely with relative ease and speed.

Barry walked into the tent and stood next to Sam where Hunter was finishing last-minute system checks. He couldn't help but notice Hunter's steel wallet poking out of his front pocket. The wheels of curiosity began churning. What was in it? Although made out of a dulled variety of steel, the wallet had always drawn maximum attention, especially from Barry. No matter how many times and the type of tact Barry had deployed, he had never gotten around for Hunter to share its contents. Barry wondered if he would ever find out what was inside.

"I'm nervous," Sam leaned over and whispered to Barry.

He looked at Sam with a blank expression.

"I don't think I can do this. I don't know what's down there," Sam added.

Barry just stood there and stared at Sam.

Hunter spoke from his control station at the back of the tent. "Your systems are fine. You are ready. Don't worry. When the time comes, you'll *know* what to do. Besides, you're being armed."

Somehow, Sam's whisper wasn't quiet enough, or Hunter's ears were too sharp whenever Barry was around.

Barry put a hand on Sam's shoulder. His outward demeanor tried to reassure him that everything would be fine, but deep down he didn't feel it was right to send him down there if he felt uncomfortable. On the same note, he also knew that the bots were designed to carry out the orders, regardless of how they felt. Like hired mercenaries, slaves to the orders of the higher-ups, no matter the personal emotional toll. Barry decided to focus on the bigger picture and tried to not let the thoughts affect his already overtaxed brain.

Eustace stared down into the darkness of the enlarged opening when a voice from behind drew his attention.

"It's not a good idea," Barry said.

"What's not a good idea?"

"I mean—" Otherwise an outspoken young man, for some reason words struggled to come out of Barry's mouth.

"What?" Eustace asked.

"I don't think we should send Sam down there."

Eustace stood there and took a deep breath.

"He's just a kid. He isn't ready for independent missions," Barry continued.

Eustace took his time before speaking. "I want Zeus."

"A much better candidate. I just can't find him."

Eustace looked over Barry's shoulder into the far distance then turned towards the cave opening and stared. A new idea had taken birth in his mind. Zeus's absence didn't bother him in that moment. In fact, he was happy that Myra and Zeus weren't around. "Sam *will* go."

Barry looked at him, trying to discern if he was serious.

"Yes, Sam will go. But not alone." Eustace moved in closer. "I'm gonna go with him."

Barry jolted back. "Wait, I thought we already decided. It's not safe for you down there."

"Maybe, but I don't wanna send Sam alone."

Barry got lost in some thought.

"Me and Sam can handle this together."

Barry stared at Eustace, long enough to make him uncomfortable. He knew Eustace had always wanted to go into the caves himself and with Myra gone, it was a perfect excuse for him to realize his fantasy.

"But it's not safe. We discussed this."

"We'll be armed, we can handle it... I'm going with Sam."

Barry took out the sat phone and just as he began dialing, Eustace stopped him. "Don't! You are not telling Myra. She would never let me. I wanna be back before they return. In fact, if she calls back, just act cool. Let them take their time," he stared at his wristwatch then continued, "Let's plan for two hours."

"But Eustace, I don't recommend you go. Maybe we can postpone the mission and send Zeus tomorrow. Sam doesn't have to go, and neither do you."

"Barry. Let's prep for the two hours, with Sam and me."

The words put a period to Barry's further inquiry. He watched as Eustace moved towards the tent where Sam was being readied. He then turned and stared into the darkness of the cave opening.

Eustace's steps were labored. The custom suit slowed him down, but not so much that he easily fatigued under its weight. It was constructed of a few separate pieces that joined together at seams with interlocking loops and sliders. The jacket, pants, shoes and the helmet all integrated and fit as one whole unit. All designed to shield the wearer well from a variety of external elements. With temperature control and its own limited oxygen supply, as well as extras like a small canteen, the suit ensured that the wearer could sustain the environment and continue their mission comfortably. It provided Eustace with great psychological protection, like having a roof overhead. Eustace welcomed the boost in his confidence.

"You're all set for two hours. There's a reserve oxygen tank for an extra thirty, but I highly recommend you don't use it and return before the main tank's out," Barry explained.

"We'll see, we might not use up O_2 all the time, some pockets might be breathable. There's got to be some good air down there. What are all those plants breathing, after all?" Eustace said.

The built-in carbon dioxide to oxygen converters in the suit gave Eustace added peace of mind that he could stay down there longer if need be, depending on the situation, but just like any complex system, there was a probability the converter might fail to perform in unknown conditions. He knew it was in their best interest to wrap up the descent within two hours.

Eustace met with Frank, who was going over the handgun with Sam.

Once he got the hang of it, Sam stored the gun securely in the holster strapped around his leg.

Frank approached Eustace with a smile. "Looking sharp!"

Eustace nodded and walked past him towards Sam. The extra time to ponder over and the company of Eustace had calmed Sam down significantly. Most of the tension and anxiety was gone. Some of it was even replaced with a flair of confidence. Having a father figure like Eustace alongside had lifted his spirits.

Eustace turned around and faced the team. Frank, Barry, Hunter, Artemis and Tori listened as he began speaking. "Time to go. We'll be back in a few hours. Well, maybe a few minutes over."

His humor didn't land as intended. The air was silent and solemn.

Sam led the way and descended down the ladder. Eustace approached the opening then turned around and put his foot on the first rung. One step at a time, he began going down the opening as the team watched from above.

A moment later, his hand came up and gave the team a big thumbs up.

15

THE CABIN

They scanned the area from behind the safety of the charred trees. Zeus zoomed in around the cabin he had spotted some two hundred feet in front. The landscape was barren of any living thing. It was as if everything that had legs or wings either left or became a victim of the flames that had engulfed the immovable trees.

Each time they inched further up, they paused and took a quick look around. To their knowledge, no human should have any business being on Chisil. There was still some time before the government approved or disapproved the contract for the companies to start their exploit. So, before that were to happen, why were there any humans? And it wasn't some temporary stay. Somebody had built a cabin.

"I'll go in first. Join me when I signal," Zeus told Myra.

She stayed back as he continued towards the cabin. He trod lightly, keeping an eye on his surroundings. Along the way, he saw more dead squirrels, something they had been noticing as they had snaked around Lake Shadow.

Zeus leaned against the cabin's side wall and peeked around the corner. The door was ajar, motionless. Even the wind didn't seem to blow. He moved a few steps in and tried looking through the small side window. It was boarded up, and the tiny cracks didn't help much. Another step or two brought him to the edge of the door. He rested his back against the wall and pulled out a tube cam from his right forearm. He bent the cable and let the camera scan the inside. The camera sent feed directly to his visual sensors. He turned on the night vision, snaked the camera around, pivoting and panning. The images left him motionless. He stood there, soaked in his thoughts.

Moments later he pulled the camera back, opened the door and stepped in.

What the hell happened here? He wondered. Suddenly, a loud gasp from behind startled him. He turned around instantly and grabbed a shocked Myra. He braced her as *she* scanned the area. The strange odor in the cabin, a mix of burnt flesh and wood, forced Myra to cover her nose.

Even though the visuals grossed her out, curiosity got the best of her, and she stepped in, eventually. Straight in front of her lay a mutilated body. Whatever clothes remained on the dead man were charred, just like the trees. The wooden floor below was visible through the big hole where his navel should have been. His heart was missing. It was as if something had plucked it out through the hole that was in his chest. The part that Myra found most disturbing was his missing head. Strands of flesh still hung out from where his head must have been separated from the rest of his body. It was hard for her to tell the color of his shirt. It was burnt, soaked in blood and flesh. The dead man's hand, knife still clutched, lay a foot or two away from his body. His other arm was nowhere to be found.

Myra took a step in and looked to her left at the second body that rested against the side wall. A sharp cut that ran through the length divided it into two halves. The intestines hung out all the way to the floor. The man's right hand held a spatula while a piece of paper dangled from the other. The blood stained the wood deep-red. Through the opening in the torso, one could see he was missing a few organs.

To Myra's right was the third body. She pressed hard on her nose and took a few steps, careful to still maintain her distance. She had never seen anything like this before. Zeus moved closer and touched the third body. Small pieces of it chipped away.

"What happened to *him*?" Myra asked.

Zeus shrugged, careful not to break more pieces off the charred body. The body had been frozen in time right at the moment when the man must have been trying to get off his small makeshift bed. Myra came closer. Skin, flesh, tendons, muscles, fat – most of it had been seared black. A few pieces that managed to escape the burns clung onto the skeleton in desperation. She looked up at the area around the body. "Only this side is burnt," she referred to the right wall of the cabin.

"A fire? But it burnt only this side?" Zeus said.

"Definitely not a regular fire."

They both studied the pattern on the burnt wall.

"A fire wouldn't burn in a circle?" he said.

Myra stood there. Thoughts entered and exited her mind. They both stared at the large circular pattern that the burn had created on the cabin wall. "It's strange, nothing outside this circle is burnt."

A tapping sound commanded her attention. She looked around at all the supplies that littered the cabin. Food cans, an outdoors stove, utensils and a few rifles that stood erect, propped against the walls. Stashed in one corner was a large metal box. She moved and opened it, cautiously. A deep frown appeared on her face.

Zeus stepped in and looked over her shoulder. "Sons of dogs."

The box was full of animal parts. Claws and polar bear hides. Pelts of winter animals such as bobcat, lynx, and remnants of a host of smaller ones. Right next to the box dangled the trapping gear. Traps, chains, ropes and other instruments of death hung silently on the wall near the door. Myra thought about the species relocation initiative. She suddenly realized that Chisil was a perfect ground for poachers like those dead men, and whether the initiative had facilitated the poaching further as islands like Chisil were seldom monitored.

The tapping sound drew her attention once again. She looked around and did a quick double-take at something sitting on the long wooden shelf on the middle wall. She hurried and moved a few clothing items around to uncover it.

She stood there, speechless.

"What in the world?" Zeus said.

"A Golden Dart Frog."

"What is *he* doing here?"

Myra just stared at the frog as he jumped around in the terrarium, desperate to get out. The small glass tank was laced with sand, artificial grass, a battery-powered heater and a plastic pond that held some feces-infested water. Along the sand bed lay the remains of some of the victims the frog may have claimed in his time inside the glass walls.

"Why would they bring something so rare out here?" Myra asked.

"Maybe they wanted company. A reminder of their home?"

"These frogs are common in South America. Mostly Colombia, I think."

"He's so bright! Or she?"

"It's a he... his brightness is his defense." She moved her face closer to the glass, looked into the frog's eyes and continued, "That gold is laced with one of the most alkaloid toxins known to mankind. A single drop's enough to stop the hearts of twenty grown men."

"Twenty?" Zeus was surprised, but if it was coming out of Myra's mouth, he knew he could believe it. A faint doubt still crept in. He knew Myra couldn't possibly know about *all* of the animals.

"Yes, the neurotoxin prevents nervous system communication. Soon, the heart stops."

She looked near the terrarium at a plastic can that had *Frog Bait* written on it in sloppy blue handwriting over a white label. She took out a few dead crickets and dropped them in.

The frog continued jumping at the wall like before.

"Maybe he isn't hungry," Zeus said.

Myra saw a small stick next to the bait can. She took out a new cricket and put it at the end of the stick. She lowered it and wiggled near the frog.

With lightning speed, the frog lunged forward at his target. The cricket now rested safely in his tiny mouth, legs still sticking out.

16

HOLES

With each careful new step, his eyes widened ever so slightly. He had dreamed about this for an eternity, and it would have been a shame to allow any moment to slip by without fully cherishing it. It was as if time had slowed down, as if nothing else mattered. The world ceased to exist. That intoxication was only interrupted by an occasional word from Sam or anyone over the radio at the remote base-camp. Some thirty minutes ago, they had stopped and observed the critters that Scout had discovered in the puddle. Eustace was still basking in the sweet feeling of having seen those tiny living things with his own eyes.

Every time Sam looked at Eustace, he wondered why couldn't he be as calm and composed. Perhaps calmness was a gift only awarded in ripened years, or just to humans. There was still quite a time for him to reach any such years. Or perhaps the reason why he couldn't keep calm was that he saw more than the middle-aged man beside him. But Sam himself couldn't put his finger on how he felt. It was some sort of an intuition. A lingering feeling of vulnerability that he couldn't shake off no matter how much he had wanted to. He realized how emotionally naked he felt. He kept one hand on his weapon, which seemed to calm his nerves, just a little.

Although Eustace preferred videos over photos, his descent into the caves had brought out the photographer in him. Nothing novel escaped without first being captured by his portable camera. Armed with a variety of modes, the camera could quickly toggle between color, IR and thermal as the sensors in its outer cage read different types of data. Eustace also took advantage of the low light sensitivity and clicked everything he possibly could.

Except for the puddle with tiny critters, the caves had been devoid of any life that they could spot, even with the help of various sensors and cameras. But Sam knew that was not going to be the case forever and without warning, they could come face to face with the monstrous plants that had robbed Scout's life. Eustace and Frank hadn't been as quick to label them monsters, but Sam didn't hesitate from sharing his feelings about it. Even with all the fear, a small part of him wanted to see them himself. To come face to face and study them. To experience being in their presence. To chop off their branches and to litter their bodies with bullet holes, if need be. What happened to Scout had affected Sam in ways he didn't even fully under-stand yet.

Eustace clicked a photo of the stalactites, sending the flash racing down deep into the dark tunnels. He stared at the screen, marveling what would seem just regular stones and rocks to an untrained eye.

"Approaching the one-hour mark. How are the levels?" a voice crackled on the radio.

Eustace checked his gauge. "I'm good. Plenty still in the tank," he replied from inside his suit.

"You guys should make a U-turn and start heading out. The tanks are half done. Time to get back," Barry's voice had a touch of command and request at the same time.

"Yes, soon," Eustace said as he continued putting one foot in front of another.

Ten minutes later, they were still inching their way deeper into the caves.

"Yo- guy- ..." some words went through, and others got lost as Barry tried to maintain communication.

"We should head back now," Sam said.

Eustace looked at Sam and then at the fork ahead of them where the cave split. It appeared similar to the one that Scout had encountered just before he came face to face with the monstrous plants. Eustace glanced at his oxygen gauge and calculated that he had solid 45 minutes, plus the backup tank for maybe another 15-20.

"Ten more minutes. We'll turn around in ten," Eustace spoke into the radio.

Sam stood there, helpless. A huge part of him felt responsible for Eustace's safety. He couldn't afford to think too much about his own and chose to follow the orders. He knew they would *have* to turn back in ten. He began moving towards the right side of the fork.

"This way," Eustace said as he pointed to the left.

Sam paused, then turned left and began walking, Eustace in tow, as fast as the suit allowed him.

"Da-..." Myra's voice screamed from the walkie. Broken but with full intent.

"Myra!" Eustace replied, hoping at least she would be able to hear him clearly.

"Dad, why are yo- down ther-? You promised you wouldn't-"

"I know, I know," he looked at Sam then continued, "I came here for Sam."

Each and every one of those words pierced deep into Sam's conscience. A wave of emotions ran through the circuits of his mechanical body.

"Frank told me you wanted Zeu- to have gone down wit- you," Myra said.

Sam looked away and stared into the darkness ahead. He knew Myra was aware he could hear her words. A feeling of smallness descended upon him. He knew Zeus was bigger, smarter and stronger. Her words only fueled his fire further to prove himself. He started walking, Eustace hung back.

"Pleas- come bac- now."

"We'll turn back soon."

"Just come bac... I lov- you Dad!"

"I love you too!"

Eustace wasn't sure if Myra heard those last words. He squinted as he tried to make sense of the path ahead. Only an occasional crack in the surface brought a rare shaft of light this far down. They were cautious not to use any of theirs to keep the attention minimum whenever they came across forks. The night vision helped Eustace, but he still had to squint. Eustace saw Sam crouched some ten feet ahead of him. "What is it?"

"Shh..." Sam gestured.

Eustace crouched next to him and stared. Sam pointed at a deep, six-inch-wide opening in one of the walls. Eustace focused on it.

A minute passed by as both tried to remain still, eyes still locked onto the hole. Sam gestured to wait a little more. There was a new sense of calm in his demeanor. But Eustace could hardly wait. He wished Sam would just tell him what it is that he had seen. Sam looked back at Eustace and pointed at the opening.

On the night vision, the darkness of the hole turned white as something began inching out. A thick tubular worm-like creature crawled out some, until a few inches of it hung out. Eustace started lifting his camera, but Sam stopped him. Perhaps there was more wisdom in witnessing it with real eyes as opposed to capturing it in images. Sam began recording on the inbuilt storage in his chassis.

The creature remained still for long before it came back to life. One by one its long tentacle-like arms began unfolding from the end that hung out. It ground its purple teeth as all six arms fanned out and revealed its face. A soft squeaking emanated from the creature's mouth. Not too loud, but enough to register on Sam's microphones and Eustace's decade-old ears. At the end of each arm was an intricate network of protrusions and finer tentacles, some pink, some purple. These nimble tentacles danced in whichever direction the creature commanded. Similar to a scorpion, the middle of each of the six arms held an amber-colored sac filled with a liquid that moved as the tentacles danced around and the sound amplified.

Eustace whispered a 'wow.'

Sam wished he could express his excitement, but his nerves had better of him. He leaned over to Eustace and whispered. "We must leave, now!"

Eustace studied his gauge one more time and pursed his lips. He nodded, then lifted his camera once again. Sam motioned him to put the camera down, but Eustace assured him. He moved the camera to within inches of the creature. As he focused on its large center teeth, a sharp voice broke the silence of the cave.

"What is that?" Myra inquired over the radio as she saw fuzzy images that Sam beamed from this far into the cave.

The sudden loud voice startled and knocked Eustace off balance. His forearm came a little too close to one of the tentacles, and before he knew it, the creature pushed a razor-sharp barb through the suit and jabbed his forearm, emptying the sack into Eustace's body.

The pain was instant, and Eustace shook his arm violently.

"We gotta go!" Sam shouted.

Suddenly, the creature began convulsing and making rodent-like sounds as it got excited. Sam looked behind him as he heard another similar sound. Then to his side. He powered up his onboard lights. One by one, the beams illuminated the walls that surrounded them. He noticed the dozens of similar six-inch-wide holes, all possibly occupied by creatures like the one Eustace had annoyed. He put Eustace's good arm over his shoulder and began walking away. They had not even gotten a few steps further when one of the creatures wriggled out of its hole and dropped straight in front of them. The creature lifted its head and stared them square in the eye.

"What do we do?" asked Sam.

"Shoot him!" Eustace yelled as he tried to bear the sharp stinging pain. The sensation clouded his thinking and the only thing he wanted in the moment was to escape, no matter what.

"I can't."

"I know, Sam! I know," Eustace kept staring at the creature. "It's survival." Eustace became edgy and angry. His inner calmness was no longer enough to keep his mind straight. "We're gonna die, Sam. Kill 'em!"

Sam unholstered his gun and removed the safety. He aimed it right at the creature's face, who was busy grinding its teeth just a foot or two away as drops of amber liquid oozed from one of its tentacles.

Sam aimed, then looked away just as he pulled the trigger. The bullet pierced the creature through the mouth and traveled the length of its body in a split second. Each revolution of the high-speed projectile creating new holes and gashes into the creature's armored body. The same amber liquid splashed everywhere as the creature burst into a dozen pieces. Some of the liquid landed on Eustace's suit and some on Sam.

The concoction of innards and the smell of the liquid agitated others. One after another, they began wriggling out of their holes and surrounding the duo. Sam put more of them to rest as he bore new holes into their bodies while still being cautious. He didn't want Eustace to come in touch with the amber liquid. He didn't know what that liquid would do.

With each passing second, Eustace felt more restless. He sensed their vulnerability. His mind raced in high gear. One part of him tried its best to deal with the pain as the other was busy plotting all the things that could go wrong. Drops of the same amber liquid started dripping from the ceiling. Sam didn't pay much attention as he kept his cameras trained at the dozens around him.

Eustace put his foot down on one of the creatures, smashing it to death. Sam punched, kicked, stomped and shot at dozens among the scores that now surrounded them. The ones that escaped their attacks began stinging. Indiscriminate in their choice of target, the creatures tried piercing Sam's metal skeleton, desperately, only to find their tentacles were no match for titanium. Sam's skin-like sensors emulated the stinging sensation as they tried to analyze the composition of the liquid. But they needed more time, something the creatures didn't want to spare them.

"Dad! Sam! What's going on there?" Desperation wreaked out in Myra's voice.

Only one in a dozen words she spoke reached this far into the cave. They had no time to reply, just to try and fight their way out. Sam quickly reloaded as they fought some thirty feet from the fork in the cave where they had turned left.

Sam shot left, and he shot right. Fear and guilt no longer

controlled him. He directed all that happened with him in the past few hours and days towards the worm creature army. The feeling of inferiority, of not being good enough. The responsibility of protecting Eustace, each and every emotion gave his bullets more aim and meaning. He noticed more frequent drops from above. He looked up at the ceiling, and it was as if time had suddenly stopped.

A much bigger worm, six feet wide, was struggling to get out of *its* hole. In a heightened, slowed down state, Sam witnessed the big worm's tentacles unfold. For those few moments, the creatures on the floor didn't matter. He knew he could handle the small ones... but the one above?

A deep, sharp gargle emanated from the ceiling as one of the massive arms descended and pinned Eustace to one of the side walls. Another two arms hit Sam hard and smashed him against the other wall. His cameras cracked and sensors battered, he felt the jolt as the tentacle pushed him with all their might. The ground creatures slowed down. Their tentacles still wriggled as they began dispersing.

Sam tried breaking free but found it impossible. The impact damaged the hydraulics of his right leg. Already the lightweight version, he found it impossible to push off the tentacles that pinned him. The cracked camera lens didn't help, either. He struggled to find his footing as Eustace lay forced against the other wall. Eustace knew it was best to keep calm, even though the stinging pain made him want to scream his lungs out, for once.

The ground creatures could hardly contain the excitement as they watched the big worm descend from its lair. They all stood patiently in some sort of anticipation as if waiting for a reward. The ones in the middle who didn't move out fast enough were crushed to death as the last bit of the big worm dropped from its burrow. Face to face with both Eustace and Sam and all tentacles spread out, the big worm dragged its six-foot-wide jaws towards Eustace. With tentacles the girth of drainage pipes, the big worm could have easily pierced Eustace's fragile body many times over in a single stroke. It chose not to. At least not yet.

Eustace fell to the ground and curled into a ball as the big worm tried to pin him. Fighting and resisting were futile. It was wise to appear small and harmless. If he could play dead maybe the creature would let him go. It took great courage to be that quiet when face to face with the strangest thing he had ever seen in his entire life as an avid nature explorer, while still carrying the stinging pain that grew every second.

The big worm chattered its teeth and snaked towards Eustace. It rotated its face a few degrees to the left and then to the right as it watched the human with as much fascination as the human watched its monstrous face. The big worm's piercing white eyes scrutinized Eustace from every angle. All eight of them. Eustace lifted his head and stared straight into a few of them. No matter how hard he tried to contain, he found it impossible to not be fascinated. Part of him was still fascinated with what was unfolding in front, although he was sure his life would be over in the next few moments as his vision became blurry and the pain stung deep. He started to feel dizzy.

"Dad! Please answer, we can't see anythin-" Myra yelled over the radio.

The strange words both startled and agitated the big worm. It charged in. Suddenly, a loud *boom* echoed in the tunnel. The bullet tore off a huge chunk of flesh from the big worm's side that faced Sam. The worm cocked its massive head back as it felt the pain. Then, it lunged towards Sam.

Sam knew. He held the gun up and fired round after round after round as the big worm closed in. All tentacles spread out, facing forward, each one impatient to grab.

Sam fired his last bullet that grazed past the worm's

mouth. The tentacles snapped in at lightning speed. Needles an inch wide pierced through Sam's metal armor and the circuits inside. The big worm dug its two massive teeth into Sam's body. One pinned the torso and other the upper thigh. One after another, all of the tentacles wrapped around the robot and with one forceful twist of the jaw, the worm split Sam's body in two. Cables and bolts struggled to keep his frame intact as the worm mauled and chewed the metal skeleton.

As the tentacles pulled, they tore off different parts. Some grabbed the head as others the legs and arms, each playing with some section that had kept Sam intact.

The big worm continued mauling the body into smaller and smaller pieces, Sam's face still recording the audio and video – whatever he was able to see or hear. Broken images and sounds were being stored somewhere deep in his memory as he was being eaten alive.

TEAM

"Dad... Dad!" Myra kept screaming into the walkie. Every time she pressed the talk switch, the tip of her finger turned white. There was no use looking at the screen. The video signal had been gone for a long time now. Only static and broken pieces of audio managed to still pass through. *Dad, please say something!* Even a single word would have been a huge sigh of relief.

At her side, Barry kept himself busy, fingers flying over his laptop keyboard. "Video non-responsive. Audio down. Touch sensors and vitals all non-responsive. Sam!" He ran his hand through his hair and then looked at Myra.

"We need to abort the mission. Get the hell outta here," Frank said.

"What? No! We're going down and bringing them back," the words left Myra's mouth with such spontaneity as if she had planned them.

"We can't. Scout, Sam and now... Eustace, all gone. We don't know what we are dealing with here. Who knows what's out there. There were so many I couldn't even count," Frank said.

"It doesn't matter. We're getting them outta there. We just need to hurry," Myra said.

"There's no point in hurrying," Frank paused then continued. "They are gone... Dead."

"Yes... Sam is!" A tear rolled down Myra's cheek as some of the audio from minutes ago replayed in her mind. "We need to save Dad!"

"I'm not sure if Sam is gone entirely. Facial power's still active," Barry said without looking away from his screen.

"What good is that gonna do us?" Frank said.

"Well, it can help locate him... Maybe," Barry said.

"Guys, we need to bring both of 'em back. Even if we have to send all of the bots," Myra told Frank.

"No! We are not sending any more bots down there. This is beyond us now. We need to get help and let the government handle this."

"No! We can't wait. Don't you understand?! They need our help, and they need it right now!" Myra explained.

"Nobody needs *your* help. You already helped us plenty when you decided to do some sightseeing with your buddy," Frank said pointing at Zeus.

It suddenly hit Myra. *This happened because of* me? *Maybe if Zeus had gone with Dad, this wouldn't have happened.* She also knew if she had been present, she wouldn't have allowed her father to go, no matter what. Myra found it hard to recover from the sudden slap of guilt. She stood there, silent.

Frank started moving away from the monitor, "We're heading back to basecamp."

"Wait!" Myra spoke to everyone. The team had already started moving. For some reason, they concurred with Frank and felt that perhaps Myra was to blame to an extent for the events. A wave of confusion hovered over in the team. With no strong direction, most gravitated towards whoever appeared to be the strongest and surest. The crew agreed that it was dangerous for them to go down there and investigate any further. Being so remote from support limited their ability to take any unnecessary risks. Frank's proposal sounded much safer and logical.

Myra walked over to Frank. "What are you doing? We have to get them back!"

"I'm doing what's best for everyone. Nobody is going to risk their life after what we just saw."

"X-corp owns all of the bots. You can't just take them with you."

"I own a quarter of X-corp, that makes me in charge now, and, I'm not forcing them, they themselves don't wanna go. They wouldn't wanna lose their lives. Especially on *your* command. Sam died because of *you*."

His words hit Myra once again. *He's right. Poor Sam. He shouldn't have had to die. If only Zeus had gone down with Dad.* Suddenly, she recalled Sam's face. His always-happy child-like demeanor and playfulness. Over the years, they had developed a special relationship that may not have had a title, but she knew what it meant for her.

Myra felt helpless. The strong desire to search for her father was still there, but she felt the water passing under the bridge fast. *I dunno what to do.* The bots seemed to be listening to Frank. She knew Artemis and Tori already were not on her side. As far as Mimi was concerned, Myra felt it justified if she also leaned towards Frank. She didn't want Mimi to feel compelled to risk her life.

Myra noticed her hand shaking as her feelings began manifesting into her body. She looked up at Zeus walking towards her.

"I'm staying with you."

A big smile appeared on Myra's face and contrasted the slow tears that had started to roll down her cheeks. "Thank you," she whispered.

Zeus nodded and turned towards Frank, "I'm staying here with Myra."

Frank shook his head, turned around. "I'm gonna start mobilizing the team. We'll evacuate Chisil. It's only a matter of time before those worms come hunting for us."

"I'm staying!" Myra said.

Frank knew he was finished convincing her. A part of him was happy that they decided to stay back. He never really liked Myra or Zeus that much. Every time there was a breakthrough at X-corp, a new leap in robotic emulation of emotions or learning, it seemed Eustace had always found a way to somehow divert the credit to Myra and saw Zeus as the leader among the bots. This was not something Frank wanted. He longed for the day when Artemis would be developed further as the apex X-corp machine.

"I'm staying, too," Barry said as he closed his laptop and walked towards Myra and Zeus. Myra knew he would support her and would never abandon Eustace.

"You will all die out here," Frank said as he turned around. His intention was not to scare the three but to tell them the truth. As a self-elected leader, he felt he could do anything. It didn't matter what happened in the future. In that moment, on Chisil, he felt the gravity of all the power in the world, the feeling one gets when holding a loaded gun.

Frank, Hunter, Artemis and Tori entered the AUV as Mimi stood by the door. She paused for a few moments then got in, eventually.

Frank turned the vehicle around and rolled down the window from the driver's side. He looked at Myra, Zeus and Barry standing in the distance, then spoke to the bots in the AUV. "Time to go, boys and girls." He rolled the window back up and thrust the AUV forward. Each bump and turn took them further away from Myra and *her* team.

18

SHRUNK

E ustace felt groggy. As the moments passed by, he slowly began coming back to his senses. The sharp pain had changed its nature. It was now only a lingering sensation, but still enough to keep drawing his attention.

He could hear the water dripping in some distance, each drop hitting the hardened cave floor and trying its best to leave its mark. A few different openings snaked around the large open area he found himself in. If one were to decide which direction to walk out from, there was nothing special that would hint at a favorable choice.

Eustace's eyes widened as he stared at his left arm. There was just enough indirect light in the area so he could make out what he was looking at. His breathing escalated as shock gripped his mind. It was difficult for him to comprehend. Instinct guided him not to express himself vocally. He caressed the affected arm with the other.

There was no sensation. It was as if he was touching a big, long-dead, calloused part of his body. The affected arm looked smaller. Was it just an illusion or lack of visibility? He couldn't be sure but felt it to have shrunk. From below the elbow all the way to the hand, the arm appeared thinner. Much feeble than before. A fine layer of a semi-solid exoskeleton, similar to one of beetles and cockroaches, seemed to have wrapped the affected arm.

Eustace sat for what seemed like an eternity, his back against the cave wall. He remained consumed in his thoughts. The pain was intermittent, but it didn't matter now. He noticed there was no sensation in the shrunken part. It was as good as dead. No movement in the fingers or the wrist. The best he could do was bend the forearm up and down from the elbow, although even that, was painful. He wondered if he would regain any movement eventually. Perhaps once the poison was cleared from his system.

He struggled to breathe. He took out a knife and began cutting the suit. He didn't want to be in it anymore, it had failed to protect him. With each slash, the sound bounced off the walls and echoed through the deep chambers of the cave system. He wondered how he got where he was and if the big worm was still around.

The absence of any gaping holes in the nearby walls helped calm him a bit.

As he cut the last sections of the suit, he caught some movement in his peripheral vision. His eyes peeled and his breathing escalated. He couldn't afford to miss any details. He got up as quietly as he could. Knife in hand, arms in an aggressive stance. Ready to put up a fight, even though he knew it would be his last. It surprised him that he was still alive. He looked around and saw a few human body parts. A severed hand, a leg, and two heads. The sight almost made him puke while adding to his nervousness at the same time. Not that he hadn't seen dead bodies before, both human and animal, but the poison and the situation amplified those emotions. He wondered whose body parts they were and what were they doing there.

A clicking sound drew his attention. He looked around, trying to locate the source as moments passed by. The sound emanated again. He squinted hard as he scanned the area. Straight ahead, in one of the dark paths, he could barely make out the faint glow of flickering lights. Intermittent but visible to hungry eyes. The glow flickered and synced with the pattern of the sound. He maintained a low profile, sticking close to the wall, but there weren't that many places to hide in the chamber he found himself in.

The wait tested his patience to its limits. Each moment felt longer than an eon. His mind had numbed itself from the pain as he focused solely in the direction of the glow. He remembered that he had a small flashlight with him. He pointed it at where the radiance was coming from. The clicking frequency increased, and the glow intensified.

"Come out!"

His demand was met with more clicking sounds. He picked up a small stone and threw it in the direction of the glow. What he saw next shocked him more than his shrunken arm had. The stone hovered some three feet above the ground, rotating, and silhouetted by the same glow. *What the...* Then, suddenly, it dropped to the ground. Eustace stood in silence, taking in everything that was unfolding in front of his eyes.

He pointed the flashlight to the edge of the corner quickly as he saw some movement. Four long tentacles, similar to those of an octopus but without the suction cups, wrapped around the rock. He raised his knife, adrenaline pumping through his veins.

The tentacles gripped the corner and pulled the rest of the body into Eustace's flashlight. His eyes widened once again, this time even more. He didn't care about the knife or any defensive stance anymore. He just stood there, struck with pure awe. *Impossible!*

The quadruped creature was approximately three feet tall. Its long slender legs extended out from an equally long bony body. The skin resembled the shell of an armored insect such as a beetle. The long neck snaked upwards and at the end sat a peculiar face as the mouth remained hidden behind tentacles. A set of large turquoise eyes embedded comfortably – not too far – above the tentacles.

Eustace made eye contact. The two communicated in silence. Just like an impatient artist, he frantically studied every inch of the exotic body. He just couldn't take his eyes off the creature's head – a big transparent dome lined with pigmented cells, changing colors with the frequency of alternating current. Inside the dome was also a network of vein-like threads that helped in amplifying and projecting the cosmic glow he saw earlier.

The creature maintained its distance. The only parts that seemed to be communicating something were the dancing tentacles and the glow in the dome that changed colors, continually. Eustace didn't feel threatened. On the contrary, he felt a sense of calm and peace as if studying a masterful painting. He found himself being lost in the feeling of cherishing what was in front of him, his own pain and condition completely pushed to the back burner... at least for now.

19

A RUSTLE

With each turn it took, the wind unloaded its chill all over Barry. It was indiscriminate towards who stood in its path. Each stroke sent tiny shivers up his spine. He wasn't dressed for this, certainly not enough to be out in the night, facing the elements head-on. But then again, he hadn't expected he would find himself in this situation.

Every new step he took felt like a struggle against the ash-coated grass beneath him. He looked back. The glow in the distant cabin kept it easily visible amid the fog that had started to grow. He realized how far he had come. The lone walk helped grant him time to process everything that had happened a few hours ago. He wondered what Myra and Zeus were doing.

To his one side was Shadow Lake, the bright moon glinting against its surface. Every now and then some sound would try to draw his attention. Each time, he let it go. The movement of branches and grass served as a peaceful melody for his journey.

Some ten feet later, he picked a spot. Something about the location suited him. It was the right distance from all the discussion in the cabin that he had been part of ever since they separated a few hours ago. He had decided to walk a little extra to take a break from Zeus and Myra's voices for a few minutes.

A small patch of grass stood aloof, separated from the rest, encircled by dry mud and soil. Barry spread his legs and undid his fly and looked up at the moon. It was barely more than half-full, bright as the highest creation of a painter. The clouds around it, the mountains, and the sound of the wind completed the serene image of nightfall. He felt as if he was in a dream, albeit for only a few moments. If a part of him cherished the moment, another remained vigilant like a sentry.

He waited some more. And then some more. More than taking a piss, he just wanted out of the cabin. He zipped his fly back up and just stared at the moon. Having been huddled in an office, cramped spaces, always staring at a screen, he realized how much of the natural world he must have missed over the years. For a moment he wondered if he had paid a heavy price for his chosen profession. It was hard for him to not feel that way. The mystic nature of the moonlit landscape tried hard to stir the artist in his technical left-brained mind.

A distant call tried to draw his attention. He scanned the horizon. The blanket of fog was still thin, and the glow from the moon provided an almost infinite view of the land. When he heard the same call again, he squinted at the small hill some ten yards away. *What's there?*

He ducked as he hid behind the hill in front of him. The moaning had grown since he last heard it. The grass cover hid whatever was the source. It was a struggle to see it without revealing himself. Suddenly, a small animal emerged from the grass and into the open. *Is that a... bobcat?* He knew the Relocation Initiative had populated the region with several animals but wasn't sure if bobcats made the cut. As the animal came closer, Barry identified it as some species of wildcat, *possibly* a bobcat.

The baby was small. Barry looked around for its mother. A depression in the grass near the baby hinted something. With each passing moment, the soft deafening screams of the bobcat baby entered his ears, just like the staccato beats of a piano, only laced with fear and desperation. Barry stepped closer, but some movement to his right stopped him, immediately. The grass rustled. He pulled back instinctively behind the safety of the small hill.

Whatever it was that rustled the grass did so erratically. Something was moving in all directions, searching for something. The bobcat kitten fell silent, the movement had triggered its natural instinct. Was it just a sitting duck? The grass rustled more until the thing that caused the stir came closer to the depression in the grass that Barry had noticed a few minutes earlier. Suddenly, the creature emerged from the grass and exposed itself – a wild thing that Barry had never seen or ever imagined before. If there were any words he would have chosen, he would have described it as a giant, strange lizard. Or some version of it. A long slender body with four short legs just like a lizard, but with floating strings for a mouth. It was as if nature had made a cross between a lizard and a jellyfish. While Barry absorbed the sight, the creature wrapped its strings around the dead body that lay in the depression in the grass and dragged it away with full force.

The bobcat baby sat quiet and still, watching its dead mother being dragged by something that was beyond comprehension. The creature went away as fast as it came. Moments later, there was no sign of it, only the trail in the grass where the body had been dragged.

Barry sat there just like the bobcat baby. Quiet and still.

Soon after, the baby began moving around, searching

again. One after another, the desperate cries echoed and called for its mother.

A new sharp movement rustled the grass, even faster than the one a few minutes earlier. The creature returned and lunged at the baby, silencing its calls.

Barry just stood and watched in shock as once again, the land returned to the same silent state it was when he had stepped out of the safety of their small wood cabin.

20

MYRA

M yra set her radio down next to the terrarium. The frog bobbed and hopped inside. She dropped a few crickets from the feeding hatch, which he didn't seem to notice. She turned around towards Zeus who was busy putting some wood into the stove. The promise of incoming heat had already started lifted Myra's spirit. The rising fire made the cabin cozy while the gas lamp that she had lit a few hours earlier provided the light.

"What do you think attacked them?" she asked as she came around and knelt next to Zeus.

"I don't know."

Myra had tried hard not to spill her emotions in front of Zeus or Barry. She knew she had to be strong on the outside. Ever since Eustace's last words over the radio, Myra only had a single thought on her mind; how to get her father back. She was sure he was still alive. He *had* to be. There was a naive confidence in her belief. All her life she had seen her father move mountains in pursuit of his ambitions. It was only natural for her to believe in the safety of her strong father.

She also knew the gravity of her situation and their

limited options. No supplies, no weapons, nothing. They couldn't just walk into a slaughter. If that strategy had even a remote guarantee of bringing Eustace back, she would have done it in a heartbeat. But as the night stretched longer, she began realizing a full charge without any planning would only further her separation from her father.

She stared at the frog as he bumped against the terrarium wall. It gave her something to focus on as she processed her thoughts. The frog was relentless. Each time he would try to jump he would slip down. *You are so strong. You have no concept of failure. Only effort...* Every now and then, the frog stopped, as if taking a small break, and then continued. Myra walked over and just stared at him from up close. Watching him struggle dragged a memory out from deep within her.

Myra left the sand behind and steered the white Toyota 4x4 onto the pitch-black road. The headlights illuminated the path ahead fifty-foot at a time as the rest of the Mojave Desert remained plunged in total darkness.

Eustace had fallen asleep in the passenger seat. As the excursion had come to an end and with the adrenaline wearing off, Eustace's body demanded what it needed so badly. Myra felt tired herself but decided to continue marching on. For now, it was just her and the open road ahead flanked by the Mojave on either side, a prime opportunity for letting the mind wander. And wander it did. With her eyes fixed on the road and the mind free, she wondered about the day now behind them as the night chill cooled the landscape. The animals they had encountered. The plants they had studied. From desert tortoise to lizards, birds of prey to cacti with flowers as bright and vivid as an impressionistic painting, each memory was still a beautiful new song.

Before she had had the time to react, it was already upon them. In an instant, she found herself steering the 4x4 hard left, going off the road and stopping abruptly when the tires skidded over loose sand and the front sunk into a small ditch. The airbag popped and yanked Eustace out from his slumber.

"Myra!"

She just sat there, in shock. She turned back and looked through the rear window but didn't see much.

Eustace turned and looked back. "What happened?"

Myra rushed out the car and treaded back carefully where the vehicle had just been. Once outside, Eustace knew. He jogged towards the spot.

As Myra approached a crouching Eustace, she had a chance to see what was in front of them. Tears started rolling down her cheeks.

"It was an accident, Myra."

She stood there with watery eyes, still staring. Eustace got up and rubbed his hand on her shoulder then walked towards the car. Myra felt alone, standing under the moonless night staring at what she had done, all of her thoughts tainted with guilt.

The shovel that Eustace raised in front of her interrupted the thought loop. She turned towards her father. He nodded and extended the shovel.

"No, I can't," Myra sobbed.

"I know you can't, but you must."

She just stood there, eyes on the road.

"You can't run from your fears forever, Myra. You're gonna have to go up close and face them."

"You do it, please!"

"No, I can't. It's yours to do. I won't always be around... You'll have to do it someday."

She wished her father hadn't said that. The words of him being gone added salt to her wound. She took one big breath, grabbed the shovel and took a few steps forward. As she got closer, she smelled the blood and innards that spread over a couple of feet on the concrete. She wanted to cover her nose but decided not to. Whatever it was in front of her, she tried to face it head-on. She crouched and lowered the shovel. It was then that her hand started shaking. She stared into the open, lifeless eyes. And the eyes stared back at her. Questioning. Myra couldn't control her emotions. Tears started spilling. Something so beautiful, young, healthy and agile, gone like this in a flash. The thought paralyzed her hands.

"Dad, can you please do it?"

Eustace shook his head.

"Please!"

"You don't wanna leave him in the middle of the road, do you? You can do it!"

"I can't. I just can't."

"Yes, you can. Believe in yourself, Myra! I believe in you!"

She looked up at her father.

"Yes, my sweet little darling baby, I do."

Myra took a deep breath and slid the shovel under the still-warm body. For a second she feared it would start moving. As the shovel went deeper, it lifted the body up. Suddenly, she pulled back.

"Aaaahhhhh!"

She waited. It's just a feeling... you can do it, Myra, she thought. She moved the shovel again and gently lifted the body with it. As she got up, strands of innards hung from the shovel's edge. You can do it, Myra, you can do it. She repeated to herself and continued walking to the side.

Once off the road, she gently put the body down behind one of the bushes that lined either side. She stood up and once again stared into the lifeless but still beautiful eyes of the hare *that lay in front of her, in silence.*

"Always remember him, Myra... you are in his debt, and you must always pay back your debts in life," said Eustace from a distance. Each word penetrated deep into Myra's conscience.

The nature of the sound changed and filled the cabin. The

frog's body slapping against the terrarium wall began sounding like a long hiss. A brief pause later, there was another. Myra's gaze deepened as a third static drew her attention to something else on the shelf. It wasn't the frog. Her frown relaxed, and with the agility of a cheetah, she lunged forward and grabbed the radio, almost knocking down the terrarium in the process.

"Dad!... Dad!" desperation and excitement wreaked out from her voice. Was the static from Eustace's radio?

Zeus walked over.

Myra pressed the talk switch harder. "Dad... Are you OK?"

"Did you hear him?"

She shook her head and clutched the radio even harder. The wait and silence were deafening. As the moments stretched on forever, her eyes began watering. She held the tears back before they had a chance to escape. She stared at the radio for some more time. The bobbing frog failing to divert her attention now. She looked up at Zeus and took a deep breath in. "I'm gonna bring him back, no matter what," she spoke after a pause.

Zeus just stood there. Even his ultra-fast processors struggled to come up with an appropriate response at that moment. It wasn't that he didn't want to bring Eustace back. He just knew it was not a simple task, if not outright impossible. Not in their current circumstance. Extreme emotions hadn't taxed his circuits like they did Myra's. He took into account the bigger picture. The reality of making it out of Chisil on their own should Frank decided to actually leave them behind. Those things were always on his mind.

"I'm bringing him back. With you and Barry, or alone!"

Zeus just nodded.

Myra began searching the cabin. She grabbed her bowgun that leaned against the wall and immediately felt its weight. It infused her with a feeling of intense power. Something inside her woke up as she studied the weapon. Then, an idea entered her mind. She turned towards Zeus. "Are you with me?"

Zeus took his time. He already knew what he was going to say. It was pointless for her to even ask that question. He nodded a *yes*.

Suddenly, the cabin door flung open, and the sound of Barry's aching lungs entered before him. He stood at the entrance staring at Zeus and Myra. He then noticed Myra's firm grip on the bowgun in her hands.

21

CARCASSES

The absence of light wasn't a problem. The creatures were masters at adapting. The darkness of the night was even darker inside the caves. A large opening allowed the moon spill several feet in. As the amber ball rose higher, even that glow began to recede.

His shadow hugged the now frequented trail, shrinking in size as he approached the opening. The lizard-like creature that Barry had encountered rushed in towards his destination, the bobcat mother and baby carcasses, clutched within his facial tentacles. There was a sense of purpose. A sense of direction. He continued deeper, navigating each turn with confidence.

Every few minutes, the creature adjusted the position of the carcasses and used the opportunity to take a break. The bodies were large for him to handle, but something drove him. They had to be delivered. It was *expected* of him. With great strain, he carried on into the deeper chambers which were infested with the alien plant growth all along the walls. The plants soaked up every molecule of the stench of decay as the creature ventured deeper. As the aroma passed, it excited the barbed vine extensions, and they started bending in the direction of the odor.

In this part of the cave, the reptilian-like creature didn't need any directions. The steady increase in the plant network and the familiar stench that was common in this part let him know he was headed in the right direction. The stink kept getting stronger as the creature moved further in, much stronger than the odor of the carcasses his strings held. It was hard for the vines to contain their excitement. The ones closer to the ground wriggled faster.

The creature stood still in front of a pitch-black path in the cave. It was too dark even for him to use sight, but his sonar sense drew a clear picture of what was ahead. He continued standing still, observing. As the branches snaked in, they weaved their way through a pile of bones littered on the floor. Some small, some big, others half-consumed – a variety scattered all over the ground. It was as if the unsavory parts were left for last. The creature stared straight ahead into the distance, still trying to map an aural picture of what was ahead. His sonar kicking in high gear. A variety of sharp staccato sounds entered his sensitive ears. Crushing, biting, dissolving, a melody of indiscernible sounds. He knew it was time. He removed the hold of his strings and dropped the carcasses on the ground. They made a *thump* as they fell on some of the bones.

The lizard creature stood there as he observed the barbed vines rushing and engulfing the carcasses one by one, an arms race for each to grab as much as possible, to jab the bodies with as many barbs as they could. Each stab injected a small dose of the hot liquid into the dead animals' bodies.

The lizard creature wondered if someday he too would meet the same fate.

As the liquid entered the body, it began moving. Pops and clicks were heard as the joints unfroze and started to loosen up. It acted fast. The dead animals began dissolving from the inside. Each passing minute aided in breaking down the tissues, muscles, tendons and anything around them. It all unfolded live in front of the lizard creature. It wasn't the first time he had witnessed it, but for some reason this time he chose to extend his stay a little longer.

Before long, in front of his, the branches began dragging the bodies towards the dark end of the cave. Inch by inch, they slipped into the darkness until nothing was left to be seen. The lizard creature turned around and started to head back. It was over. He knew he had to continue doing this. There was no rest. No breaks.

With the same urgency in his stride, he tracked his way out of the cave and stepped into the cool of the moon at the entrance. He looked around as if sensing the lay of the land once again, and scanned it for any movement. He wasn't sure which direction to head in, but he was sure he *had* to go. He knew his survival depended on it.

He chose a random direction and started on his way.

22

SEQUENCE

The carcasses had made their way through the plant system, as with each passing minute, the chemicals broke every piece down to its very essence. Each part was eventually reduced to its building blocks. The system had absorbed the elements with remarkable efficiency with minimum wastage. What was not usable was ejected out by one of the several openings in the extensive plant network. Even the discards weren't made to go to waste. Another much smaller plant system worked diligently to grab nutrients out of the rejects. Guessing the extent of the plant network was difficult. At one end, it started from where the lizard creature had dropped the carcasses, and at the other, it reached as far as where Scout spent his last moments. Between the two ends were a lot of caves and in those tunnels, a vast, intricate network of the predatory plants.

Somewhere in the middle and in another deep chamber, there were things that were *more* than plants. The branches of the plants clutched the walls even here, just as they did in the other parts. Somewhere along the network, a plant-bulb like lump, the size of a refrigerator, rested on the floor. Several branches extended from its tall, oval shape. At its center was a long opening with ridges. Although the branches and the outer area of the lump were made of hard bark like trees, the center opening was made of soft organic materials, a stark contrast to the rest of its solid structure. There were several such lumps distributed across the chamber.

A few feet from the lump, two soldiers kept themselves busy tending to a large body that lay on a makeshift resting podium made of rough black clay-like organic material. The clay bed may not have looked like much, but the body that lay in a deep sleep must have felt it to be comfortable. The soldiers kept circling the body. Every now and then one of them would go towards the head and gaze into the body's transparent dome just above the skull. The soldiers themselves had portions of their skulls transparent, each emanating a bright flickering glow. The glow from their domes cast colorful hues in various corners of the large area they were in.

The body may have been asleep, but laying on the clay bed, it emanated power. A quadruped and the bigger version of the friendly creature Eustace had encountered, it still commanded respect.

The soldier creatures, although identical in anatomy, differed in appearance. Green pigmented cells lined the body of the one smaller in size. The spine, outer portion of the limbs, and even denser formations around the face were all covered in green. The second soldier had similar markings except in bright red. They differed not just in appearance, but personalities too. The green soldier paced around cautiously, thinking through every move, while the red thrashed around, at will.

The red soldier strode on his quadruped frame and moved an arm over the resting body. He exposed a barb that extended out, just like a retractable feline claw. The barb was sharp and needle-like but firm. He hovered it several inches below the long neck of the resting body. He waited a moment, looked up at the green soldier, then pushed it into the rigid exoskeleton of the body. The red soldier retracted the barb immediately and took a step back. The green soldier also pulled back, instinctively. They both waited as the body lay there, still motionless.

A sound drew the soldiers' attention. They saw a familiar glow coming from a passageway at the far end of the open area. A moment later, a familiar face that was similar to theirs greeted them. Then, the soldiers noticed someone very alien to them: Eustace.

They stood taller and revealed their full size. Standing on their hind legs, they were towering and menacing. The red soldier moved closer and stared square into Eustace's eyes. Eustace just stood still, in disbelief. For him, it seemed that the mission was already a success. After all, he *did* manage to find new creatures in the cave system, just not the Earthlings he was after.

The red soldier produced a series of sharp clicking sounds. It was as if he was using ultrasound waves to read through the human. Then, without any notice, the soldier lunged towards Eustace. The creature who had accompanied Eustace blocked the red soldier's charge and saved him from being jabbed by the sharp venom-laced barbs at the red soldier's disposal. The red soldier stared at the creature with Eustace and emitted sharp clicks as it cocked its face higher. His mouth widened, teeth exposed as he expressed his dissatisfaction.

Eustace realized that although he enjoyed the view, it was only time before he would meet his fate in this foreign company. In that moment, he would have given anything to be able to understand what these creatures were conversing about.

The creature next to Eustace managed to calm the red soldier down. The soldier no longer inflated his body or projected his size and gradually slowed down. Eustace loved being in the presence of the creature who had brought him to this area – only a few feet tall, but playful and friendly. Full of energy and life, just like a human child. For Eustace, that creature was the alien child.

As the tension dissipated, Eustace noticed the massive body that lay dormant on the black clay bed. How the green soldier guarded it let Eustace know its status. Perhaps it was someone higher up in the hierarchy. He wanted to go closer and inspect, but he hesitated. He knew any wrong move would be his last.

The alien child moved towards the podium, followed by the red soldier. Once there was some distance, Eustace joined them as well, as quietly as his excitement would have allowed him. The glow from the alien child's dome scattered in all directions, tainting the dull cave walls in dazzling hues as he studied the resting body.

A series of clicks emanated from cavities around the child's mouth, increasing in intensity as seconds passed. Even his glow brightened and flickered. Then suddenly, everything began slowing down. The colors lost their passion, and things went dull.

The soldiers continued staring at Eustace.

He could almost hear the faint clicks coming in his direction. The foreign sounds that emanated from the soldiers' bodies sent chills down Eustace's spine.

23

BASECAMP

The moon continued climbing higher, spilling its light on the basecamp beneath. The holographic projections the team had deployed to mask their operations had been turned off. Frank had decided it wasn't needed anymore. The two engineers were deep asleep in the foldout beds located inside the *Whale*. Although they were loyal to Eustace and X-corp, their immediate task was to make sure the *Whale* was in top condition. After the day's events, they figured the best they could do was to get some sleep for their flight out the next morning.

The occasional cloud cover had allowed enough sun throughout the day to charge the battery banks for powering things like the pumps for portable showers, which nobody cared about. The thought that prevailed at the camp was to abandon Chisil at first light. The batteries still held enough juice to power through the night.

Behind the northern mountain of the basecamp channel, the RUV struggled to navigate the terrain. It was running on its last fumes. Its hybrid engine either needed more fuel or a strong charge. The three passengers of the RUV had none. They had turned the headlights off both to conserve juice and to avoid detection.

Back at basecamp, Mimi faced the open path of the valley as she sat on one of the folding chairs bolted in the inner of the *Whale*. Despite her continuous attempts, she seemed unable to shake out the feeling of how the day had made her feel. Sam's death and Eustace's disappearance still consumed her mind. The cold air struck against her sensors as the night critters sang. She looked up when a large shadow came into her view.

Tori was almost silhouetted by the soft glow of the moon behind her. "You better juice up."

All the bots at basecamp had already recharged their batteries. It was a good time to do so. Their next destination was unpredictable, and they didn't know how long the battery banks would last in case they had to recharge the *Whale* consistently after short flights. The chopper had a maximum upper range of 200 miles on a full charge. Attu, the nearest island was 175 miles east. They would be pushing the limits of the batteries. With no midair refueling option, their plan consisted of letting the *Whale* use hybrid power and as soon as the cells dipped to the 75% mark, to burn fuel and make the engines recharge the batteries. Only if the combination of fuel and batteries allowed them to reach the next island, would they figure out their next step.

Tori knew Mimi's charging would not take as much juice but nonetheless, it would have been wise for her to be ready. She moved in towards the AUV that stood chained to the *Whale's* floor.

Mimi just sat at the rear hatch, still engrossed in some thoughts.

. . .

Past the northern mountain, Myra, Zeus and Barry shook back and forth as the RUV finally ran out of power. Zeus sat in the driver seat, trying to restart the machine, but it had already given up on them. He looked over at Myra in the passenger's seat and then Barry in the rear. The rifle in Barry's hands was already looking like a mistake. Even Barry believed he wasn't the one who would shoot anybody, for any reason, ever. A computer in his hands was more potent than a high-powered rifle.

Tori checked on the two engineers snoring inside the *Whale*. She came back out and sat next to Mimi. "Still thinking?"

Mimi nodded.

"Look, what happened was terrible. We all are sad about it, but we can't do anything. If it was not for Myra, maybe Eustace could have been saved... And Sam!"

Sam's name sent a violent wave of emotion through Mimi's circuits. She had been thinking about him more than Eustace and just hearing his name from someone else reminded her how much she was going to miss him. She looked up. "And their bodies?"

"There is no way to retrieve them. I know it's going to be difficult, but you should forget about them."

No matter how much Tori tried to console her, Mimi could sense something was off about her words. But she also knew what she was hearing was probably right. She couldn't imagine Frank taking the team back to retrieve the bodies and risking more lives.

"I'm also thinking about Myra, Zeus, and Barry."

"Forget about them. If it weren't for *Myra*, we would all *still* be together. Eustace and Sam would have returned unharmed and be eating dinner." Tori put a hand on Mimi's shoulder. "We have very short lives. Seven years are not long. You should just live your life and not worry too much about others. Yes, we lost them, but they had their own destiny. You can't waste your life worrying about others. Your hours are precious. I'm sure Frank has a plan to get us all out of here. We'll be back home, soon. I'm sure they will create more of us. You'll have new friends. Don't look back – you have to move forward, and this is the only way now. Myra and her friends... they chose to stay behind."

Mimi maintained her silence. She was at a loss for words as moments passed by.

"Make sure to charge up before we fly out." Tori got up and headed out the rear hatch.

Mimi watched her leave, but her own thoughts refused to leave her mind.

The trio sat behind the mountain just at the north edge of the basecamp valley. Myra adjusted the strap of her bowgun on her shoulder and peeked around the corner. She clearly saw the *Whale* in the distance as moonlight reflected off its military green paint. A few areas around it were lit. She noticed, in particular, the intense glow some 50 feet away. Behind her, Zeus adjusted the rifle that was slung over his shoulder and peeked around the corner. His night vision capabilities and zoom presented them with the details they needed.

Myra began explaining. "We definitely need food packets, water filters and we *must* get our hands on one of the battery banks and the solar strip-" She stopped abruptly as the ground under her rattled. They stared at each other. "Did you guys feel that?"

Zeus didn't, Barry nodded. It was a low rumble. Just enough to make her notice. Her hyper-alert state made her more perceptive to any signals around her.

Zeus reported seeing Tori walking towards the big glow

that Myra had noticed a minute ago near the nose of the *Whale*.

A bright glow emanated from the modest tent as soft wind rattled its fabric. Frank and Hunter occupied the two folding chairs, continuing their discussion. Outside the tent, Artemis noticed Tori walking towards him. She ran her finger over his face and whispered something. They both left the area. Frank and Hunter didn't seem to notice.

A sound drew Mimi's attention. She scanned the horizon in front of her. Moments later another stone rolled down the hill and caught her attention. She got up and walked to the edge of the rear hatch and looked around. Her gaze froze at the sight of a faint glow of Zeus's metal body peeking from behind the hill at the far end of the channel. She looked around, then started walking towards him.

Frank took a quick sip of his chamomile tea and set it back down on the small equipment case in front of him. He stepped out of the tent, angled the antenna of his sat phone towards the sky and tried the number once again. Hunter watched as Frank waited for the other end to pick up. A few seconds later he got the same message he had been getting for hours: "Please check the number you have dialed. Goodbye."

"Damn it, Emerson!" Frank yelled as he threw the phone. It hit the equipment case, almost knocking the tea over.

"Told ya, we can't trust nobody. He isn't coming to get us. Good idea... poor planning," Hunter said as he picked up his steel wallet from the top of the equipment case and shoved it back in his pocket. He didn't want Frank's anger to befall on it.

Frank just stared at the ground, breathing fast, hands on his waist.

"Good old Captain Emerson, probably on course to Thailand raining *your* money on hookers." Hunter never missed an opportunity to rub salt on fresh wounds. "Again, you sure you have the right number?"

Frank didn't respond. He came back and sat in his chair. He kept thinking about Captain Emerson and what went wrong. The reality of having the wrong number hit him. If the digits were indeed wrong, that would change the whole game. This was the last problem he had expected.

A low rumble in the ground drew his attention. He looked at his teacup then at Hunter, who was just as clueless.

"But Frank told us it was because of *you* that Eustace didn't come back," Mimi said to Myra with some hesitation.

"You really think I would let Dad go? If I had known..."

It suddenly dawned on Mimi. It was so simple, but somehow she managed to not think it through and had taken Frank's words for it.

"He doesn't wanna help me bring them back. He would rather leave us here, dying than help. Ten hours ago, he was under my father's command. If my Dad said sit, he would sit. If he told him to stand, he would stand. And now... he just wants everything." Myra expressed her frustration for the first time. She had spent all her energy thinking about what to do next to help her father. She had decided she would deal with Frank later. Bringing her father back was her priority number one.

There was an awkward silence as the four of them sat in

a corner near the mountain. Nobody knew what to say. Nobody seemed to be in a rush to speak.

"I don't like Frank. I want to be with you guys," Mimi said.

Myra looked at her then smiled.

Mimi strode down the valley towards the rear of the *Whale*. She was careful not to draw attention and flaunt the large cloth bag that Myra had given her, which the trio had found in one of the compartments in the RUV. Mimi knew she was inside as soon as she heard the snoring concert of the sleeping engineers. She quietly walked over to the pallet that was densely packed with Ready to Eat meals and started shoving them in the bag. The noise didn't seem to bother the engineers. Mimi picked up some fire-starting supplies and put them in, as well. She filled the bag with whatever she thought they might need.

Myra, Zeus and Barry made their way to the *Whale*, some 50 feet from the tent where Frank still vented his anger at one of the sat phones. The trio came upon one of the battery banks. It was smaller than the main one that provided the core power for everything, but still the size of a small refrigerator. Besides it lay the solar strips neatly packed and tucked in their case. Myra pointed at the strips as Zeus and Barry closed in.

Frank hung up the sat phone, folded its antenna and opened its storage case. The steel teacup rolled over and fell with an almost inaudible *thud* on the soil. He put the phone back in its slot next to three more. He closed the case and moved the numbers of the lock. He stepped out of the tent, lit a cigarette and gazed at the moon. Behind him, Hunter still sat in the folding chair, his bulging stomach rested against his thighs. He popped open his fourth beer and took a big chug.

Zeus removed last of the wheel brakes that held the battery bank in place. It was finally ready to be moved. Barry wondered how they would transport the bank all the way back to the cabin with the RUV dead, out of charge. Weighing at 100 pounds, it would be a real struggle to drag it several miles out to the cabin. He felt lucky to have Zeus around. Zeus pulled the bank out and began dragging it, then he stopped. They felt the same low rumble under them. Suddenly, with the reflex of a cat, he dodged to his side, averting a solid metal punch that would have landed on the back of his head. He turned around and saw Artemis and Tori, fists clenched.

"Not so easily," Artemis said as he lunged forward and drew a punch straight for Zeus's face. He blocked and landed a side kick to Artemis's torso. The sound of titanium against titanium roared through the valley. Artemis grabbed Zeus by his shoulder and swung him around. Myra, Barry, Mimi and Tori all stepped aside. They had no business being amidst all that machine male energy.

The commotion drew Frank's attention. He threw his cigarette and dashed while Hunter decided to stay behind in the comfy chair. He wasn't sure if the sounds were something to be bothered with or not. He wasn't even sure if he heard anything. Maybe it was all an illusion. But, he definitely felt the second rumble beneath him. This time it was stronger.

Zeus swung around and threw Artemis towards the *Whale*. The force of impact created a dent in its hull. Artemis recovered and charged, pushing Zeus away towards the mountain. He landed on top of Zeus and delivered a punch straight to his face.

A gunshot drew everyone's attention as the bots continued their bout. Myra spotted Frank in the distance, gun drawn, silhouetted by the amber glow from the big tent lamp behind him. Myra, Barry, Mimi and Tori took cover behind the rear of the *Whale*.

Barry pointed his rifle towards Frank and pulled the trigger. Nothing happened. He looked puzzled. Another shot came from Frank's direction. Myra opened her hands, and Barry passed on the rifle in a flash. She undid the safety and fired a shot. It hit the ground several inches away from Frank, which is precisely what she wanted. Frank took cover behind the *Whale*.

The engineers came rushing out through the rear hatch.

"Stay in!" Myra yelled as she kept the rifle pointed in Frank's direction.

She felt a rumble under her feet. Frank felt it stronger. The bots didn't care. Back in the tent, Hunter noticed it the most. The ground under him began to shake and rattle. He finally decided something was up and tried to get out of his saggy chair. He was too slow. The ground started caving in as if something was swallowing from underneath. Everything began falling into the center. Hunter's chair slipped backward, and he began sliding into the vanishing center. A large hole about six feet wide started swallowing him in.

"Frank!" The desperate word escaped his mouth as he went down the hole.

Frank rushed back towards the tent. "Hunter!" He yelled into the darkness. "Hunter!" The ground was still shaking. He heard a muffled scream. "Hunter!" Frank yelled again as he opened fire. Shot after shot, he emptied the whole magazine. He loaded a new clip and continued. Each round flashed and illuminated a small portion of the dark hole, but not enough.

Myra saw Frank shooting down in the ground from her position. She rushed towards him, careful not to bump into the bots who still struggled to establish dominance. Barry followed behind her.

Frank took his flashlight and inspected. The beam only reached so far. Standing at the edge, he struggled to get a clear view. He bent over as far as he could and looked deeper. "Hunter!"

"Frank," Myra spoke from behind him.

He turned around and pointed his gun at her. Myra and Barry pointed their rifles back at Frank.

"What do you want?" Frank asked.

"The thing that *you* don't want," Myra replied.

"Hunter... the hole swallowed Hunter," he explained, his voice stuttering, visibly shaken.

Myra took a step closer and lifted herself on her toes as she tried to look inside the hole.

Frank yelled Hunter's name one more time. Then he unloaded the remaining of his clip into the void. Each shot was mixed with a yell. He didn't know what else to do. Watching Hunter go down right in front of his eyes still had him shaking. He loaded a new clip and was about to start.

"Stop. You're wasting bullets," Myra said.

Frank turned around. She had lowered her rifle, but Barry still had his weapon aimed.

As Frank was about to reply to Myra, he fell on his face as his left foot was yanked from behind. His eyes widened as he saw his foot clutched firmly into the long tentacle of the big worm. He pointed his gun and began shooting while trying not to go down, at the same time being careful not to shoot his own leg.

Myra and Barry lunged forward. She grabbed Frank's free arm while Barry pulled with his arthritis-free left hand with all his might. The big worm's limb straightened with tension. It tugged harder. Frank's body began inching deeper into the void. Myra and Barry pulled with all their might.

"Zeus!" Myra yelled at the top of her lungs and hoped he would hear her.

Barry pulled as hard as he could. A second tentacle emerged from the hole and grabbed Frank's other foot. He began slipping down, faster. Myra looked around. She quickly grabbed the gun from Frank, walked over and started shooting at the tentacles. The bullets landed and ripped holes right through the alien flesh. Bullet after bullet, she unloaded the whole magazine. The tension in the arms released as they began limping and twitching. It felt as if the base that they were connected to no longer existed. Barry realized he didn't have to pull anymore.

Zeus rushed and dragged Frank out and away from the hole. Mimi and Tori stood outside the tent, watching.

As Zeus dragged Frank further out, the tentacles that clutched his feet came out with him. All six feet of them, severed from the base that they were connected to a few seconds ago.

24

WORM HOLE

A tiny crack in the ceiling let a narrow shaft of light penetrate the area where the creatures were wandering, aimlessly. Dozens of them squabbled and fought to claim a small space as their territory, teeth exposed whenever one of their siblings dared come too close. Enclosed on all sides with only a single six-foot-wide hole for entrance, the tiny worms chose to keep themselves busy stripping pieces of flesh from the decaying carcasses that lay on the floor. The horrid stench only helped excite their appetites, and conflict was inevitable. When the remnants of the bodies ceased to satiate their ever-increasing hunger, they would start nibbling at each other only to be met with hissing and more show of teeth.

Not everyone was destined to survive. Abundance always leads to wastage and the law of nature demands that out of many, only a few get to pass on their genes. Whenever one of them started giving up on life either due to injury, too much competition for food or attack by its own sibling, others didn't hesitate to tear apart one of their own kind. It wasn't an act of evil for the sake of being evil, only necessity. The stronger seeds were determined to move on, whatever the cost may have been. Perhaps some of them wondered when they would be big enough to crawl out of that monstrous opening into an unknown world. They were only a few days old, but the accelerated growth trigger their parent initiated was speeding up the process, much faster than they would have grown on their own planet. At only six inches in diameter, the grubs didn't have too long of a wait before they would be able to make their own journey out. At least the ones who survived the sibling rivalry.

All around them was the same intricate network of plant-like branches. Intermixed with them were the same refrigerator-sized lumps with gaping mouths. All four of the lumps lay dormant, awaiting some sort of trigger.

A small group in the center fought over the last few strands of meat attached to a leg bone of some creature. As one of them dug its teeth, its neighbor grabbed the strand in the middle, and they both tugged towards each other. The little force they exerted wasn't strong enough to split the flesh, but the weaker grub found itself being dragged towards the one with the stronger pull. In a corner, another group tried to nibble on a piece of titanium that looked like a part of a skull. No matter how hard they bit, they couldn't strip any of it. Desperate hunger pushed them to try one more time. They were too young to have developed the ability to leech acid through their mouths. In a few weeks, they would be able to master that as well.

A vibration roared through the entire area. The weaker worm who was fighting for the meat strand let it go and hurried towards safety, close to the wall. The rest wriggled their way through the pile of bones as they too sought shelter close to the walls. The plant lumps closed their long oval openings. Their outer shells could withstand extreme impact, but their delicate insides needed protection.

The rumbling vibrations got stronger as the *big* worm crawled through the hole. It stopped right when its face reached the opening. All of its eight remaining arms were folded into the center. Part of its face was visible through the gap where a pair of arms was missing.

The big worm shook its body and crawled forward towards the center of the opening. Inch by inch, all six feet of it dropped out of the hole. As its tail was about to leave the tunnel, one of the smaller grubs decided to cross over to the other side. It hurried as fast as it could, but the weight of the 100-pound big worm tail flattened the little one into the ground. The little worm didn't even get a chance to squeal.

The big worm moved around as if checking on the smaller ones. It then jerked its body and regurgitated a piece of a human torso with part of a thigh still attached. The chunks of human remains were large, opened up, guts spilling. Blood splattered over a large area as the remains hit the litter of bones. The stench pulled the tiny ones in like a magnet. They opened their mouths and lunged forward. The sounds of chomping flesh, screams and show of dominance filled the worm hole.

The big worm moved closer to one of the plant lumps that still stayed closed and positioned itself. It rolled its body *away* from the lump and exposed a long tube on its underside. A green gas emitted from the tube. As the gas rose up and engulfed the lump, it began to open. Over the next minute, the bulb opened up its oval. The big worm moved closer and inserted the tube into the now fully open oval opening. In clutches of ten, it started laying its eggs. Each jerk of its body deposited a new batch, ready to be nurtured. Once saturating a spot, the big worm rolled around to a fresh site within the lump.

The big worm began turning around. Several minutes of egg-laying had saturated the lump. The smaller worms were still shoving their lunches down. As the big worm hurriedly turned, it squished a few of the unlucky ones. The ones who survived didn't seem to bother. Each death equaled more nutrition. The big worm grabbed the sides of the hole with its arms and started crawling out.

The army of smaller worms continued to tear apart the human remains their parent had brought as the egg-saturated lump closed shut, gradually, guarding the future of dozens of new eggs in its care.

25

AWAKE

The two soldiers found themselves amused with the small flashlight that Eustace had given them. They had figured out how to turn it on and off. Eustace wondered how long the soldiers would play with it before they got bored. Then he realized the soldiers were as curious about his gadgets as he was about them. The alien child seemed more intelligent to him than the soldiers. The child's fascination for the flashlight had faded much quicker.

The red soldier turned the flashlight on and off in patterns. The button clicks sounded like a crude melody yet entertaining enough and of almost a universal tone in terms of how it was perceived. However, Eustace knew he had no idea how these soldiers were processing all the information. He decided any analysis would be heavily filtered through his own anthropomorphic-colored glasses.

Ever since he had met the alien child, the burning question that lingered in his mind was, *how did they get here?* As soon as he tried to answer that, more inquiries would pop up unannounced. *Where is their spaceship? Are they hostile? What do they want?* A barrage of questions entered and exited his mind constantly. He sat in a somewhat comfortable area of the cave – as comfortable as a solidified lava rock bed could be for him. He found himself calculating how long he would survive before they chopped and ate him, or burned him with lasers, or used some other fantastical new way of delivering death.

Eustace noticed the child still standing next to the comatose body. He could hear clicks coming from his right as the soldiers played with the flashlight. The glow from the child's dome was dynamic. Was he mourning? Eustace knew from his study of animals, at least on Earth, a vibrant display of color could indicate expression of emotions. The long stretched clicks and vocals seemed to confirm his theory that the child was experiencing some deep sentiments as it stood next to the body. It was impossible to know what the child was thinking or feeling, but that didn't stop him from guessing. The one thing he knew for sure was that the emotions were strong, and those feelings penetrated every pore of the sleeping body.

The thought of making his way out of the caves had crossed his mind several times. He felt vulnerable in the presence of the two soldiers, who seemed unpredictable and full of energy, like a trigger-happy band of teenagers looking for trouble, eager to explore and take more risks. However, he could not shake the feeling of immense fascination from watching what was in front of his eyes. He realized he had started the mission in hopes of discovering new species of earth creatures but never in a million years had he imagined something like this. And they had been *friendly*. At least so far. He wished he still had his camera with him.

The child put one arm around the middle of the resting body's torso and the colors of his dome dazzled with even brighter shades and vibrant displays. Bright light scattered and lit the whole area.

A clicking sound from close proximity drew Eustace's attention. He turned and saw the two soldiers standing a foot from him. They tilted their heads as they scanned his body up and down. The red soldier eyed the walkie that hung around Eustace's waist. Only half of it remained as the other half, the part with the battery, was lost somewhere between him being grabbed by the big worm and where Eustace was now. It was surprising how they were so keen about any electronics or mechanical objects that Eustace carried. Could they discern the difference between organic parts such as body and things made of metal/technology? Another set of fascinating questions for Eustace ponder. He looked behind the soldiers and didn't see the flashlight. He wasn't sure what they did with it.

The red soldier tilted his head as he took a better look at the walkie, his pigments flashing a deep red. Eustace had no way of knowing what that meant. The soldier let out a clicking sound and took a small step forward. Eustace inched back into the wall, as far as he could. The red soldier extended his long neck.

"Hey!" Eustace warned.

He figured what worked for the animal kingdom as a warning could also work here. In any case, he didn't have any other strategy. He knew he didn't want to give the walkie. The red soldier extended his neck a little more. Eustace inched further back and cupped the walkie with his good hand. The other hand was useless for anything except as possible food for the soldiers should they suddenly found it appetizing.

Eustace looked at the child and found him shaking his head violently as the rate of vibration of the colors and glow increased tremendously. The sounds that emanated from the child were clear indications of the expression of deep emotions. Positive or negative, Eustace wasn't sure. He wondered if the child would help in case the soldiers decided to jump, bite or do some other horrible thing that he hadn't even thought of yet.

A sudden sensation of tentacles on his hand that cupped the walkie drew his attention back to the soldiers. He didn't know what to do. Any fast move could equal death. He chose to just keep calm, still firmly grabbing the radio. Inch by inch the tentacles engulfed his hand. He felt tiny barbs around the leather-like texture. He just waited to be stung. Then, something happened. He felt as if he had lost total control of his hand. His hand loosened its grip over the walkie. He couldn't discern what was happening. The process of controlling the body with the mind is so intuitive that he apparently never had the need to think about how the muscles in his hand worked. If he wanted to move his hand, it always just happened, but now even if he gave specific, deliberate commands for it to tighten its grip, the muscles didn't respond. He saw his hand open up and release its hold over the walkie. He felt no sensations as the hand opened up on its own. Only by watching it happen was he sure he still had a hand attached at the end of his arm.

The soldiers played with their new toy, emanating a variety of rapid clicks. They tried to push every button on it just like the flashlight, but the same tactile click wasn't there. It was much more silent. The soldiers' fading chatter indicated their excitement had declined.

A loud scream commanded Eustace's attention. His eyes widened. The child lay in a corner, its body jerking and shaking like an animal in search of shelter under lightning. The body that had been resting was no longer still. In a slow, dragged-out sequence, it rose up, just like an elephant rising from its side. The big alien got up and moved its head around as it scanned the area. Eustace sat still. He knew this one didn't seem as friendly as the child. The big alien stood up on all fours and immediately went for the child. With exact anatomical design, the two aliens looked like big and baby version of the same species. Was that the parent? For now, that assumption was enough to make sense for him.

The big alien towered seven feet over the child. The display of colors and glow that emanated from the big alien's dome put the alien child's displays Eustace had seen earlier to shame. The intensity lit every corner. The big alien nudged and inspected the child with long tentacles under its face. The child slowly recovered from the exhaustion and stood up. The loud, emotion-filled calls that echoed in the cave solidified Eustace's assumption that they were indeed parent and child. Maybe *mother* and child? He knew such a show of emotion could only happen between a mother and a child. Even though in the wild not all mothers were that attached to their offspring, this pair seemed to have a deep, primal bond.

The sounds grew louder and the emotions intensified. The child rubbed himself against his mother's towering frame as she caressed him with her tentacles and arms.

The alien mother looked around. She spotted Eustace. She lifted her neck and spread out her facial tentacles as she let out a deafening roar. The child came and took shelter under her legs just like elephant babies do. Eustace shrunk as much as he possibly could. He had never felt so vulnerable before. He turned around, the soldiers were nowhere to be seen. Eustace felt a soft rumble in the ground. As he turned back towards the child, he saw the full might of the alien mother charging towards him.

26

TRUCE

B arry's fingers raced over his laptop keyboard. Sometimes fast, other times slow and deliberate. His guard key was plugged into the USB port, and the frown behind his glasses let Zeus know the work was serious.

"How much longer?" Zeus asked.

Barry just nodded. He knew it was futile to give an answer. Any estimate would be wrong as the laptop didn't have the full computing power of the bigger station, and they never had the chance to set it up before he had gotten separated from the main group to be with Myra. He needed more time.

He was using the X-corp proprietary machine management software, a sophisticated interface designed to alter and maintain the AI associated with the many bots they had manufactured. The software would only function in the presence of a guard key such as the one he was using. Without the key, any new modifications could not be applied, a safety mechanism designed to prevent unauthorized adjustments to how the AI responded. Only Barry and Hunter had the keys on this expedition. Barry knew Hunter had tinkered with the AI, which explained some of the behavior Artemis had engaged in. He was glad that he had implemented a secretive firewall that prevented Hunter from manipulating any other bots. He was surprised how Tori had aligned herself completely with Artemis and followed his lead. But he was sure that wasn't due to any software manipulation. The bots were complex sentient machines who had minds and choices of their own, and they may act differently from time to time than how their makers had intended. That was the risk associated with this cutting edge technology. Great technology brought great risks.

Zeus stared at his forearms and legs, the small dents and scratches kept drawing his attention. He wasn't into vanity, but outside of training back at X-corp headquarters, it was the first time he had had to actually fight with someone. Let alone Artemis, who was as much an adversary as himself. Then again, when he saw Artemis's body lying by his side, with even more significant dents and scratches, he didn't feel so bad. Although there was a negative feeling that lingered in his mind after fighting his own kind, he also felt good that he had come out on top. It reinforced his status as the pack leader and stroked his ego.

Barry looked at Artemis, who still lay motionless. The frown behind his glasses deepened as he buried himself again into his laptop. It was then Zeus understood it would be a slow process. He wondered if he had damaged Artemis beyond recovery.

Not too far, on the other side of the *Whale*, Myra was busy studying the map along with the two engineers. "I agree. Your best bet is to fly out to Attu."

They had been discussing the proposed plan with her. After what had happened last night, Myra knew Frank and the team would have no problem sharing a few supplies with them. When the engineers started discussing the plans with her, she had naturally gotten curious and joined in to go over different scenarios.

With the satellite phones case gone down the sinkhole, the team knew there was no way for them to communicate for a possible rescue or to even alert the authorities. On the one hand, they commanded the most advanced sentient bots, and on the other, their simple satellite Internet devices had kept failing them. The satellite vendors were still reluctant to provide any reliable web services in a place as remote as the Aleutians. The team knew they wouldn't be able to bank on any connectivity once on Chisil. It was still worthwhile to bring in the gear though, just in case. Their only chance now was to fly out to Attu and, if needed, recharge there using solar and then fly out to the next island.

The engineers couldn't wait to fly out of Chisil. They were not at all interested in staying any longer than they had to. For them, it was just a matter of time before their team flew out. Even with a decade of piloting experience under the senior engineer's belt, the *Whale* was infamous for being particularly difficult to handle in unexpected conditions, and they were not sure what the weather forecast was for that day. They hoped that once the cloud cover granted them a break or upon reaching Attu, they would find some connectivity and be able to use the satellite communication onboard the *Whale* to alert the X-corp base in Hawthorne, California and call for assistance or rescue. Regardless, they knew they had to leave Chisil now. Help or no help.

The heat that rose from Frank's coffee attempted to warm the cold interior of the *Whale*. The strain and lingering pain in his right foot were the least of the worries on his mind. He knew soon he would have to go out and face the team. Each sip of the warm liquid gave him a few extra seconds to procrastinate on what he knew he had to do. The events of last night had changed something inside of him. For most of his life, he had hidden his feelings from the outer world. Always reluctant to share too much, he found himself vulnerable after a long time to emotions such as anger and self-pity.

Barry felt the pressure rising as all eyes locked onto him. Mimi and Tori had straddled closer a few minutes earlier to be part of the staring team, too. Barry was busy punching keys when some loud words pulled him out.

"He's back!" Mimi shouted as she saw Artemis starting to wake up and look around.

Tori rushed as Artemis tried to get his bearings. The whole team cheered and looked at Barry. He milked his fine moment of glory. With the system booted and core data files restored, Barry had utter confidence that Artemis would start behaving normally. At least that was the theory he was banking his procedure on.

"Myra!" A voice from behind managed to fall on her ears amid the cheering.

She turned back and stared at Frank. "How's the foot?"

Frank gave a casual nod.

"We were discussing the route you planned. I think Attu is a good idea."

"We're not flying out," Frank said coldly. He didn't know how else to put it. Frank figured it was easier to be lean and mean rather than drag things out. He was always weak in facing emotions. Better to get it over with quickly.

"You are not?"

"No... I think the team wants to stay back with you."

Myra giggled internally. She found it amusing to watch him try to express while trying to maintain his image.

"What about the safety of the team? You forgot last night? It's dangerous out here."

"We're safer when we are together. As for last night, we'll get that son of a bitch!"

The two of them had such intensity and intimacy in their conversation that they became oblivious to the noise others made around them. It was like a private bubble that they conversed in.

"That *son of a bitch* is not my priority. I want my father back, first. That's goal number one."

Frank took a pause as he finally stared long enough into Myra's eyes. He knew he didn't want to apologize.

"Aye aye, Commander," he said with a soft smile and a tone that was his version of accepting a truce.

FIRE

Myra was surprised that Frank had finally decided to join and support her. She hadn't expected this, even after having saved his life. Ever since they had started working together on the Chisil mission at X-corp, there had been some tension. Myra knew Eustace favoring her never rubbed well with Frank. It was a hit to his ego when Eustace would put her in charge of specific responsibilities or demote Frank unintentionally. In the back of her mind, she always wondered if Frank would incite a mutiny or try to sabotage the project. Ever since she had seen Artemis following Frank's orders for the first time onboard the *Polar Explorer*, her suspicions had grown, and she could almost anticipate the problems coming. The immediacy of the mission had kept her attention elsewhere.

Myra stared at the terrarium that was now brought and stored in a somewhat deeper part of the *Whale*. They had sent Mimi and Tori to fetch the frog and its food from the cabin, along with all the ammunition they could find for the three rifles that Myra, Barry and Zeus had brought earlier. The frog was surprisingly calm, no longer trying to escape. Myra figured he must be tired, just like her. Myra was good at hiding her feelings, and she had managed to mask her stress ever since Eustace went missing. But deep down, all of the tension was manifesting into something bigger. She stared at the ready-to-eat rice and beans she held in her hand. For some reason, she didn't feel hungry. She figured that the uneasy stomach she had was probably due to all the tension of the past 48 hours. She tossed the unfinished food packet into a special garbage bag which the team would torch once full. The bags were made of a non-plastic material that was designed to be burned without releasing toxic fumes into the atmosphere.

Myra stepped out of the *Whale*. The setting sun in the distance helped amplify her uneasiness. There was something about that sunset that didn't feel quite right. She figured she must be facing the resistance that had plagued her in the past every time she was about to start something big. She remembered all of the times when she had a paper due in college or had to meet a strict deadline with any task at X-corp. The uneasiness of the moments before something big was about to happen was all too familiar to her. She knew she was about to start perhaps the biggest challenge of her life.

The three robots stood next to each other as they watched Mimi throw more dry wood onto the pile that was already several feet high. Fire was particularly fascinating to the bots. They may not have ever understood the primal connection with this force of nature like humans had, but they still found themselves profoundly attracted to it. The bots had tossed a coin to decide who would start the fire. Although they all would have loved to win, even if they hadn't it was still mesmerizing for them to watch the process.

Mimi finished tossing the last pieces of freshly collected

dry wood onto the pile and kneeled next to it. She broke a few branches and ground smaller pieces into a powder that fell on one part of the stack. Mimi may have been an embodiment of a new frontier in technological development, but her method of choice was ancient. Once she had enough wood dust, she grabbed the flint stone and striker that she had already set up some time ago. Mimi began striking the magnesium stone with the striker. Sparks flew out of the surface and landed onto the pile. Some stronger ones landed on the wood powder and ignited it. She continued striking as more and more sparks ignited the fine dust. Soon, a fire began to rise.

Everybody focused on Frank as he inspected the camoed out rifle as the sound of the now-raging fire filled the silence near the tent by the *Whale*. Designed to easily blend in an environment like Chisil, the matte finish rifle was perfect for remaining invisible in warmer weather with sunshine and green grass against towering brown mountains. As the sun dipped lower, the fire the bots had started a few feet away helped in bringing back warm feelings at basecamp.

"Fifty rounds?! That's all?" Frank asked.

"That's all," replied Barry.

"They were skilled poachers. One shot one kill," Frank whispered as he ran his fingers through the bullet hole in one of the polar bear hides that rested on top of a few more, each one with its own such wound.

Barry nodded as he tried to put the rounds back in their box as neatly as he had found them in the first place. He wondered if he would be able to make a kill with every shot when the time came. Barry didn't even know the target yet. For him to have felt assured, he would have had to know what or who he would be shooting at.

"Every shot matters," Myra said as she approached the tent. Frank's loud voice had let her in on the conversation.

"We're gonna need more," Frank said.

"And the bot guns?" Myra asked.

"Only two... Two guns for four machines."

"Give them to Mimi and Tori. We've got three rifles between us. And my bowgun. Zeus and Artemis will need something else."

"Knives and axes!" Barry interjected.

"Yes," Frank mocked.

"No... They'll lead. We need something bigger. These low-lives don't die easily. Cutting 'em up still leaves rest of their bodies wriggling to fight back," Myra said.

"I wish we had something bigger. Something like those propellers," Barry pointed towards the *Whale*, then continued, "to chop these dirt crawlers into pieces."

A frown appeared on Frank's forehead as he gazed at Barry. He noticed there was an air of excitement in his voice, something he had seldom observed. To be fair, he rarely had a chance to study Barry as most of the time he had found him glued to a computer screen.

Myra shook her head, staring at the crackling fire just outside the tent. She grabbed one of the polar bear hides and immediately felt its weight. Myra then gazed into the raging flames that now reached several feet high. With a mighty swing of her arms, she tossed the hide into the fire. As each strand of fur started burning, it enraged the flames, and black smoke ascended higher into the air.

Myra stared at the popping polar bear hide. "We'll burn those fuckers!"

28

HEARTBEAT

E ustace pressed his neck to relieve the pain. He still hadn't gotten over the urge to use his calloused hand. As the hours had passed, he had begun to accept his condition, but it was still surreal for him to see part of one of his arm turned into something that resembled the exterior of a hard-shelled beetle.

As he tended to the pain, he continued hearing the clicks and sounds of the alien mother and her child communicating. The glow from their head domes let him know they were both excited, both in some sort of a heightened state. *Are they high on something like adrenaline?* The two soldiers were nowhere to be seen. Did they run off after the mother woke up?

The hit that knocked Eustace down when the mother had charged had given him a glimpse of the power she was capable of unleashing. If it weren't for the child to intervene and stop his mother after Eustace had fallen, he was sure he would have been dead. He knew he could trust the child; he was protecting him from his own mother. He wished he could find out what the mother and the child were conversing about.

Eustace was missing Myra. He wished to see her again. He wondered how she was doing and if the whole team was worried about him and if they were trying to come and rescue him. The mother's unwarranted charge had shaken him off-center. He knew he could be gone at any moment. He wondered if he was perceived as a threat. After all, the mother had been in some sort of hibernation, and she could just have been protective of her child and her own kind. There was no way for him to know.

He noticed the mother moving towards him. There was an air of edginess in her behavior despite the child trying to hold her back. The stride was different this time. Her pace was slow and steady. The glow in her head not as vibrant as it had been a few minutes ago. There was something about her gait that made Eustace feel less threatened, and he didn't pull back this time. The mother was now only a foot from him. Her towering frame stared down at him. Only from this close could he really appreciate her full size. Dwarfed, Eustace was left both humbled and in awe.

The mother kept staring down as she studied him. Then, her massive head began descending. Inch by inch, she lowered her head. Eustace felt as if a giraffe was coming for him. Her eyes were now at the same level as his, scrutinizing every move Eustace's blue eyes made. He was hesitant to make eye contact for long, but there was something about the mother's eyes that prevented him from looking away. He was surprised to see how small they were. *Can she even see with those? Maybe she has weak eyesight... She doesn't use them much.* In her world, she may not have had to navigate through darker areas, or she may have a whole range of other senses that augmented her vision in rendering the environment, he thought.

As she got even closer, Eustace noticed her eyes were turquoise blue with a dozen small black dots. He wondered if those were similar to the colored part of human eyes.

Eustace was so transfixed that he hadn't noticed the tentacles that were now inching towards him. When they finally touched his neck, his focus shifted to the sensation of the alien touch he felt. He also noticed the child moving closer through his peripheral vision.

He felt the foreign texture as the tentacles touched his neck. An odd mix of reptilian-like scales with hundreds of tiny ridges, grooves, and indentations. He felt as if he was being molested with a leathered sandpaper. Slowly, the tentacles wrapped around his neck and then snaked down. As they found the heart, they stopped. All of the more than half a dozen of them stayed on the heart and expanded their surface area as if being filled with air. He knew he shouldn't show excitement or any fear, but he could not suppress the adrenaline that coursed through his veins and made his heart *thump* like the pistons of a race car.

The tentacles continued wrapping around his chest, feeling the rhythm. He noticed the glow from the mother's dome was matching the rhythm of his heartbeat. With each short beat, her bloom flickered. The mother shifted her gaze and stared straight into Eustace's eyes. He stared back. As the heart beat faster and the glow flickered, he began to feel some pain. A strange pain germinating in his head. Something he had never felt before. He wondered if he should look away, but he didn't. Her gaze kept him transfixed. As the seconds passed by, the pain increased. He focused so intently on her eyes that he ceased to feel his heartbeat anymore. Instead, he could almost hear the faint high-pitched sound that he thought was emanating from a small cavity in the mother's forehead.

Was she mapping out his brain?

29

PLAN

The two engineers hunched over the makeshift drawing board inside the *Whale* as they remained engrossed in the same thought. The tactical feel and flexibility of old school pen and paper still beat the complexity of using a tablet when prototyping rapidly. Myra sat in one of the three cushy seats on top of Falkor as she observed the engineers working below. Still non-operational and useless, the chained quadruped bot served as a good couch for her if nothing else.

"We can certainly arrange the pipes for the delivery tube," the senior engineer said.

"And the ignition and pilot flame won't be an issue. There's enough butane to last for weeks," the junior engineer spoke as he looked over at the rest of the team.

"We'll find a way to deliver the pressurized gas and give the flames some range," the senior engineer added.

"We'll also need a frame to deliver the fire," interjected Frank, who wanted to make sure they would be able to carry them with ease, that they were light and mobile – something like a gun.

"We'll build a frame around them," the junior engineer assured.

To maintain and fly a copter as big as the *Whale*, the engineers had to keep a small army of parts and supplies for regular maintenance on site, as well as troubleshooting and replacements. For a mission like Chisil, they had had to pack extras. They may not have known how right off the bat, but, in the back of their minds, the engineers knew they would be able to fashion the throwers Myra and Frank were thinking about.

"No! No..." Leroy Higgins screamed as he stumbled on his way close to the fire near the tent by the *Whale*. His voice didn't reach far externally but, internally, he could feel the weight of his own words piercing through his brain. Leroy moved closer and saw the polar bear skull sizzling as the last bits of skin, fur and remnants of attached meat burned off. Not too far from that, he saw the other two heads which he knew very well. He moved closer to the tent and gazed into the six-foot-wide hole that reached far deep into the earth. As he turned around, he noticed a dip in the valley and amidst the fog, he could make out something that looked like propeller blades far in the distance. He started in that direction as his excitement thrust him forward, quickly.

The junior engineer cradled a few different sizes of small pipes and hoses and brought it to the makeshift command center inside the *Whale*. He put down the supplies on the equipment cases. The other engineer joined him in inspecting the goods.

"Myra!" A familiar voice beamed from the rear of the *Whale*.

Myra turned and looked at the bots standing at the hatch. For a second, she didn't know why Zeus was shouting her name, but then she noticed the man in torn, dirt-caked clothes standing among them.

Leroy appeared as confused and surprised as her. "What's going on here?"

There was an urgency and loudness in his voice. Something about his look and tone didn't appeal to Myra as much as she had wanted to when she first set eyes on this stranger. Her subconscious must have detected something about him that was off-putting. The tone of Leroy's question, his clothes, the long salt-and-pepper beard, and weather-hardened face with deep valleys – everything made her feel uncomfortable. "Well... who are *you*?"

Leroy looked at the bots and then started walking towards Myra and the team. The engineers, Frank, and Barry, got up. Frank's eyes widened a little as he opened up his body towards Leroy. Myra remained seated comfortably on top of Falkor, the frown continuing to grace her forehead.

"What the fuck you guys think you doing here? How dare you burn those bear hides?" Leroy snarled as he tried to figure out who to direct his words to.

The frown on Myra's forehead released as she straightened up and cocked her head back.

"Those were *your* hides?" Barry asked.

Myra knew that question was unnecessary. For all his brightness, she knew Barry could be slow at times when deciphering human behavior.

"Yeah, asshole. You're damn right. Mine!" Leroy pointed at himself with his right index finger and continued. "And you destroyed them!"

"*I* burned them," Myra said almost immediately before Barry even had a chance to think about what Leroy had said and come up with a response.

"Why?" Leroy asked as he walked towards Myra, the decibels of his voice pierced her ears.

Frank and Barry moved over and stood near Myra, stopping Leroy in his tracks.

"You have any idea how much they were worth? You destroyed everything!"

"Yes, so that you wouldn't be able to sell them," Myra said.

"You know how much money we sunk into this? Me, Blake, Carter and John? Twenty thousand fucking dollars! To rent the plane, to get supplies, to make multiple trips. Do you have any idea??"

Myra suddenly realized the extent of his state. She knew instantly he was still in shock. She understood some of his anger was not directed at her but the situation he was in. "So, you guys spend twenty thousand dollars to come *all* the way out here so you can kill some innocent bears? You know they are protected. Parts of Chisil are bear sanctuaries."

"I don't give a damn about your fucking bear sanctuary. Each one of those white coats is fifty grand."

"Well, there you go. Your hundred fifty grand is sizzling up in smoke outside."

Before Leroy could say another word, a tapping sound from the side drew his attention. He noticed the frog jumping against the terrarium wall. "Titi!" He shouted as he started towards in his direction.

Myra moved and blocked his path.

Leroy gave her a good stare down. "That's my frog."

"Not anymore."

"What do you mean, 'not anymore'? Fuck you!"

"He's mine now. You abandoned him."

"He has a name. Titan! And I didn't abandon him. I thought those damn creatures got him. Just like how they got my buds."

"What happened?" Frank asked.

Leroy looked at Frank and let out a sigh. All his life, the only time he had broken down was when his mother had died when he was ten years old. Ever since it was almost as if he had lost the ability to express his emotions. They still rose inside him but seldom broke the surface. A long, drawn-out sigh had always stood in as a generic representation for many of his feelings. He just stared at Titi. "You don't wanna know."

"Tell us!" Frank said.

"What you guys doing out here?" His tone was much calmer now.

"None of your business," Myra replied.

As Leroy looked back at Myra, he noticed the rifles propped against one of the equipment cases. "You guys took the guns, too. What else have you taken?"

"Nothing. Just those and Titan," Myra said.

"Well, I'm taking what's mine. The guns *and* Titan."

"That's not happening."

Leroy stared at Myra and then at others. "You all gonna die." He looked around inside the *Whale* and continued, "Leave when you have a chance. Power up your big bird and fly away... You won't survive otherwise. Not against *them*."

"I'm sure we can handle ourselves," Myra said.

"And what about you? How do *you* plan to survive?" Barry asked.

Leroy looked at him, then back at Myra. "Gimme my guns and my boy, and I'm outta here."

"You mentioned renting a plane," Barry said.

Leroy was surprised that Barry had paid attention. "Of course, we had to rent the damn plane to get here. The best way in, but not the easiest. We just had to tuck it outta sight," he looked at Myra. "You know, it is *illegal* to hunt those damn bears. It's a fucking sanctuary!"

Whatever Myra felt inside, she tried not to reveal it.

"Where did you hide the plane?" Frank asked.

Leroy took a long pause as he recalled Frank's question from a few minutes ago about what had happened in the cabin. He looked at Frank and Myra, then smiled.

"Gimme my guns *and* Titan and maybe... I'll tell you guys what happened."

EXPLORATION

E ustace stumbled as his foot landed in a groove in the uneven cave floor. The amber glow of the dying sun painted his face warm as he took a few more steps out, letting the soft breeze rustle his dirt-ridden hair. A smile appeared on his face as his eyes widened ever so slightly. He tried to remember after how long he had seen a view such as this, but he found it to be a difficult task. His head still buzzed from the sharp pain that he experienced when the mother had decided to be extra curious towards him. The movement from behind compelled him to keep marching, although he wished he could just stand there, at the edge of the cave and take in the view for few more seconds.

The cave opening was large, wide enough to fit a few people at the same time. Eustace wondered why his team hadn't discovered this entry point. Had they found it, they wouldn't have had to blast their way into the cave system. As he moved further out, he noticed the almost razor-sharp edges along the entrance. He ran his finger over them. *So sharp. And precise.* There was very little dirt or grime along the edges. The elements must not have had enough time to darken them yet. *Did the aliens make this opening?* He wondered.

He noticed footprints. There was heavy traffic in and out of the cave. None of it was human. A sharp burst of clicks compelled him to continue. He finally stepped onto the volcanic soil that decorated the outside. The alien mother stepped out right behind, followed by her child. She stood on all fours with Eustace on one side and the child on other. The mother took deep breaths as she scanned the horizon. With each new breath, she analyzed the air composition. Both aliens labored as fresh air entered their bodies. The mother didn't react. Since they had landed, they had been primarily inside the caves, with only the soldiers venturing out along with other smaller creatures from their party. The mother and child's lungs were already adjusted to the air inside the caves. It was only a matter of time before they adapted to what was beyond.

The mother looked back into the cave and heard some sort of a fight. When she saw the two soldiers run out towards her, she figured they must have been just playing. She let it go. She didn't feel the need to discipline them. The world in front of her commanded all her attention. She looked to her left and stood up on her hind legs, now towering more than ten feet high. She sniffed something and dropped back down on all fours. Eustace felt the mild rumble as her feet touched the ground.

The alien mother dropped her head and sniffed the calm water as the soft breeze continued sending gentle ripples across Shadow Lake. Soon after, she lowered one of her tentacles and dipped it in. It absorbed some of the liquid as everyone waited. The child looked up at his mother, noting her behavior, learning from her. Eustace looked around. He knew Myra and the rest of the team were just on the other side of the lake. He also knew it was twenty miles around. Not something walkable, easily. Nonetheless, he wondered what his daughter must be doing. Was she coming to get him?

One by one, the mother dipped all of her tentacles into the lake's water and began drinking. They expanded in size as water was sucked up through tiny openings at their ends. The child drank as well. The two soldiers didn't seem that interested. It was not the first time they had seen the lake or been around it. Eustace noticed their feet and realized the footsteps he had seen earlier at the cave entrance mainly belonged to them.

A squeaking sound interrupted the mother's drinking. She immediately rose up and listened as water dripped from her moist tentacles. She stood still, like a rock, as no part of her body moved. The child followed. The soldiers, having witnessed the tenseness in the mother's body, cleaned up their act and listened intently. The same squeaky sound originated again from her right, and the mother immediately turned and locked her eyes onto the source. As soon as she knew the direction, she pointed the hole on top of her nose towards the target and with the precision of a laser, shot out a high-frequency wave. The squeak ended abruptly. Everyone stood in silence for a few moments. When she heard no more sounds, she started in the direction of her victim.

The squirrel's lifeless body looked very odd to the mother. Long, with four legs, a furry tail, and small face, strange but still very fascinating. The mother tilted her head as she studied the dead one. There was an opening in the carcass. A hole that was created when its body had quickly released the internal pressure as the precision microwaves cooked it alive. Eustace arrived last and stared at the remains. *Cooked alive*. He looked up at the mother. He couldn't see her eyes but had a good view of the tentacles, which moved up and down, in excitement. The mother lowered her head. She examined the body with the same curiosity she had shown towards Eustace inside the cave. A few moments later, she pulled her head back and stood up on all fours. She looked around and scanned the area, then charged towards a small hill near the lake. The child followed, but the mother looked back and signaled him to stay put. The soldiers rushed in and flanked her offspring.

The speed with which the mother had crossed the distance from where they stood to the hill left Eustace in awe. At one hand, every moment he spent with these beings left him awestruck while on the other, deep down, he knew the power they possessed, and he still didn't know the extent of what all they were capable of. What was their agenda for being here on Earth?

The mother climbed the hill with high speed and reached the top to get a clear view of the surroundings. She could see the perimeter of the lake stretched far into the distance with the towering volcano on one side. The longer she spent there, the more of the fresh wind she felt on her face. The sun was fading, but she could still feel its warmth. Then, suddenly she stood on her hind legs and made herself taller. She filled her lungs with all the air she could and let out a loud, almost deafening roar.

Eustace watched the mother in the distance screaming her lungs out. For a moment, he thought she was growing in size. Was she stretching her cells? It amazed him once again as the vibrations of the roar passed through him. Almost instantly, his thought went to Myra and the rest of the team. He wondered if they would ever encounter these creatures. A fast movement close to him broke his trance, and he noticed the child running towards his mother. The two soldiers followed, each letting out clicking sounds, trying to contain the child's enthusiasm, who was now charging full speed towards his mother.

In no time, the little one reached his mother and stood next to her. She looked down at her baby then scanned the horizon again and let herself be heard with another colossal roar. The child tried to mimic. Together, they created the large force field that echoed through the land as it bounced back from distant cliffs. The glow in their domes sent bright, beaming colors in all directions. The child rubbed his head against his mother's leg. The mother looked back at the two soldiers standing near the base of the hill now. The soldiers climbed up and also stared at the lake.

Suddenly, the alien mother turned around and did a high-resolution horizontal scan.

Eustace was gone!

SEARCH

The red soldier sniffed the water as he stood on the shore of Lake Shadow. His red pigments flashed bright, in excitement, but he hesitated. He turned around and looked back. The green soldier leaned his body towards him without moving. Red knew it was time. Even though he had almost always been the one taking the initiative, this time it wasn't the case of bravado or dominance. Red knew he had lost the argument they had had in the cave and to settle the score; it was his turn to be the first.

It was almost as if the wait was over in an instant. Red was done thinking about it. He sniffed the water once more and started moving in. The temperature sent a chilling wave up his bodily sensors. As he went deeper, the cells along his body began warming. Soon, it didn't matter how cold the water had been. Neck deep in water, the red soldier turned and looked back at his brother. Green stood there as if trying to make him think. A few moments later, the green soldier started moving in, too. Red took a deep breath and submerged himself.

. . .

The red soldier struggled to see through all the murk that was in the water. The visibility was at best five feet. Every now and then he turned back and saw Green behind him, which was reassuring. He had lost Green a few times as they ventured towards the center of the massive lake. Twenty miles in perimeter, fifty to hundred feet deep – it wasn't difficult to get lost. As they approached the center, more and more dead fish banged against them, especially whenever they surfaced to take a breath. The soldiers had already sealed the openings in their skins to resist any transmission of oils or any other potentially harmful chemicals. Whenever the water got too murky, they relied on their subsonic sonar to maintain communication. If only the sonar would work in locating what they were after.

Most of the craft had been damaged by the explosion and the fire that had eventually taken it down. Large pieces of their remote home lay at the bottom of the lake. Whatever remained was hard to make sense of. The soldiers surfaced, looked around and took deep breaths before going back in. As they descended, they saw a more extensive section of the craft in front of them.

The large section was what would have been the center when their vehicle was intact. The construction of the vessel was such that the center was guarded by several redundant layers of protection. The outer shell, when it was intact and functional, was constructed of a metal-like substance, an alloy comprised of naturally occurring metals mixed with an organic, carbon-based hard shell substance. That same organic substance also made parts of the soldiers' exoskeletons.

The soldiers dove deeper and came around the first layer of the exoskeleton of the large centerpiece. As they went further, several rows of structures became visible. It was as if they had entered the sleeping chamber of the craft. There were several platforms constructed out of the same hard shell material. The berths extended from either side of the punctured oval hull. Their pointy edges appeared uncomfortable but for the soldiers, berths such as these must have been comfortable. Once they were ready to rest, the soldiers or others of their kind would slip into each of these slots, and the indentations on the berths would line up perfectly with the grooves in their bodies. It was as if each bed was paired to a specific soldier. They moved past the sleeping platforms and deeper into the hull.

As they ventured further, they came across an area that narrowed towards the center. In front of them, there was a large hole that lead to a lower floor of the craft. The soldiers were getting close to running out of breath, but they realized they had found the opening they had been looking for. If they rose up to get more air now, they would have to come this far again, and there was no guarantee they would find the hole right away, as visibility was still a challenge. They looked at each other for a moment. The red soldier went in first, and Green followed, immediately.

They found the bottom level to be even darker. There were no openings, and the fading sun failed to penetrate this far through the hole. A sealed chamber lay isolated from the rest. The soldiers flashed their pigments as brightly as they could, producing enough glow to barely make things out. The red and green bloom was non-directional. It emanated randomly from cells that lined their bodies. As much as they would have liked something equivalent to Eustace's flashlight, they had to settle for the tools they had, the visibility that their glow provided, and the sonar. The chamber walls were barely an arm's length away, and it made the sonar rather ineffective. They decided to fall back on good old tactile feedback.

The red soldier signaled and they both started searching

the opposite sides. Their arms moved with urgency as their bodies showed increasing signs of excitement. They knew they had to finish fast. Red ran his arm against the wall, trying to feel for the groove that should have held what he was looking for. Green did the same but on the opposite end.

The green soldier suddenly turned back as he heard a sharp click that Red sent his way. He hurried and saw that Red had his arm extended as he touched a part of the curved wall. Almost zero visibility even after the glow, made it impossible for Green to see what his partner was doing. He extended his arm to where Red's was and found himself touching a hole in the wall, an empty cavity where the object of their search would have been. Red fired off several clicks, his pigments flashing and flickering in rage. Their trip had been for nothing. What they were looking for was gone. Green let Red know it was time to go.

Without any more thoughts, red began swimming back towards the hole that separated the upper and lower level. Green followed. As Green swam behind Red, he noticed something from the corner of his eyes. He turned around and moved towards what had caught his attention.

Red was so desperate for air, he didn't even look back to check on Green as he made it out of the lower level. He continued to swim out the way he had come in, thinking all this time that Green was right behind him. As he left the opening in the central oval shell into more water, he turned around, quickly. He looked hard to see through the murk then shook his body and began moving *back* towards the craft. Just as he was about to enter the shell once again, something grabbed his attention. He immediately knew what it was. He shifted his focus from worrying about Green and moved towards an oval object that floated nearby. The object was dark, almost black in color, constructed from a similar beetle-shell like substance like the berths. Red immediately grabbed it and turned it around. The other half of the oval was missing. He looked closely. There was nothing inside. The half that Red held had six deep grooves, precisely crafted to hold tube-like objects. If both halves had been present, there would have been twelve groves, with tubes. He let go of the cover and looked around frantically, almost bursting from lack of air and barely surviving on the last bit that was trapped in his body. He searched the area for those missing tubes. He dove deeper towards the lake bed and searched there, too.

A tap from behind compelled him to turn around. He was almost shocked to see Green. He had forgotten about him altogether. Just as he began explaining that he had found the oval object, but the tubes were missing, the green soldier raised two large pieces made out of a clay-like substance that he held in his hands. They were not the tubes the red soldier was after, but, when he saw those pieces, he couldn't contain his excitement.

32

THE DESCENT

Myra looked directly up as she saw Barry climb down one rung at a time. The rope and wood ladder that hung down into the hole that had swallowed Hunter wasn't as sturdy as the other ladder the team had used from which Eustace and Sam had entered the cave system. To retrieve the other ladder, the team would have had to first go to the other site and bring it back. It was faster to construct a new, lightweight version. Ever since Leroy had left them, the group had chosen to spend all their time planning and fashioning the new gear they were so eager to put to good use.

The ladder swayed back and forth as Barry climbed down another rung. Myra thought maybe it would have been better to anchor it at the base. To tie it with something so it wouldn't swing. It wasn't big, but the swing was enough to let the butane canister on Barry's back hit the walls, occasionally. Myra hoped it wouldn't explode. Frank, Zeus, and Artemis had a surprisingly less difficult time coming down.

The ladder reached some ten feet deep into the hole, which curved beyond a certain point. The big worm had taken a horizontal path before turning up and shooting out under the tent and dragging Hunter down with it. As Barry reached the last rung, he observed Myra, Frank and the bots standing a few feet deeper right where the hole curved. At first he hesitated, but eventually, he jumped. The jump made his knees bend all the way *in,* and Barry almost rolled over before being caught by Myra and others. "Thanks," Barry said as he regained his footing. He tightened his wrist guard and adjusted his glasses before looking straight into the long dark tunnel ahead of them.

The flashlight beams bounced against the huge tunnel walls as the team ventured deeper. The soil under their feet was loose, not as hard and densely packed as Myra would have expected. She wondered why it was so. Were there any chemicals oozing from the big worm's body, making the soil softer? Was the big worm eating away at dirt and rocks, boring tunnels? She had a hard time believing that, but it was one explanation she could come up with.

Barry sneezed, and the sound echoed deep into the worm tunnel. Besides his sneeze, there was hardly any talking, only whispers. There was no way for them to know how deep the hole ran and if the big worm was just around the corner. The small pilot flame from Myra's thrower didn't make much of a sound as she led the way. Frank and Barry kept theirs off. Even with plenty of butane supplies aboveground, they had no idea how much of it they would need.

With every passing minute, as they ventured deeper, Myra kept wondering about the soil. She couldn't get over why it was so loose. Occasionally, the soil would break loose from the ceiling and fall in front of them, the flashlight beams making them glitter. It wasn't the first time Myra had seen unusual things in nature. Growing up in southern California since the age of five, she had accompanied Eustace on several nature exploration trips and remembered seeing the odd pairing of geography sometimes. She recalled one instance vividly when she and Eustace had been exploring a desert in California. The desert sand was fine and made tall dunes, their barrenness was only broken by a random bush here and there. As they had pushed their 4x4 higher on one of the sand hills and come down on the other side, there was a bend that hugged a butte. She remembered seeing several trees lined up around that bend and along the road. She had had a hard time believing that so many trees could exist somewhat randomly in the middle of the desert.

Myra felt the same watching the loose sand as they continued down the worm tunnel.

The throwers they fashioned were rather clumsy, long metal tubes outfitted with Butane canister along with CO_2 cans. The mechanical levers used for switches to control the fuel supply added to the bulk. As the team spent more and more time having them slung over their shoulders, the weight started to drag them down. There was an impending sense of hurry – no time for fancying their makeshift weapons. Leroy's recollection of the incident of what had happened to his mates at the cabin at the hands of the alien soldiers, and how he had managed to escape, had put the whole team on edge. Frank was very reluctant to give the rifles back to Leroy. They needed those guns. Having never used a thrower, he just felt more comfortable with traditional weapons as compared to something the team had fashioned in only a few hours. There was no guarantee the throwers would work as intended. They all tested fine, but when they were underground, in the hole, with possible areas without any oxygen, there was no guarantee they would work. As the bulk felt heavier, he just wished Myra had given the damn frog back to Leroy, instead of the guns.

The lack of oxygen was another possible challenge the team had thought about. There weren't enough kits for everyone to be fitted with O2 masks and cylinders. Both Zeus and Artemis carried small O2 canisters slung over their shoulders. These canisters would be the last-minute hack that could save the humans' lives in case they found themselves in a tight spot without air, although the vast hole that the big worm had created assured them that enough air must have traveled down to keep them alive. They just weren't sure how much deeper they would still have to go.

Myra stopped as she came at another bend in the hole. She noticed that whenever there was a turn, it was always around after ten feet. She shone her light into the opening ahead, and the darkness of the hole consumed all of it. Her thoughts went to Mimi, Tori and the two engineers who had stayed back at basecamp. She wondered if Leroy had actually left, or if it was just a ruse. She unclipped her radio and pressed the talk switch.

"Basecamp, come in."

33

START

The animal's distress calls echoed deeper into the cave as they bounced off the walls. Intermixed with them were the occasional clicking sounds. The cacophony kept entering Eustace's ears but had failed to wake him up yet. If it weren't for that final, deep, laborious wail, he would not have woken up. As the massive sound knocked on his ears again, he began coming back to his senses. As he gradually came back, things became more evident. A few moments later, he was able to discern the clicks and wails along with a few other sounds. All this before his eyes began opening. His subconscious had been processing all the information in the background.

Millimeter by millimeter, he opened his eyes. The scene in front of him gradually came into focus as he tried to adjust. At first, what he saw appeared strange. For a moment, he wondered if he was still in his groggy state. He thought he saw a moose in front of him. A big, strong bull moose in his prime. The massive antlers dragging across the cave floor as he struggled. He wondered if the animal was injured and needed help. *How did he get here?* Only after noticing the strong, black, clay-like substance that bound the moose's ankles, he realized the animal didn't get there on his own. The glow that filled the cave started bothering him now that he was fully awake. He squinted and wondered if the light show also bothered the animal.

A moving body commanded his attention as he saw the red soldier walk towards the head of the moose. The green soldier stood a few feet away, watching as the animal struggled to break free from the bindings the soldiers had restrained him with. As the enormous antlers scraped against the cave floor, they began digging into wherever it was soft. In the areas where the antlers couldn't break through, they produced an uncomfortable scraping sound, like dragging nails on a chalkboard. The red soldier grabbed one of the antlers as he tried to restrain and hold the bull in place. Red applied even more force as the moose agitated further. The young bull pulled away, harder, swaying Red back and forth.

Eustace noticed the alien mother and her child nearby. The entire glow came from the mother. The intensity from her child paled in comparison to how excited the mother appeared. Whatever they were doing with the moose held Eustace's attention. None of the aliens had noticed that he had awoken. A sharp pain in the head drew Eustace's attention inward. He tried to remember what had happened when they all visited the lake. He recalled the part where they had left him behind as they went for the hill. He remembered thinking about Myra as he had witnessed the tender moments between the alien mother and her child. He had known he couldn't possibly outrun the quadruped giants. His heart had been beating fast. Fast enough that it could have fallen out of his chest as he had plotted his escape. Out of options, there was only one possibility that he could have considered. That idea may not have been the smartest, but out of the two options, it was indeed the better one. He had started moving back towards the cave they had come out from. He recalled focusing hard, trying to remember the geography, but had soon realized he didn't know anything about how the caves connected. He had thought about figuring out the layout once he was deeper inside and away from the alien mother. He had been only fifty feet away from the cave opening. Fifty feet away from freedom. As he had put more hurried steps towards the entrance, he recalled being knocked down. It was as if a force field had hit and threw him off balance. Had the alien mother sent a wave of energy to knock him down? Sharp pain in the spine had followed. His body had convulsed as he had turned. The dying sun had still been too bright in his eyes to quickly see what was happening or who was behind him. He remembered the last thing he had seen was the giant seven-foot silhouette of the alien mother charging towards him.

Eustace didn't know how much time had passed since his escape attempt. Whatever they had done to get the moose in the cave, he figured it must have taken at least a few hours. He noticed the green soldier walking towards the moose's head as Red still tried to hang on to the antlers in a desperate attempt to restrain the energy of the young bull.

What the fuck are they doing?

MEMORY

M yra's flashlight beam bounced off the big worm tunnel the group was walking through. She covered her nose as the stench got stronger every moment they inched further. Not unbearable, but enough to make everyone uneasy. She squinted. "I think there's an opening up ahead."

Barry moved up from the back of the line and checked. He focused intently on the faint sounds coming from straight ahead. "Are you guys hearing that?"

Everyone stood still as they listened. A cacophony of cricket-like sounds entered their ears. Myra strained to make out details of what was up ahead.

Myra approached the edge of the worm opening, taking her last steps ever so carefully. The stench was extreme and sounds blaring. She inched towards the end and pointed her light straight down. Her eyes widened.

One by after another, each member came closer and stared down at what she was looking at.

"Damn," Frank said.

"At least fifty of them," Barry said.

Myra continued staring down. "Fifty stinkers?" She noticed the small piles of white deposits all over the area, each adding to the stench. It bothered her less and less as minutes passed. The little worms got excited and produced more clicks every time light hit them. Myra adjusted her flashlight dial and made the pattern bigger. The worms expressed their excitement vocally. "They love the light."

"Maybe it's annoying them," Barry said.

Myra turned it off and asked others to do the same. Almost immediately, the sounds lowered in intensity. She thought Barry might be right after all.

"Look at all the bones," Frank said pointing at a small pile towards the left side in the opening below them. He had turned his light back on and narrowed the beam into a tight pattern.

"They've been eating animals," Barry said.

"No. Somebody has been *feeding* them animals," Myra said as she looked around the area and the little stinkers.

They turned their flashlights back on and scanned the opening. The clicks and ringing amplified again as the beams moved across the area.

"It's not a good idea to stay here long. We should move on," Zeus said.

"Hang on," Barry said as he discovered the two large plant bulbs towards the right side of the opening. The one in which the big worm had deposited its eggs was closed while the other was still open.

"What the fuck are those? They look like plant vaginas," Frank said.

"Well... They could be part of the same plants that Scout encountered... Not sure," Barry said.

"Is that metal?" Myra asked as she pointed her light

towards the far end of the opening and caught the glint of something shiny.

Barry and Frank pointed their lights and looked.

Barry squinted as his brows tensed. A few moments later, the tension in his expression released. "Its a chassis,"

"A chassis? For what?" Frank asked.

"We should take a closer look."

"Sure, you wanna jump in?"

Barry looked back at Frank and let out a sigh.

"I'll go," Myra volunteered.

"Wait. Me and Artemis will go," Zeus said as he moved from the back to the front.

Artemis followed.

The little stinkers clicked and squealed as they pulled away from where the two bots walked. Zeus looked back up at the rest of the group then continued moving towards the shiny metal. He moved ahead as Artemis hung back near the open plant bulb.

Artemis crouched to eye level with the open plant bulb. He thought about what Frank had said earlier. The lump did indeed look like female genitalia. He stared at it, perusing every detail. He had never seen such a bizarre thing in his whole short life.

Zeus jerked his foot as he tried to get rid of one the stinker that had attached itself to him. He was sure they were no threat to him. Zeus didn't feel the need to hurt or kill them. As he came closer, he saw a more giant pile of bones surrounding the piece of metal. He bent down and moved some of them to reveal more of it.

"What is it?" Myra asked.

Zeus didn't reply. He continued staring at the object. At first, it was hard for him to make sense of what it was. He noticed the damage. Parts of it appeared to be burned as if a strong acid had eaten through it. He saw some of the bones around the metal had similar traces of acidification. For a moment he hesitated to touch it. He worried the acid would burn his own exoskeleton. As he cleared more bones, he saw an area of the metal the acid hadn't touched. He grabbed the whole piece from the unburned area and tried to lift it. It didn't budge. He applied more force, but the object didn't slide, at all. He tilted his head and zoomed in on the ground where the metal laid. He noticed part of the object was going inside the floor along with some of the bones. It was as if that area was fused solid with the metal and the bones. He wondered how was that even possible.

"Zeus, what is it? Tell me," Myra said.

"Wait a second."

He scraped the rounded metal, about the size of a football. No longer worried about the dried-up acid, he rubbed the surface and suddenly stopped when a large portion of the object became visible from underneath the layer of acid.

"Zeus," said Myra.

"Sam!" Zeus whispered.

"What?" Myra asked.

Zeus looked back at the team. "It's Sam."

Myra's shoulders dropped. "Sam?" There was a brief silence in the area, with only the stinkers buzzing.

Barry looked around, thinking. "Bring him here."

"I can't. It's stuck to the ground."

"What do you mean stuck? Just yank it," Barry said.

Zeus stood up. He noticed one of the stinkers was too close to him. Zeus pushed it away with his foot then bent down and held onto one of the grooves in Sam's skull, and pulled hard. He struggled, but the piece didn't budge. He adjusted his posture then tried again, even harder this time. Suddenly, it worked, and the sheer power of his pull threw him back as something gave way. He landed and delivered death to the few stinkers who had gotten squished under him. Zeus sat up and noticed a small piece of the skull had chipped, but he hadn't managed to pull the whole thing out. He studied the broken section in his hand. Zeus felt some sensation on his back and removed the wriggling bodies of the squished stinkers. Zeus saw other worms rushing in to feast on the dead bodies he had just thrown in. He looked back at Myra, shook his head, and then noticed Artemis was still gazing at the open plant bulb. Zeus wasn't sure what his co-bot had found so alluring about the lump. But, he ignored him.

"Wait," Barry said as he removed his thrower and set it on the ground.

"Where you going?" Myra asked.

"Hang on. We need this," Barry said and lowered himself down from the worm tunnel into the opening before Myra even got a chance to throw another word at him. She looked at Frank and then lowered herself behind Barry. Frank followed shortly.

The group noticed the grubs were far more interested in them than the robots. As the three walked, they saw the little creatures turning their heads towards them. Some of them began extending one of their ten arms like open hands, ready to receive. Ready to grab.

"They can smell us. Or something," Myra said.

"Pheromones. Gosh, these guys must be really perceptive," Barry said as he hurried towards Sam's skull.

Frank held back and crouched next to Artemis and joined him in studying the bulb. Like Artemis, Frank also found the object fascinating. He squinted as he focused on a faint glow that emanated from deep inside it. Perhaps that glow was what had kept Artemis glued to it.

Barry crouched next to Sam's skull and lowered himself to look inside. The acid had damaged most of it. Upon closer inspection, he figured it was no longer unsafe as the acid had dried. He took his flashlight and looked deeper.

Myra kept an eye on the stinkers. Each time one tried to come close, she pushed it away using the long barrel of her flamethrower.

Barry's eyes widened. He looked up at Myra.

"What?" She asked.

For a second he was at a loss for words. "The mem-" he swallowed and continued, "the memory is still intact."

"The memory is still intact?" Myra asked.

"Yes! I knew these things were indestructible."

"Let's take it out."

Barry bent down again and undid two of the six latches that secured Sam's memory in place. He tried to pull it out but didn't budge. "I don't think its gonna come out. I removed the two latches but can't reach the other four." He pointed his light deeper and continued, "I think the other latches are fused with the metal casing. We can't pull it out."

Myra pushed another grub away. "What do we do now?" It was getting harder for her to keep them at bay as their curiosity kept bringing them back.

A few feet away, Frank did the same. However, fewer bothered him.

Barry quickly pulled out a portable tablet from one of the long pockets in his cargo pants and searched his others. Shirt pockets, all the pockets in his pants. Finally, he pulled out a small cable. He looked up at Myra. She smiled as she flicked another stinker away.

"I think it might work," Barry said as he plugged the cable into a tiny slot on the memory and the other end to his tablet. He played with the screen and entered a few commands.

Myra leaned over towards him. "There's a lot of data," she said as she looked at the content of Sam's memory bank.

"Yeah, but we don't need all of it. We just need Sam-specific files. No need to copy the base database, which is the same throughout. But we can't replace what Sam learned and saw."

Suddenly, it dawned on Myra. If they were able to extract as many memories as they can, then they would be able to know more about what had happened to Eustace. "We'll know what happened to Dad?"

Barry gave her a blank look. "Maybe."

"How long will it take?!" Myra asked.

"Hours." Barry canceled the transfer and went back into the memory files. His eyes remained squinted.

Myra heard clicking and ringing. She turned back and saw a gang of five stinkers near her. She aimed the thrower at them, then changed the angled towards the ceiling and pulled the trigger. A five feet long streak of fire blazed from the nozzle, lighting the area and sending all the grubs away into the far corner.

"We gotta hurry up," Myra said.

Barry was watching the screen. "I'm only transferring the last two days of data. That's all the space I have," He shook his head.

"How long that's gonna take?" Myra asked.

"A few minutes. It's pretty fast."

Zeus stood up and headed back towards the worm hole. He grabbed the thrower that Barry had dropped earlier and slung it over his shoulder then returned to Barry and Myra.

Frank and Artemis also moved over. Zeus and Frank shot out two more burst of flames into the air. The stinkers ran as far back to the other wall as they could.

Myra looked at Barry and saw a tear drop onto the tablet screen. Barry was trying to hold it all back. She leaned over and watched some of the images that he was pulling as the files were being transferred. As he scrolled through the thumbnails, he saw some selfies that Sam had taken with the rest of the bots. Images of the crew. The *Whale*. Several photos at basecamp intermixed with others of the team.

Barry pressed a key, and an image of Eustace came on his screen. The picture was taken from Sam's POV when Eustace was descending down the ladder into the cave. Eustace wore a calm smile in the photo, looking back at Sam. Barry felt a drop of liquid on his arm. He didn't look up at Myra. A moment later the rest of the team huddled around the tablet, eager to get a glimpse of more images. It was as if the whole team had fallen into a trance. Each new image brought back a host of memories and germinated questions.

A sudden loud grunt yanked everyone out of the trance. Frank jerked his leg as he shook one of the stinkers that had latched onto him. He rubbed his ankle quickly then looked at the nuisance who was still charging towards him. "You son of a bitch," Frank said as he aimed his thrower and pulled the trigger hard. A hot flame wrapped the grub and instantly started burning it. It squealed. The desperate cries were deafening. They echoed in the open area and went deep down into the hole the team had come from. Frank turned around and saw another stinker heading his way. "You too. Take this," he said as he got up and burned the other bugger alive. The squeals intensified. He looked around, aimed the thrower and with one grand sweeping motion, he torched dozens of the little grubs. They all struggled, scampered around as they tried to escape their fiery deaths. Frank breathed heavily and in short bursts as he watched the pests burn.

"Frank!" Myra yelled.

"What?"

"We are not here to kill."

"Well, you should tell *them* that."

Myra watched a few of the stinkers slowly get charred to black. The desperate cries faded as they became motionless. The rest of them had moved far away to the other side. It seemed they had learned their lesson.

"How much longer?" Myra asked.

Barry stared at his screen. He didn't reply. A second later he lifted his head up. "Did you feel that?"

"Feel what?"

"Everyone stay still."

The whole team stayed put and tried to feel what Barry was pointing at. A low rumble shook the ground beneath them.

"That!" Barry said.

Myra looked around and up. There was nothing, just cave walls. She looked at the plant bulbs; they were exactly the same they had been earlier. Another rumble shook the ground. "How much longer? We gotta go."

"Almost done. Fifty seconds," Barry said.

Frank and the bots stood up keeping an eye on the stinkers, but they no longer appeared to be of any threat. One of the grubs moved towards the charred ones. It sniffed the darkened bodies of its siblings. Uninterested, it looked around. "You have no idea how that feels," Frank said staring down at the grub who was sniffing the body. His finger ready on the trigger.

"Thirty seconds," Barry said as another rumble passed underneath them. The pattern had changed to a wave. A more continuous vibration with shorter pauses.

"Almost..." Barry said. He yanked the cable hard from Sam's memory bank and shoved the tablet back into his pocket. For a moment, there was some hesitation, but he gave Sam's remains a final look and got up.

Frank moved towards the big worm tunnel, and the rest followed. He had his eyes fixated on the stinkers. The rumble was much stronger now. Each wave shook the ground with ever-increasing intensity.

With all his attention on transferring the files, Barry hadn't had a chance to pay attention to the little stinkers. As they crawled, he looked around at the charred ones as well as ones on the other side. As the flashlight beams moved around, Barry noticed another shiny object behind a cluster of grubs to the side. He looked at the team in front of him heading back to the tunnel and quickly turned towards the shiny new object.

"Barry!" Frank yelled.

"Just a second," Barry said as he tiptoed, avoiding the litter of bones and any angry worm. He walked a few feet and came upon the cluster of stinkers who guarded the object. Barry waved his hands as he tried to shoo them away. "Move!" he said, still waving. Suddenly, he felt the heat near him as he saw a beam of fire launched towards the cluster. The grubs squealed and rushed around.

"You're outta your mind. Let's go!" Frank yelled.

Barry hurried towards the object. As he bent down to pick it up, he realized what it was. His eyes widened, and hand started trembling. He finally had what he had wanted for such a long time. Hunter's steel wallet was scarred by acid, but most of it was still intact. Barry shoved it in his pocket and followed behind Frank.

As they came upon the big worm tunnel above them, Frank turned around and gave one last look at the stinkers. The worms had started to move towards the team once again. He aimed his thrower and pulled the trigger hard, this time pointing in the air. Once again, the fire scared them away.

Suddenly, Myra saw Frank being yanked up and away from behind and deep into the big worm hole. The sudden shock made him pull the trigger harder, and a big flame shot out as he was sucked from behind, deeper into the hole. The team couldn't see anything until the flame burst subsided.

"Frank!" Myra yelled. She rushed towards him and climbed up into the worm tunnel. Myra saw him in front of her, clutched in one of the arms of the *big worm*. "Frank!"

She hollered at the top of her lungs as the rest of the team rushed in. Myra's instincts told her there was no time. The big worm held Frank in one of his eight remaining arms. Frank's legs were spread wide, propped against the corner of the grub's mouth. Between his legs, down below, he could see the rows of teeth waiting for him. The monster worm had a firm hold of his upper body, rendering his arms useless, but his legs were still free. He knew if he moved even slightly, he would lose his balance and be shredded to pieces. He had been in many hairy situations in his life, but this had to be unquestionably the worst.

Myra raced towards the big worm, aimed her thrower right at its mouth and pulled the trigger hard, being careful not to hit Frank's legs. She knew it would be a miracle if she didn't burn him. The burst of flame toasted the center of the worm's mouth directly. The big worm immediately let go of Frank and rubbed its mouth with all its arms. Frank's legs were burning. He rolled over on the ground, desperately. He Stood up and took off his shoes and pants faster than a lightning strike.

Barry and the bots climbed up into the hole and helped Frank. Myra stepped in and aimed her thrower once again at its mouth as the big grub tried to relieve itself of the burn. She knew this time she would be able to damage all the arms. She pulled the trigger in and waved the thrower around as flames started licking each and every part of the big worm's body. It let out deafening squeals as it squirmed and convulsed. The worm desperately tried to rub its face, but now even the arms had caught fire. No matter how much it tried to get rid of the flames, it made it worst.

The big worm wriggled back and forth in the hole. First, it retracted, trying to find an escape route, its instinct preventing it from going forward and burning all of its offspring with it. It had moved back some hundred feet, but when it was unable to find a route tracking backward, it looked straight ahead. It saw Myra and Barry and the bots aiming their throwers at it. The worm let out a big roar and charged forward at full speed. Myra, Barry and the bots pulled their triggers, and a ball of fire raced towards the big worm. As it opened its gaping mouth, the fire went deep into its body. The team didn't let go of their triggers and unloaded all the fuel they had onto the ten-foot-long monster's body. It convulsed, screamed, roared and moved, but a few short moments later, it slowed down, then stilled, finally.

The worm's six-foot-thick body burned in front of the group, blocking their only way out. The smoke rushed towards them and in the direction of the stinkers. The team retreated and jumped back down into the area with the little ones. As they hurried to the far end, Artemis noticed the second plant bulb had also closed. Was that to prevent smoke damage?

Myra, Barry, and Frank took turns in sniffing the oxygen from the small portable cylinders they had brought in. They didn't talk. Even though their hearts were racing, they tried to take shorter breaths and conserve the energy.

"We're gonna go move it out of the way. You guys stay put. Come on," Zeus said as he motioned Artemis to follow.

It had been a minute or two since the bots entered the hole and left the rest of the team behind with the stinkers. Myra knew the oxygen tank would not last forever. Not with three people using it. She looked at the convulsing grubs. Most of them were struggling. The smoke had already claimed some of their lives. Their burning parent had given death to them as their very last gift.

Suddenly, Myra remembered something. She took a long deep breath from the tank and raced towards the hole, gesturing Barry and Frank to follow her.

The trio climbed up.

Myra turned around and looked back one last time as the last one of the stinkers jerked its body. She brought her focus back to the sizzling big worm and concentrated on what she was about to do next.

35

FAILED

Eustace's face tensed as he watched the two soldiers forcefully restrain the large head of the moose that lay on his side. No matter how much the animal struggled, he couldn't break free from the bindings that held his limbs. Once the soldiers had a firm grip of the head, he ceased to move. Every now and then the soldiers would move along as he swung the head back and forth, scraping the cave floor, but Eustace noticed the animal was getting tired. He had no way of knowing how long the moose had been tied up, struggling. He figured it must have been a while since an animal that size wouldn't tire that quickly, especially in a dire situation like this.

Eustace noticed a tube that hung near the center of the mother's belly as she inched her way closer to the moose. He didn't remember seeing it earlier. It was about a foot long, but Eustace noticed it was retractable and the mother could control how much it extended.

The mother looked down at the moose as the glow from her dome radiated vibrant colors. Eustace knew she was excited. She positioned herself to stand directly above the animal's tiring body as he lay on his side, no longer struggling. His foamy mouth touched the ground as his tongue licked the floor, occasionally. The mother moved two legs over and stood directly above him. Then, she started lowering herself.

In the moments that passed, Eustace understood what she was about to do. He knew the mother had all the intention of piercing the bull's body with that sharp needle-like tube. He knew he could only observe. From the corner of his eyes, Eustace noticed the alien child standing nearby. The glow from his head was much duller. He didn't seem to be nearly as excited as his mother.

The mother lowered herself even further. Her legs bent as she came closer and closer until the needle was only a few inches from the moose's body. Eustace noticed that the base, where the needle was attached, was moving. It was as if the needle was secured to a lump of skin that could rotate and in turn move it a few inches left or right to find its target. He was still processing the thought when suddenly he noticed the mother jabbing the needle into the moose's testicles. Eustace's eyes widened as the moose let out a deafening cry for help. He tensed his face as he witnessed the animal trying hard to kick and move his head with no luck. The only free body part, the tail, flicked up and down furiously as the tube pierced the testicles deeper.

The mother wiggled the needle as she fine-tuned its position. The moose kept trying to kick and move his body, but Eustace was surprised to notice the needle didn't shift or pull out from its target. It compensated for movement and stayed on point. *Is she extracting his sperm?!* Eustace thought. He was both shocked and surprised at the same time. He was surprised how the alien mother had pinpointed the location of sperm without even opening up the body or doing anything else to it. He wondered how she knew she could find sperm there. *She knows about sperm. They must procreate similarly.* Was she trying to mate with the moose?

He figured the alien mother was very dumb if mating was what she had on her mind. Eustace knew there was no way the alien's biochemistry and body would be designed to mate with earth species. From all his work and study as a naturalist, Eustace understood humans had failed in inter-species mating. There was no way the alien mother was going to have any luck trying to mate with this moose. Eustace's fertile brain had distracted him away from his surroundings for a few brief moments. As soon as he heard another loud moan, he returned to the present.

The alien mother retracted the needle as she stood up and moved away. Eustace fixated his gaze on the animal, hoping they would let him go after she had gotten what she wanted. He noticed the glow from the mother pulsated and flashed brightly. Eustace tried to look at the part of the body where her needle had protruded from. With the needle now fully retracted, there was only a small hole left, but he did notice the cells that lined that area emanating a light blue color as they pulsated. He saw the mother had her head bent down as she stared at her belly.

The child approached his mother, cautiously. He produced a series of clicks, conveying some message to his mother, but she never bothered to spare him any attention. She was fixated on the pulsating aqua blue pigments on her belly. The two soldiers let go of the antlers as the animal no longer struggled. His stomach rose up and down rapidly as he tried to recover. As the moose exhaled, the force of his breath pushed any loose soil away.

A series of loud grunts drew Eustace's attention to the mother. She moved her head up and produced a burst of short but loud clicks, loud enough to make Eustace cover his ears. He noticed her glowing cells still pulsated aqua blue. He pulled himself back as the mother sprung into action and lunged across the area to the other end. She appeared angry. Eustace wondered why.

The mother grabbed one of the large pieces of the semi-solid substance the soldiers had recovered from their underwater search of the craft. She slid her right arm through the clay-like material, which immediately wrapped around it and began solidifying. The solidified substance fit around her arm like a long glove that extended to almost a quarter of its length. Eustace noticed there were several holes in the now-hardened clay glove. To him, it appeared as if she had wielded some sort of a gun. His thought was confirmed shortly when he saw the mother move in and point her weapon at the recovering animal. A few seconds after that, he saw the lower half of the moose burst into a thousand tiny pieces. Some parts remained intact, but most of him had spread open. There was no smoke, no flash, just a big blast of flesh.

Blood and body parts splattered all across the area. He looked down at the strands of flesh and stains of blood on his clothes. His focus shifted to the moose, whose face was still intact. The lifeless eyes stared back at him. He noticed the tongue that was plopped to one side, licking the dirt, and the massive head that still rested on the equally massive antlers.

Eustace breathed heavy as he felt a deep ache in his heart.

36

EUSTACE

Myra and the team trudged carefully as they navigated the cave system. Barry still couldn't believe they had gotten out from the worm hole, alive. When he had seen the big worm light up, he was confident they would die there. If Myra hadn't spotted the side opening in the tunnel, they all would have perished. Both of the bots had tried pushing the sizzling big worm back and deeper into the hole in hopes of creating a path for the humans to walk out of, but even with their strength, the ten footer was impossible to move. Its large body had gotten stuck in corners and made it unmovable. Even with their heat resistant coatings, the bots couldn't possibly have stayed in contact with the fire for too long either. Time was what they didn't have. Zeus remembered seeing Myra run towards them and pointing at the crack in the tunnel that neither of the bots had managed to notice. Once they had found it, the bots moved in, quickly, punching through and making it bigger.

"We sure this is the right way?" Barry asked.

"There's no right way. We don't have a map. Let's just hope this will lead us out," Myra replied.

Each fork they encountered, they just took their chances and followed the path that felt right. The group no longer had any trouble breathing, which gave them some hope that fresh air must be coming in from somewhere and they could be getting closer to an exit. Their flashlight beams bounced off the cave walls as they continued advancing.

"Basecamp, come in," Myra spoke into her radio. They had been trying to get in touch with the rest of the team aboveground, but so far hadn't received any replies.

"They aren't getting us," Frank said as he shined his light up and noticed the shark tooth stalactites formation protruding from the ceiling. He felt as if he was walking into the mouth of an animal too big for their comprehension.

"Which way?" Barry asked as he stood at a fork with three narrow openings.

Myra walked past him and picked the one that was the furthest to the right. She had only taken a few steps in when she turned around, walked over and went for the one on far left. Barry shook his head, then followed.

"Guys!" Frank said from a few feet behind them. Myra and Barry turned and noticed him studying an object in his hand. Myra rushed towards him.

As she came closer the squint of her eyes relaxed. Frank looked at her as he handed the front part of a battered flashlight to her, gently. She inspected the object with all her attention.

Barry came and stood nearby while the bots hung back, on guard. "Eustace!" Barry whispered.

"We are close," Myra said as she felt the coldness of her father's flashlight in her hands, at the same time restraining the tears with all her might that wanted to roll down her now dirt-covered face.

. . .

There was an urgency in each new step they took. The presence of plant growth along the walls had made them extra careful. They figured as long as the plants didn't trouble the group, they didn't have to bother them. However, Myra was surprised to see the extent of their growth. She wondered how those plants survived; if it weren't for their flashlights, the cave would be pitch dark. How did they get any sunlight? Myra noticed the similar plant vagina lumps near the bottom, all along the path. She bent down and stared at one of the closed ones. The indentations and texture kept her attention. It wasn't quite like wood, but something softer and glossier. She moved her finger to touch it but then retracted. Myra looked to her side and noticed Artemis also staring deep down into another bulb, this one open. He didn't need the flashlight. She saw a faint blue glow emanating from it. She kneeled next to Artemis and pointed her light directly into the bulb. In an instant, a spray of liquid shot out and hit Artemis directly on his face. He immediately pulled back, trying to rub it off. Myra noticed the smoke that was rising from his face. The whole team rushed.

"Wipe with these," Barry said as he handed Artemis some old crumpled up tissues from his pocket. Unable to see, the bot managed to grab them and rubbed his face furiously. He moved his head around as his vision restored. Most of the liquid had hit towards one side, and if it weren't for Barry's used tissues, Artemis would have lost his sight as the burn was too close to his lenses.

"Damn," Frank said as he studied Artemis's face under his flashlight.

"Are you OK?" Myra asked.

Artemis nodded as he tried to wipe off the last bits.

"Let's not touch anything," Myra said as the familiar sound of a thrower caught her attention.

Everyone pulled back as they saw a hot burst of fire hit

the bulb that had attacked Artemis. Frank let go of the trigger once the flames engulfed the doomed lump.

"Frank!" Myra said as she covered her eyes.

Frank looked back at Myra. "We won't be touching that one anymore!"

Myra jerked her head as she honed on a very faint but familiar sound. She closed her eyes and tried to listen as the team stared at the charring bulb. "Shhh..." She decided to concentrate.

The team looked in the direction and tried to listen as Frank tightened his grip on his thrower.

Myra heard it again. Suddenly, her eyes sprung open. "Dad!!" She got up and dashed in the direction of her father's distant faint words.

Eustace's words got louder and louder as Myra and others closed in. Even though they were now audible, she could still only barely hear him. Myra came into a long stretch of the cave with several side pathways.

"No...no!" Eustace's screams reached her ears.

"Dad!... Dad, are you OK?" Myra shrieked as she put her ear against one of the cave walls.

"Eustace, can you hear us?" Barry asked as he tried to reach him on the other side of the thick wall.

"Get off me!... No, nooo..."

"Dad!... we need to get to him," Myra pleaded to Zeus, desperately.

Both Zeus and Artemis paced around the area, rushing up and down the pathway in search of an opening that could let them to the other side.

Frank and Barry just stood still, listening. There wasn't much anyone could do unless the bots were able to find a way to get to the other side.

"Aaahhh..." Eustace's desperate and deafening cry traveled through the wall.

"Dad!... Dad!" Myra yelled as she broke down. She couldn't hold it anymore. Myra looked around as the bots dashed back and forth, still searching. She turned to Barry and Frank. They stared at her, blankly. Then, there was silence. Myra leaned hard against the wall and tried to listen. She heard nothing. "Dad!!" She looked around, hoping that the bots had found a way. Myra hurried in one direction in an attempt to help them, desperate to find a way. Somehow, she thought that maybe they weren't looking hard enough. She could look better and would find a way. A big explosion stopped her dead in her tracks. She rushed back to the wall and listened. "Dad!!!"

"This area is sealed – there's no way in," Artemis said as he returned.

"Can you break this?" Barry asked as he moved forward and touched the wall.

Artemis thought for a second. "Myra, step back."

A powerful impact roared across the cave as Artemis punched at the stone wall. A small piece of it broke loose. He stepped back and rammed straight into it. All he did was break another small part. He looked at Myra and knew what she must have been feeling. He found a small piece of rock and tried to break the wall with it. It smashed into pieces before managing to only chip a small section. He pulled back one more time and was about to charge when some words stopped him.

"This way!" Zeus said from the far end of the area.

Myra rushed in with the rest of the team in tow.

Zeus and Artemis took a few steps back and charged at the wall in front of them. The full force of their combined impact shattered the thinner section, and large chunks of it fell on the other side. Zeus was glad Artemis was there to help as he knew he wouldn't be able to do it by himself.

Myra stepped over the fallen rocks and entered the other side. Immediately, she noticed the other side was much brighter and open compared to the rest of the cave. She looked around, then rushed to her left. Myra saw what she thought was a dead end in front of her. As she got closer, she realized there was a bend in the path. She took the turn. The rest of the team followed soon behind. As Myra came to the end of the turn, she froze. The whole squad stared in the same direction. For a split second, Myra couldn't comprehend what was in front of her. But her subconscious knew. Her hands covered her mouth, instinctively. Myra started breaking down as she took slow and heavy steps towards her father.

All this time she had been searching for him. There had been nothing else on her mind but to see her father again, and yet, the sight of him only brought unimaginable pain. A pain so deep the full extent of which she didn't even know in that moment. Each step she took got heavier and heavier.

The human mind is an incredibly adaptable machine. Although at first glance, Myra did see half of her father's body splattered around, her mind automatically chose to focus on his face and tried to ignore what was too painful to think about or even look at. Myra concentrated solely on Eustace's face as she inched closer. The rest of the team hung back. Her sobbing had gone silent. Tears flowed quietly as if trying not to disturb her, as she was having a quiet moment with her father. Myra lowered herself slowly and sat next to her Dad. Her breath started skipping as more of the sobbing remained contained. Eustace's eyes were closed and expression of unease. Myra took her time in studying her father's face. She observed every detail. His lips. His nose. His bushy brows. His chin. Every inch of his face was the object of her fascination. Myra ran her hand over Eustace's forehead and onto his hair. She wondered when was the last time she had observed her father's face in such detail. She couldn't recall. Myra felt guilty of not having done that often or in recent times. As her hand soaked in the warmth of her father's face, she thought about when was the last time she had touched him like that. That also she couldn't recall.

Myra moved closer and took her father's face in her lap. In the horrid scene with flesh and blood splattered all over the area and the dead body of her father in front of her, she felt a strange momentary calm as she felt the weight of her Dad's face in her lap.

Myra lowered and kissed her father on his forehead. She remained there, with him.

All the emotions that had been building inside her burst out like an unruly flood as Myra's tears began washing the dirt off her father's face.

37

DEPARTURE

Myra sat on one of the folding chairs and just stared at the floor. The flurry of activity around her couldn't manage to break her concentration. The footsteps that rushed in and out created hollow echoes as they struck the metal floor of the *Whale*. The pattern was random, the energy rushed. Occasionally, a tear or two rolled down her face and landed on the tarp that lay still near her. The weather of Chisil was notorious for being overcast, and rain would come unannounced. The team had prepared extensively for any weather condition that they might encounter during their mission. Tarps, umbrellas, rain gear – they had carried everything they could think of. Just as the tarp was designed to prevent the rain from seeping in, it kept her tears from reaching her father.

Barry stepped in through the rear hatch, hard drives and cables in hand. He stopped and looked at Myra. His shoulders sagged. He walked around Myra and stowed the gadgets in one of the bolted containers then turned back and crouched next to her. Barry stared at Myra for a few silent moments, then put his hand over hers. "There's nothing you could have done."

Myra continued staring at the tarp.

"We came here on Eustace's mission to discover new species," Barry continued as he looked at the tarp, "and we *did* find them. They were just not earthlings. Imagine how he must have felt when he spent time with them. He was the kind of man who had a sense of wonder and awe in him. If you take away the pain that he endured, it must have been a thrill of a lifetime. It truly must have been."

Myra's gaze shifted ever so slightly as Barry's words managed to break her thought pattern. She wasn't sure if what he said was appropriate or not. But she had known him for long. She knew he was just trying to put a positive spin on the event without discounting its magnitude.

Barry was about to say something when he suddenly restrained his words. "I say his mission was successful," he said after some thought. He looked at Myra, trying to gauge her reaction. Barry knew his statement could be inappropriate in this moment, but nonetheless, he felt the desire to say it. He knew Myra would take his words in the correct light. "Rest assured, they are not gonna be giving the contract to those companies anymore. Once we get back, they'll bring everything in their arsenal and burn these fuckers to ash. These intruders stand no chance against the government. Once these monsters are wiped out, the world will know what Eustace wanted and what he had stood and sacrificed for. Chisil *will* be protected, for *good*. There's no way people will let this place be raped once again after the aliens are dealt with... It was the ultimate sacrifice, but I think he did what he set out to do."

He spent a few more moments crouched next to Myra. She didn't feel any need to reply, and he fully understood. He wasn't looking for one. He felt lighter having shared what was on his mind. Barry got up and headed down the rear hatch ramp. He stopped right at the edge and turned back.

"We're almost ready."

It was time for the team to leave the present behind. All the years of preparation, sweat, blood, and dreams had come to this finale. When the mission started just barely a week ago, no one could have predicted it would end this way. They all did intend to make it off the island, but not in this way. Not carrying a dead body wrapped in a tarp of the man who in the first place dreamed of discovering new species and showing the significance of the island and its biodiversity to prevent selling its resources. But, just like how all good things must come to an end, this mission was also over for X-corp. It was good while it was good – until it turned ugly. The team was tired and ready to go home. Although impossible, they all wanted to somehow put this behind them. For some it would be easier, for others, impossible. And the rest might not be ready to put the past behind just yet.

There was no time to wrap up and collect all the gear. The mission had spread out in two different camps. Frank wanted both the AUV and the RUV onboard just in case they needed them on the next island. It was best for them to load in the vehicles and just get out of dodge. Less gear onboard would also help extend the flight range. They needed every extra mile that the *Whale* would be able to fly. There was a ray of hope when Myra had finally agreed to leave Chisil behind. Even though she never explicitly said yes or no, both Frank and Barry had taken her silence as her confirmation. They wanted to get out before Myra changed her mind or had a chance to come out of her shock.

The rear hatch closed shut and was locked from inside. Even though the *Whale* stood in a valley surrounded by two towering hills, its massive size prevented it from getting diminished by the landscape. The morning was quite foggy. Not the best of the weather to fly out in, but it had to be done now. The sun wasn't strong enough to melt the fog just yet. The silence of the early part of the day began breaking as one by one the four rotors started churning. Minute by minute, the roar got bolder and the constant *chuck chuck* amplified as it bounced off the towering hills. Pieces of trash and other things left behind rolled as the draft hit them. In a perfect mission, they would have never left anything behind. Leaving Chisil just the way they had found it was one of the mission's goals, but then again, this wasn't a perfect mission. Nobody had time to worry about such things.

As the rotors approached the takeoff speed, the *Whale* started shaking. It swayed left and right as the engineers maneuvered it. Soon, it was steadied, and in a smooth upward stroke, the bird began rising from the valley. It climbed higher and hovered over the top of the channel, briefly.

The rotors tilted down and propelled the craft forward, increasing the distance between Chisil and the humans and robots who cared for it so very much.

CURIOUS

The green soldier woke up with a start. He shook his head and searched around. When he didn't find what he was looking for, he jumped up with lightning speed and began exploring. As he continued walking, the darkness of the cave started diminishing. He knew he was getting close to the opening. As he navigated around, the realization of how big the cave system was hit upon him once again, but he didn't let it stop him. He had a goal and was eager to find what it is he was looking for.

As he neared the cave opening, the green soldier stopped in his tracks and noticed the child standing in the distance, just at the edge. The child's curiosity about the outside world kept him oblivious of Green's presence right behind him. Without much hesitation and thinking, the green soldier charged towards the child while releasing a series of high-pitched clicks. The child turned. As Green approached, the uncomfortable clicks became increasingly unbearable. The child stepped away from the opening and made his body smaller as he pushed back against the wall, in preparation for whatever was about to happen next. As quickly as the soldier had charged, he stopped, instantly, mere inches from the frightened child.

The clicks almost made the child deaf, and he produced low-pitch whines in reply. A few moments later, the soldier began calming down, and the clicks started fading too. The soldier moved to the opening and studied the horizon. The child still kept staring at the outside world from a distance. Once satisfied that there were no threats, the soldier returned to the child. Green lowered his face and made eye contact with the child, who was no longer as frightened. A lot was communicated in those brief moments. The child knew his mother had assigned the soldier to guard and look after him. It was the soldier's duty and responsibility to keep him safe. In a way, Green's anger was justified. If anything were to happen to the child, his mother would undoubtedly kill the soldier. But, on the other hand, the child also wondered had his mother been closer to him and not out there somewhere, doing who knows what, this soldier would never have dared to vent his anger like that.

In those brief moments, when the soldier stared and projected his dominance and power, there was nothing the child wanted more than to see his mother once again. In those moments, there was nothing that was on his mind except to feel the touch of his mother. The child knew he was always safe and protected when his mother was around; nothing could dare touch him in her presence. He knew he could trust her completely. His mother was his shield. And, as long as she was around, he was king. But, the child also wondered where she had gone and when would she and the red soldier return?

AIRBORNE

The *Whale* was too slow. Too slow compared to when the squad was inbound to Chisil after they had taken off from the *Polar Explorer*. The speed was slow enough that everyone noticed, but nobody cared. If a leisurely speed meant saving fuel and having a chance of making it out to Attu, then they were all for it.

Myra sat alone by the window, her head leaned to one side observing the stunning landscape under her as it drifted away at a snail's pace. She turned slightly to angle herself for a better view of the land. She squinted. *Is that a moose?* She wondered. She wasn't sure, but the big unmoving lump of something she saw did look like a dead moose to her. She could only hope it wasn't another dead animal. She thought about the one they had found in the cave next to her father. She still remembered the look in his eyes as they dragged and had left his half-body by the lake, to be returned back to nature. The thoughts about her father hadn't left her mind even for a brief moment and the sight of another dead body only aided in amplifying her pain.

She again thought about the moose they had left by the

lake. *What happened to him? Did the other animals get to him?* A few minutes had passed when suddenly there was a new energy in her. The idea that had just entered her mind filled her with a new sense of direction. She looked away from the window and into the Whale's large cabin. Barry and Frank were fast asleep while the robots were docked in their charging bays, essentially also asleep. The engineers were busy in the cockpit. They worked in silence, laser focused. She got up from her seat and headed towards them.

The engineers tried to establish communication with the FAA once again, but it wasn't working. They were flying on their own until they heard back from somebody.

Myra tried to get a solid footing as she navigated the path that led directly to the front of the helicopter. She hung onto the edge of the cockpit door as the *Whale* shook a little from the violent Chisil winds. The noise of her shoes shifting on the metal floor drew the engineers' attention. Even with their headsets, they were able to sense her approach.

"We need to turn around," Myra said.

The junior engineer on the right took off his headset as the look on his face indicated he would have liked to hear once more what she had said, just to make sure.

"We must turn around!"

The tone of Myra's voice indicated desperation. The junior engineer stared at her then at the senior engineer, who also had his headset off by this time. The senior engineer was still focused on flying for the most part. Whale's autopilot was nothing similar to a commercial jet. With its four rotors and its size, it was nearly impossible to rely on computers alone. Human intervention and attention were necessary. The engineers knew very well that the *Osprey* had been notorious for crashes and had claimed many lives before a safe version was finally iterated. The *Whale* was no different. If anything, it was even more complicated in its design. It was mostly unsuitable for autopilot work.

"Turn around? But why?" the junior engineer asked.

"Please, just do as I say. We must turn or land somewhere on Chisil."

"Myra, you know we can't do that. We are already en route. It's dangerous to go back there."

"I know. I know. There's something I need to do. Can you guys *please* turn around?"

The conversation didn't escape the cockpit. It also helped that the *Whale* was unusually noisy. With Barry and Frank both asleep, there was no chance of them waking up or overhearing even a word of what Myra and the engineers were arguing about.

"But why do you want to turn around? I thought we decided we are leaving this mess behind." the senior engineer asked.

"I know and yes, we are, there's just one last thing I must do before we leave. Just please listen to me... Please land."

The engineers looked at each other. The senior engineer whispered something to the other. The junior engineer shook his head and looked up at Myra. "I'm sorry. We can't do that. We can't risk going back and put everyone in danger. I'm sorry."

Myra could see the engineer was indeed sorry. She knew if it was possible for him to make the decision, he probably would have done it. It was evident he had to follow what his senior whispered into his ear. And she was sure it was a resounding *NO*. But, she also knew herself. Eustace had spoiled her enough to never take a NO for an answer.

Myra stood in front of Barry as she watched him enjoy his slumber. She could tell he was in deep even though she knew he had never found the seats comfortable. It didn't matter; he was dead tired. She glanced over at Frank and saw him too in REM state. She figured she didn't want to wake either of them. What if they concurred with the engineers? Right now, she only had to convince the senior engineer to give in. She looked around and saw the robots hanging still in their charging bays.

The engineers kept their attention fixated on their instruments and the view outside of the cockpit windows. The thick fog, occasional fast wind, and hills made for a very attentive flight. They continually checked back and forth between their gizmos and the view ahead. The senior engineer stretched his arm as he reached out for the air flow knob. All that pressure was starting to make him sweat. As the airflow increased, a sense of calm descended upon his face. Right when he pulled his arm back, he felt a tap on his shoulder. He turned around and saw Zeus standing in the cockpit, next to Myra. Their presence caught both engineers off-guard.

"Can I help you?" The senior engineer asked.

"Yes, you may. By granting a small request," Zeus tried a softer, more elegant approach. Myra looked at him as the words came out of his mouth.

"I can't do that. I already told her. I can't risk everyone's life." The senior engineer turned his attention back to his instruments as he gave his final verdict.

The other engineer shrugged and turned back to his panels too.

Myra pursed her lips and looked at Zeus. He ducked and moved into the cockpit. Zeus reached over and yanked on the lever next to the senior engineer's seat and pulled. The seat rolled back, along with the engineer in it.

Zeus bent down face to face with the senior engineer.

"What are you doing?" the engineer yelped.

"I haven't done anything yet."

The engineer looked at Myra then back at Zeus. He peeked over their shoulder into the main cabin, but the cockpit door obstructed his view. Myra shifted her lean to her other side and blocked whatever he was able to see.

"Frank!" the senior engineer shouted.

"Aaahhh... No!" Zeus whispered as his big titanium hand silenced the senior engineer's mouth.

The engineer looked at Myra. She stood still, standing her ground.

"How much do you weigh?" Zeus asked.

"What?"

"About 175?" Zeus guessed as he studied the engineer's body.

"More."

Zeus moved his hand down from the engineer's mouth towards his neck.

"Have you ever been lifted by just your neck? All 175-plus pounds of you? Imagine all the weight of your body pulling down as I lift you up. It'll be a lot of strain on this area." Zeus rubbed his fingers along his neck. "And, I'm certain you are not made like me. What do you say, we give it a try?"

A large bead of sweat rolled down the senior engineer's face. He stared into Zeus's lenses then looked up at Myra, who stood squarely in the cockpit doorway, arms crossed across her chest.

40

MERCY

The alien child bent down and sniffed at the patch of grass in front of him. With highly tuned senses and a much more nuanced perception than humans, the child was indeed capable of smelling individual blades of grass at a much higher level, even other things that humans couldn't. He found it fascinating. There was something alluring about the aroma. Although there was plenty of it around, every new patch they came across he would try to check it out as if he wasn't already distracted by the myriad of new things in front of him.

The green soldier didn't take him anywhere new. Nowhere he hadn't been already, but this time the child had a new relationship with the environment. With nobody to look over their shoulders and monitor them, he felt free. His random, haphazard movements and occasional bolting into a direction to inspect something that had caught his attention were all signs of the newfound freedom he was enjoying so much.

The green soldier had no way of knowing when the mother would return, and he found it was harder and harder to control the child without her. It was a significant risk to let the child wander about like this. But, in his mind, there was nothing to be afraid of. In their exploration, they hadn't yet found any species that was threatening enough to them, no species that they couldn't handle easily. Why not explore? The soldier would get some fresh air all the while keeping the little bastard's mouth shut.

They had reached the edge of the lake. The child sniffed the water as the soldier kept him on a short leash. Suddenly, a faint sound caught the child's attention. He lifted his neck and looked in the direction then leaped closer to the source. The green soldier bolted behind him.

The child noticed something was wounded at the edge of the water. As the animal saw the child approaching, it growled and hissed. That display of strength was enough to stop the child in his tracks.

The soldier finally arrived. He realized perhaps he was getting old, or that the child was too young. Clearly, the child was capable of outrunning him, a fact the soldier didn't like much. As he neared the child, he let out a series of clicks, warning him to stay put and not approach whatever was in front of them.

Both of them stood there, still, and observed as the animal convulsed in pain. The big wound in its stomach was leaking blood fast. It was starting to lose consciousness but was still determined to hiss and put up a front until its last mindful breath. The child turned around abruptly. The soldier looked at him, trying to figure out what that meant. They communicated briefly. The soldier understood that it was uncomfortable for the child to witness the animal in pain. The soldier kept staring at the creature as it tried to stay conscious. The child turned towards the soldier once again and let out a series of clicks. The soldier just stared back at him.

A few moments later, the soldier began moving towards the struggling animal. His approach was slow and cautious.

It was still too dangerous to approach new species about which they didn't know much and didn't understand their behavior. A few steps later, the soldier was nearly standing at the top of the downed animal, which no longer hissed. Its eyes still moved. Life hadn't entirely left its body just yet. The green soldier bent down and brought himself closer to the animal. He let out a long series of waves. The animal convulsed one last time but then fell silent. As life faded away, its tensed body uncoiled ever so slightly.

The soldier stared at the lifeless being for a few moments, then turned back. He searched the horizon, frantically.

The child was nowhere to be seen.

41

ELEMENTS

I f anyone had looked up at the sky near the lake, they certainly would have noticed the *Whale* was getting bigger in size as it descended towards a chosen spot.

Barry opened his eyes wide. The drop in altitude forced him out of his sleep. He got up from his seat and walked around the cabin towards Myra, who sat near the cockpit along with Zeus. "What's happening?"

"Uh... Nothing, we're landing," Myra replied.

"Landing? Are we already on Attu?" Barry asked as he stood on his toes trying to get a view outside the cockpit window.

"We are landing on Chisil."

Barry shook his head, came around fast and sat near Myra. She looked at him. He noticed Zeus wasn't in his charging bay and just from the way things looked, he began to read clues. "Why?"

"I have something to take care of," Myra said after a pause.

"Take care of what?"

The worry in his voice was legitimate. Myra understood his concern. Nobody wanted to go back there. They all had seen what the creatures were capable of, and for a second she hated the idea of putting everyone through the ordeal. Nevertheless, deep down she knew she had the right reason for risking everything.

"Myra, you know that's not a good idea. We can't just go back."

She looked at him, then away. She took a deep breath in and just sat still, like a castle door bracing for impact.

After Barry saw the look on her face, he understood she wasn't going to tell him why. He knew if she had wanted to discuss it with him, she would have by now. She would have even woken and told him if she had felt like it. He looked at Zeus, who sat still and patient like a crane in pursuit of fish. Barry knew all he could do now is to wait. He looked down the window and saw the ground coming closer.

Water rose and churned as the strong draft hit it at full speed. The *Whale* hovered briefly before touching down near the lake. Seconds later, the engineers cut the engines. Gradually the propellers began to slow and were coming to a stop. The rear hatch began to open.

Zeus stood inside followed by Myra, Barry, and Frank, who was also awake by now. As soon as the hatch opened, Zeus stepped out and looked around. Not sensing any danger, he motioned for others. Myra saw the lake in front of her. She felt a sense of freedom, but she wasn't sure why.

"OK, we're here. Now what?" Frank asked. He had had similar questions as Barry and was not at all happy about re-landing on Chisil. As far as Frank was concerned, they were done with this damn place. He wanted a one-way ticket out. Frank was okay letting the authorities come in and take care of those fucking aliens who had caused so much misery and robbed them of Eustace, Sam, and Hunter. The tone of his voice reminded Myra that he was not at all OK with re-landing.

Myra again chose to remain silent. She looked at Zeus. He nodded and then went back inside.

Frank watched him go, then focused his attention back on Myra. "Myra. Whatever it is you want, can you finish quickly so we can be on our way?"

"Yes. I will."

They all turned as Zeus emerged out from the *Whale*.

A deep frown appeared on Frank's face as he noticed what Zeus was carrying. "What? What are you doing with him?"

"Just following orders," Zeus replied with a faint touch of sarcasm.

Zeus came and stood next to Myra, carrying in his arms the tarp with Eustace's body inside.

Myra looked at the tarp and then at Frank and Barry. "I've decided something," she took a deep breath and contin-ued, "I'm going to leave Dad right here, on Chisil."

"What? Are you crazy, Myra?" Frank said.

"Listen-"

"No, there's nothing to listen. Why would you want to leave your father's body here?" Frank didn't let her finish.

For a second, hearing the word *body* brought back the wave of pain. Myra still saw him as her father, and not just a bag full of flesh and bones. "I know this is gonna sound crazy to you, but Dad would have wanted to stay here, on Chisil. This is where he belongs."

Frank remained silent. He had a few things on his tongue, but he was thinking for a moment at what Myra had just said.

"For seven years, he gave all his time, blood, and sweat to fulfill this dream. To come out here into the lap of nature and search for new species. New life. Things nobody has ever seen before. To discover something magical. Even though we were in California, I can assure you, for all those seven years, his heart was in here, in Chisil. He had dreamt about this place, every single day. He lived and breathed it. I know... I know I was his most beloved thing in the whole world and for all those years I had very stiff competition. This damn island was like his stepdaughter, always fighting for attention." She began to break down as she was unable to continue.

Frank and Barry listened with rapt attention. None of her words were new to them, but the gravity of the situation and hearing them from Myra had a whole another level of impact.

Myra collected herself. "There is no other place Dad would have wanted to be in. I know he will be most at peace right here."

"Where would you like us to bury him?" Barry finally spoke in as polite a tone as he could muster. While initially he had had the same reaction as Frank and disagreed with her choice, somehow whatever Myra had said made total sense to him. He agreed there was no other place his boss would have rather been. The place about which Eustace used to bug him with hundreds of questions, often times beginning as technical queries then leading into philosophical debates and discussions about the meaning of life. Suddenly, Barry missed his boss a lot more. A mountain of memories began flashing in his mind.

"Nowhere," Myra replied.

Barry stared at her, expecting an explanation.

"We are leaving him as he is."

"Oh come on, Myra. You know we can't do that," Frank interjected. He could understand her viewpoint of leaving her father behind on Chisil, but there was no way he wanted Eustace to be left out in the open, vulnerable to the elements and the aliens.

"Why not? Dad will just go back to nature. The elements

will get to him. The animals will derive nourishment from his body." Whatever emotions Myra had, she restrained them as she said those words.

"No, Myra! OK, if you want to leave him here, I can understand that, but please, let's bury him," Frank said.

Myra gave the idea another thought. "If we leave him out, he will return to nature faster,"

"Myra." A voice from inside the *Whale* made the group turn. Myra stared at the senior engineer who stood at the rear hatch, resting his elbow on the metal frame.

"You remember Dorkis?" the senior engineer asked.

Myra frowned for a second, then remembered.

"I remember what you did with her body. We were sure it wasn't you who left the heater on accidentally, but you were inconsolable... Why not do the same with him as you did with Dorkis?"

As those words entered Myra's ears, she remembered how big Dorkis was. A unique parrot fish that had earned a big scar when another fish tried to bite her at the aquarium shop. On a visit to meet a friend, Eustace had noticed the fish. He had seen that Dorkis was in a separate tank and was about to become lunch for another bigger fish, as the unsightly scar rendered her unsellable. In an instant, Eustace had adopted Dorkis and brought her into the X-corp office. He even had a large custom aquarium built where she had grown to monstrous proportions and lived out her life peacefully until the heater incident happened.

Myra remembered how much Eustace had loved Dorkis and how much it meant to him when Myra did the right thing after Dorkis got cooked alive.

Myra let out a sigh as she ruminated upon what the senior engineer had said.

42

THE DEBT

The caravan moved slowly. Myra, Barry, Frank, and Zeus sat near Eustace's body in the back of the AUV as the squad navigated the rugged terrain. The junior engineer drove while the senior stayed back with the *Whale*. By this time, Frank was not as opposed to the idea of leaving Eustace behind on Chisil, but he was still unhappy about them spending all this extra time. As far as he was concerned, anything could happen at any time. He shook his leg as he stared out the window.

"Right here?" the engineer asked.

"A little more," Myra said as she continually scanned the area around them. They had come about a mile out from where the Whale had touched down, and the new zone was littered with small hills and buttes. They were still hugging the lake shoreline, none of them had explored this area before. The engineer continued driving. He wondered what Myra was looking for. The junior engineer couldn't understand what specific location she had in mind. Perhaps Myra herself didn't know. He settled for the understanding that maybe Myra didn't know what she wanted, but she definitely knew what she didn't want.

"Right there. Can you go closer to that hill?" Myra asked pointing towards her right.

"OK," the engineer said and steered the AUV to his right.

Zeus had spent the last twenty minutes digging. Frank was happy Zeus was around, as he would have hated to be the one doing all the work. Frank wasn't exactly young anymore, and besides, he hated any sort of physical labor. Frank preferred mental chores any day over strenuous physical activity. He did take pride in keeping himself fit, but anything outside of what he wanted to do was somewhat off-limits.

While Frank gave some attention to what Zeus was doing, he kept a sharp eye on the surrounding area. Every now and then he would scan the horizon and look behind them. There was a lingering sense of fear in him that day. It was almost as if he could sense there was something out there to get them. Maybe out there *just* to get him?

Zeus stepped out of the grave and moved towards Eustace's body, which was still in the back of the AUV. Myra sat next to it. As Zeus approached the vehicle, he looked at Myra. She looked back at him and nodded, it was time. Zeus pulled the body out and carried it.

Zeus lowered Eustace's body into the grave as gently as he could. Myra knew her father was safe in his arms. When Zeus looked back at Myra, he noticed her tears had dried. As he stepped out of the grave, Myra moved closer and stood at the edge, staring at the tarp.

Frank continued scanning the horizon and wished Myra would finish sooner. He did a double take as something caught his attention. Frank wondered if he had seen a glint of reflection on one of the hills to his right. He studied the various buttes, searching back and forth between them, hoping to catch something. Suddenly, his frown disappeared as he focused on one particular hill.

"It's time to go, Myra," Barry said as he put his hand over her shoulder.

Myra stood still for a few moments, then bent down and began pushing the dug out soil back into the grave. Barry and Zeus joined in.

Myra stood back up and watched as Zeus continued filling the rest. "I've become an orphan... once again."

Barry leaned closer to her. "Any father would have been proud of adopting a daughter like you, Myra! I'm sure Eustace felt the same and was beyond happy about it."

Myra stood there, in silence for moments that seemed to stretch for eternity. She stared long at her father's grave as Zeus worked. "I have to pay back my debt of life."

Frank turned a corner around the hill where he thought he had seen the reflection. He took every step with caution, gun drawn. Step by step, Frank inched his way closer. He made sure he didn't do anything too fast or stumble upon any rocks. He was in no mood for taking any chances.

Frank propped his back against the hill and prepared himself. Whatever it was he was going to find, he was ready for it. He took a few deep breaths in and then circled around the corner, gun pointed straight ahead. As he lay eyes on the small thing in front of him, he lost the stiffness in his arm and started lowering his weapon. At only a couple of feet tall, the alien child was in no way a directly perceived threat. Frank knew he could easily tackle the small creature if needed.

A small rock rolled down the hill as Frank lost his balance for a moment. The noise startled the alien child. He turned back and stared at Frank. At this moment, both Frank and the child were equally amused by the sight of each other. The child noticed Frank had something targeted towards him. He knew Frank was the same species as Eustace. The child felt no threat from him, but, Frank had something pointed at him and just like how Frank could gauge the level of danger instantly, the child felt threatened with something aimed directly at him. Perhaps the act of pointing had cosmic similarities. Whenever someone aims something at another, it is almost as if an energy transfer is about to happen. Something from the pointer travels in the direction of the one being pointed at.

Frank noticed the child had a transparent shell for a skull, the inside of which was filled with some sort of glowing gel which was clearly visible even in the bright light of the morning sun.

The child sat utterly still, staring at Frank, who in turn stared back at him.

Then out of nowhere, a thought entered Frank's mind. Freeze!" Frank yelled at he cocked the gun and aimed at the child's head.

Zeus had finished most of the grave except for the area near the face. Myra walked up and moved the tarp from Eustace's face. She stared at her father and once again studied every feature of his face.

"Guys!" Frank yelled from behind.

"Whoa, whoa whoa..." Barry said as he looked back at Frank and the alien child.

"What?" Myra said.

Zeus covered Myra and the rest.

"He was hiding behind that hill. I think he was watching us," Frank said.

"Or she?" Barry said.

Myra stared at the alien child sternly. She noticed his front legs were zip-tied and he moved as a biped for now.

"How many of these are out there?" Barry asked.

"How would I know?" Frank replied.

"So far we have only seen the worms," Barry thought for a second. "Wait, I also saw a lizard-like creature near the cabin at night when I went out to take a piss."

"Did *he* kill-" Zeus stopped mid-sentence, as he realized it wasn't a good idea to bring that up.

Frank got a hint of what Zeus was about to say. The child leaned over to a side as he noticed the grave in front of him. As soon as he lay eyes on Eustace's exposed face, his dome started glowing brightly. A series of clicks emanated from cavities near his mouth as he bounced on the spot.

"What the fuck does he want?" Barry asked.

Frank observed the child, keenly.

The alien child grew louder and appeared agitated and excited. Frank put the gun against his transparent head. "Stop it! Or I'll blow your alien head off!"

The child didn't pay any attention.

"I don't think he knows what it means what you just said. I'm also sure he doesn't care about your gun," Barry said.

The child made a series of clicks, hums and drawn out sounds.

"Let him go," Myra said.

"What? No!" Frank said.

"Frank, just step aside for a second."

Barry and Frank stared at Myra and back at the child as he got more agitated and continued staring at Eustace.

"Please!" Myra urged again.

Frank stepped aside. It was hard for him to let go of his control, but he was also curious about what was up with this creature and why he was so agitated looking at Eustace.

The alien child looked back and forth at Myra, Barry, and Frank, and when none of them seemed as menacing as they did a few moments ago, he started moving towards Eustace's body.

Zeus moved over and stood near the grave as the child approached. Myra and the rest followed along with the engineer who had come out of the AUV.

The child stared down at Eustace's face. The glow in his skull was intense and the colors bright. The nature of his long, drawn-out sounds hinted he was wailing.

He's mourning, Myra thought. She knew there was no way of knowing for sure, but deep down she could feel it.

The whole squad stood there and watched as the alien child continued his self-expression.

Zeus once again thought about the words he had wanted to say a few minutes ago, but watching the alien child mourn like this had changed his opinion. "He did not kill Eustace," Zeus confirmed, staring at the child.

43

WAR

The AUV bounced up and down as the junior engineer steered it back towards the *Whale*. The team had come a few miles out to bury Eustace and as everyone knew these miles were slow. The last thing anyone wanted was to walk the distance should anything broke on the vehicle. But, none of the passengers seemed to mind the slow burn. Their whole attention was focused on the small prisoner that sat next to them.

In the cabin, the alien child was huddled in a corner, near the driver. His arms were still zip-tied. Myra, Frank, and Barry sat on the opposite side while Zeus kept close to the child, on guard.

Frank stared at the little prisoner, "What are we gonna do with this fucker?"

"What *are* we gonna do with him?" Myra asked, looking at the child who pushed himself as far back into the corner as he could. His glow had significantly reduced as if he had turned it off. A good strategy.

"I say we drill a hole in his body, insert one of the blast canisters, and have him experience what Eustace must have felt," Frank said. He looked at the child then Myra as the last words rolled off his tongue. He could not wait to see what effect his words had on her.

Myra continued staring at the child. "He didn't kill my father."

"Yeah yeah, maybe he didn't. Or maybe he did. You don't know for sure," Frank leaned in towards Myra as he finished.

Myra could sense he was ready for some action. Some sort of retribution. For a second she wondered how come her own blood wasn't boiling – it was *her* father, after all. She was the one who lost the most, but why was Frank more up for doing something than her? She tried to figure out why, but her mind was still clouded. No matter how hard she strained, she couldn't think clearly. "He didn't. I know."

"Well, you are just a coward. What kind of daughter are you? These sons of bitches killed your father, and you are still defending them?"

Myra maintained her silence as she looked away.

"Frank. Leave her alone. You don't know what's going on in her mind," Barry interjected.

"Oh Yeah! I'm sure *you* know what's on *her* mind."

Frank leaned back in his seat, and everyone curbed their banter. A brief silence lingered. The only sounds they heard were the ones the AUV made as well as the occasional scrapes it received as the engineer tried to navigate it around a rocky surface.

Frank kept staring at the child. "You're right, Myra. He didn't kill your father. He is the good one. We shouldn't kill him. We shouldn't do other people's dirty work."

"Huh?"

"A fast death is too easy. I have a better plan for him. I'll let the government handle him. They'll cut and dissect every inch of his ugly body and won't stop until he takes his last breath. If we don't kill him, that's the other option he can have."

"You are not gonna do anything. You don't have any

rights over him. As of right now, he belongs to X-corp. Heck, even you belong to X-corp. After my father, I get to choose what to do with him."

"Oh come on! Are you serious? You really think that's gonna fly when the government finds out we have a fucking *alien* in our custody?"

"I don't care about the government. Right now I get to choose what happens to him, and it's not the same as you want for him."

"What do you want, then?"

"I don't know."

Suddenly, Frank pressed against his temples and closed his eyes hard. The pain was unbearable. He shook his head, looked at the alien child and saw that the glow in his head was coming back. Several different vibrant colors started emitting. He looked around. Myra and Barry were also experiencing some sort of discomfort in their heads.

"Aaahh..." the engineer moaned as he pressed the side of his head with one hand while continuing to drive.

Frank noticed the child was no longer in a defensive position and began sitting up.

"You son of a bitch!" Frank charged towards the child, gun drawn. Midway his move, he and everyone else except Zeus felt even more intense pain followed by a crescendoing high-pitched sound and then suddenly, there was a blast!

The blast hit the AUV from near the front, and the whole five-ton vehicle toppled and rolled on its side. It did a full circle and continued sliding before coming to a stop, passenger side up. Smoke billowed from its engine as the wheelbase near where the blast had hit lay bent. Dents and scrapes scarred the vehicle, and the side that was under had crushed steel beams as they took the whole weight.

With a loud thud, Zeus forced open the jammed rear door. He tried propping the top half open, but it didn't stay; gravity kept closing it shut. Zeus stepped out, jumped on top of the vehicle and grabbed the door from near its hinges. He yanked at it with all his might, and the joints popped one by one and the door detached from the body.

Zeus stepped back in the vehicle and pulled out Myra. She was bruised, dizzy and confused. He lay her on the ground and went back in again for Barry and Frank. Barry had suffered a similar concussion, and he stumbled as he was helped out. Frank's shirt was stained with blood as something had hit him on his head. It could have been his gun, which he had been holding right before the blast.

Zeus went in for the third time and moved to the front. He looked at the driver's seat. The junior engineer's body lay covered in a pool of blood. There was a big hole in his forehead. Zeus moved towards the alien child, who appeared to be unharmed. He carried him out and let him stand near the rest of the group as they were beginning to get back to their senses.

"And Chad?" Myra asked as she began to recover.

Zeus stood silent as Myra covered her mouth, her hand trembling. The junior engineer's face flashed in her mind.

"What happened?" Barry asked.

Frank started going around the vehicle, followed by Zeus. They froze in their tracks as they saw the green alien soldier right in front of them, his pigments flashing their brightest. Both Frank and Zeus found themselves transfixed as they just tried to make sense of what it was in front of them. The green soldier stood on his hind legs and made himself bigger. The extra flap of skin that surrounded his neck had moved to form a disk-like shape, and Frank noticed the large cavity near the soldier's nose. They just didn't know what the soldier was doing.

Then, without warning, the soldier pushed off from his powerful hind legs and in one sweep jumped on top of the downed vehicle. The soldier growled at Frank and Zeus who stood frozen, unsure of what to do next. There was no way for them to predict what this strange creature would or could do. The soldier took a step forward and noticed Barry and Myra on the ground, who were at this point stepping back to have a better look at this creature who was on top of the AUV. Their eyes widened as they looked up at this alien quadruped standing on top, staring down at them.

The soldier looked back and forth between Barry and Myra, Frank, and Zeus. He expanded his disk-like flap and released another one of those high-frequency tones. The humans suddenly felt the same headache. They couldn't do anything but hold their heads and hoped it would end soon.

The soldier stopped producing the sound as soon as he lay his eyes on the child, who took a few steps back so that he could be seen. The green soldier retracted his flap, and with it the disk shape returned to its previous form of just a lump of skin. The soldier began stepping towards the alien child when suddenly Zeus jumped on top of the vehicle and blocked his path.

The soldier cocked his head back and then leaned forward and growled hard at the robot, revealing the multiple layers of teeth buried under extra skin around his mouth.

"Aaaahhh!" Zeus screamed as he punched the alien soldier straight in the face.

The soldier's massive head jerked to one direction, and his green blood spilled over the vehicle as he felt the power of the titanium blow. The soldier hissed again and jumped in, knocking Zeus down. Zeus and the soldier interlocked with each other. The soldier tried to bite Zeus but soon realized his teeth couldn't do any damage. The soldier had Zeus in a tight embrace, and they were matched in power. Zeus found it hard to let himself out of the alien's grip.

The soldier pulled back and punched Zeus right in the face. Zeus didn't feel it as hard as the soldier had earlier, but the concussing force overloaded his sensors for a few seconds. It enraged him.

Zeus moved in again and grabbed the soldier's arm and began twisting it. If it had been an arm of a human, he would have had no problem breaking it in a snap, but he was surprised at how powerful the soldier's was. He added more and more pressure, but it was quite hard to twist and take control of this beast.

The soldier stiffened his body and did his best to grab Zeus with his free arm. Suddenly, Zeus felt a sharp hit in his stomach as the soldier kicked him with his powerful hind leg. He felt as if an enraged kangaroo had delivered his paw right to his stomach. The impact pushed the robot a few feet away. He took a second to recover and then charged.

As Zeus charged, the soldier jumped over him and came around fast, grabbing Zeus by the neck while standing behind him. The soldier now had him in a choke hold, and he tried to put more and more pressure on Zeus's head.

Zeus grabbed the soldier's arm and tried hard to break free. He noticed a burning sensation on his skin sensors as the soldier's grip tightened. Smoke began rising as the acid from the alien's mouth fell on Zeus's hands. With each passing second, he felt the strong acid dripping over his arm and on other areas, burning anything it touched. He tried to kick back at the soldier's legs, but the soldier's wide stance made it impossible.

Suddenly, the passenger door opened and Zeus saw Myra emerge out of it.

"Turn!" Myra shouted.

Zeus turned, immediately, exposing the back of the green soldier to Myra.

Myra aimed the gun right at the soldier's torso and pulled the trigger. A hot canister launched at lightning speed and embedded itself into the alien soldier's body.

Barely a split second later, the shell exploded and so did the green body of the soldier.

Alien flesh rained from the sky all over the AUV and everyone standing around it, decorating Myra's face with exotic green blood. Her breathing was now heavy. Very heavy.

As Zeus recovered, he noticed he was still holding a part of the soldier's arm. He immediately threw it away and turned towards Myra. She climbed out of the passenger seat on top of the vehicle and walked around. Myra stared down at Frank, Barry, and the alien child standing below, her face now painted green.

Something boiled inside of her as she locked eyes with Frank.

"It's war!" Myra said as she raised the canister gun high up in the air.

44

THE SCENT

The alien mother lay silent against the clear view of everything below in one direction from her position higher up on the slope of the Chisil volcano. The volcano had been active for thousands of years. For all of those years, at different stages, it had spewed its lava at the outer world and created impressive artwork with the power of its scorching hot snot wherever it went or whatever it touched.

Over the years as the lava had flowed down, it covered the solid rocks at the lower side of the volcanic slope and managed to carve out some cave-like openings. The alien mother, along with the red soldier, had found one such cliff opening safe and they secured it as their second home – at least until they realized that the volcano was active and could wipe out their existence from this planet in a flash. For now, the cliff provided a much-needed resting place. The duo had been busy. They had spent the past day or so exploring and understanding this new landscape, which had kept their minds and bodies occupied.

The red soldier was on duty. Being a subordinate to his master, he was entitled to even less rest than her. He figured once they were back at their original cave basecamp, he would trade places with Green and get his much-needed break. That idea reminded him of something. He moved around the sleeping mother and towards the edge of the cliff. He smelled the air deep and analyzed it, didn't get the whiff he was after. The soldier enjoyed the stroke of soft cold breeze, a contrast to the warm air inside where the mother was asleep. By the looks of how she was sleeping, the extra heat that radiated from the volcanic cliff didn't seem to bother her. The soldier continued enjoying the blast of fresh air standing at the edge.

He stood there for several minutes as he monitored the direction of the wind, noticing the pattern as time went by. Sometimes it would be downwind, other times up. There was no specific direction. As soon as he sensed the downwind beginning to turn, he knew it was time, and he had to do it now, or he could miss his chance should the direction changed again. Red pointed his nose up towards the sky, pulled back his stomach and shot out a waft of spray. The liquid rose several feet high in the air. The flowing wind swept the particles in various directions. He knew if the conditions were right, what he was after shouldn't take long, only a few minutes. He hoped the conditions *were* right in that moment. All he had to do now was wait.

As he waited, he scanned the area in front of him. If he looked in a particular direction, he could point from where they had started. He couldn't see the cave opening but knew which direction it was in, where the green soldier and the child would be now. A dense network of clouds and island geography masked his vision. As he stared in a particular direction, he remembered the moment when their ship was about to crash in the lake and precisely the moment when they had ejected out. He recalled watching the mothership going down and exploding near the water as their smaller craft had broken free. The soldier tried to shake away that memory, as it brought an uncomfortable sensation. It was fascinating to him that their mothership was still underwater. He wished he could visit there again. He thought about exploring it more with his brother. When they didn't find what the alien mother had sent them to retrieve, it had brought a sense of shame upon him. He knew they might never find the tubes that were most likely lost or dissolved in the water, but he knew they could certainly retrieve more items from the ship.

As he looked ahead, he also remembered all the various new creatures they had encountered in the last day. He remembered the faces of some of these animals the alien mother had sacrificed for her curiosity. At times he did feel for the creatures, but his first and foremost loyalty was to his master. A permanent commitment that he had no control over. A servitude that was his duty and for which soldiers like him were bred, born as slaves to remain slaves.

He knew the alien mother's wish was his command and he was designed to not mix emotions with his duty. He knew maybe some of the killings were senseless and could have been avoided, but he also knew that what his master was doing was very novel and there was a need for experimentation if there was any hope of achieving the grand ambitions that the mother had dreamed of. He felt the same dilemma as his master. How would she get pregnant? The random mating acts with these creatures from this new planet had almost zero chance of success. He turned around and looked at her. She was still resting, soundly. The alien mother looked calm and harmless, but he knew all too well of her power, and it was only a matter of time that she would return to her ways.

The red soldier sniffed the air deeply, hoping to catch the chemical reply he was after. After a short break, he smelled again. Then again and again. Several minutes later, he still couldn't catch the scent he was looking for. His pigments flashed bright red, and his breathing escalated. With his restless energy, the red soldier turned around and wondered if it was finally time to wake up his master.

45

PLAN

M yra took the final few steps towards the zone where the *Whale* had landed. The team was beginning to feel out of breath. The few miles of uneven surface and lugging any necessary gear from the AUV took most of the energy out of them. There were no signs of exhaustion in the alien child. He walked in silence at the end of the line, flanked by Frank, and Zeus on either side, his hands still zip-tied behind him.

As the senior engineer watched them approach, he jumped out of the rear hatch and rushed over. The look on his face was the most intense Myra had seen throughout the mission. The lead engineer knew something had happened to the team, but he felt there was no time for questions. His first priority became to bring everyone on board in a relatively safer zone and then he would get his chance to inquire. One by one, the team boarded the *Whale* as the lead engineer stared at the alien child. The look on the engineer's face was blank. No words came out of his mouth. If someone were to peek inside his brain, they would definitely have seen a foggy mess. Even though he knew about the alien presence on Chisil, nothing could have prepared him for the shock of seeing an actual one in real life, with his own two eyes. As everyone boarded, the engineer looked around, wondering where the other engineer was.

The lead engineer sat in his cockpit seat. He stared down at one of the instrument panels as he let his thoughts wander. The chatter that came from the cabin behind him didn't bother or interrupt his thoughts. A hand on his shoulder took him out of dreamland. He looked up and saw Frank.

"I'm sorry. There's nothing we could have done. It happened too fast for anyone to anticipate anything."

The lead engineer let out a big sigh as he tried to hold back whatever emotions welled under the surface.

"Let's leave this fucking place behind. I promise these monsters will be wiped off the face of this planet. Once the government knows about it, these aliens won't stand a chance."

"I'm staying back. But you guys are all welcome to leave," Myra said.

Frank and the lead engineer turned and saw Myra taking her last step towards the cockpit door.

"Again? Come on, Myra," Frank said.

"No. I've decided. I'm staying."

"Why? And for what?"

Myra took a long pause. She stared at Frank and then at the lead engineer.

"I have to finish this. Not the government, not you, or you... just me." Myra knew she would have a hard time saying those words. She knew she couldn't possibly do this alone, but the overbearing guilt of forcing the team into her mission gave her the courage to say what she was saying. Deep down Myra hoped she wouldn't be doing this alone. She knew she couldn't.

"What do you mean 'just you'? Are you serious?" Frank said.

Myra took a long pause. "I don't wanna force this upon any of you. This won't be exactly safe."

"Of course! You think you can stand against them all by yourself?"

Myra kept quiet as the silence filled the cockpit. Frank noticed her hesitation as words came at the edge of her lips.

"Will you guys join me?" Myra asked.

Frank let out a sigh as he looked at Myra and then at the lead engineer. He could see the emotions in her eyes. "This isn't our fight, Myra."

"I'm sure it's not yours, but *it is* mine!" The force in her words took Frank by surprise.

"We already discussed this, remember? We decided, for everybody, it's best to get the fuck outta here."

"I changed my mind. I don't wanna leave anymore... Not until I finish what *they* started."

"Myra, listen," Frank moved a little closer to her and continued, "We can't be emotional about this. Staying here has serious consequences. We'll put everyone's life in danger."

"Eustace was my father! My only father. I never met my biological one, and neither did I see my mother. Both mother and father, he was my everything. He gave me every-thing... I have to give him something. It was *his* dream to protect Chisil, and I can assure you I'll do whatever I can in my power to make sure that happens. I'm driving these fuckers outta here. I'll shoot them, burn them, blow them up, whatever I can do... I will! One thing is certain: they won't have Chisil. I don't wanna ask again and again. Are you with me, or not?"

Frank paused for a moment. He was surprised to see the heat in her emotions. He wondered why Myra wasn't as enraged when she had first seen Eustace's body and why her blood didn't boil then. Nevertheless, there was a strange seduction in her words. A call to action Frank was subconsciously looking for. The roar in her voice helped ignite the rage inside him, too. It wasn't that he hadn't thought about killing these aliens when they murdered his long-term partner, who was just like family to him. He just wasn't sure if it was a good enough idea to put everyone's life on the line to pursue something that was most likely going to result in failure and possible death. Myra's words acted as a fresh waft of wind, stoking that inner rage that Frank had been restraining for so long.

"You realize we can't fight these monsters? What we have isn't gonna cut it."

Myra looked Frank in the eye, her heart racing. "I have a pla-"

Just as she was about to finish her words, both she and Frank felt a sudden jolt of force as the alien child rushed and squeezed through the gap between them towards the cockpit. Frank fell back on the lead engineer who was still in his pilot seat, while Myra fell on the other chair.

Frank regained his balance and lunged towards the child who was butting his head against the cockpit windshield. With each thud of the impact, more and more of the glass cracked. The child moved to the other side just as Frank was about to catch him. Zeus appeared at the cockpit door but found himself too big to be able to squeeze in there fast enough. Myra stepped out to give Frank some more room.

The alien child, hands still tied behind him, jumped up and down on various instrument panels as he tried to break through the windshield. His small size and incredible agility made it impossible to control him. Each jump landed hard and damaged the instrument clusters. The lead engineer got up and left his seat too.

The alien child cocked his head back and smashed it against the cracked windshield. A large section of the glass fell off. Finally, he could escape. He squeezed his head through the hole and tried to force himself out, but Frank had gotten a hold of his short tail. The child gave it all he had and exerted pressure with all his might. Frank pulled harder on the tail. As his force increased, he began dragging the alien child towards him.

Suddenly, Frank fell back and slammed against the cockpit door. He noticed he still had a part of the child's tail in his hands. Through the cracked windshield, he saw the alien child running off into the distance.

Frank turned back, Zeus was already dashing out the rear hatch.

46

PURSUIT

Zeus jogged at a steady pace as he kept his cameras and sensors honed in for any signs of the alien child. There was no point in running frantically, as he didn't know exactly which way the child had run off. The occasional footstep in the loose damp soil helped guide him, but the terrain wasn't consistent. Sooner or later, the markers faded as the ground changed.

The area was surrounded by many buttes rising high from the ground. There were plenty of places to hide and considering the small size of the creature, Zeus knew it won't be too easy to find him. He remembered the flashing pigments of the green alien soldier at the AUV crash site. It was not too far-fetched for Zeus to believe the alien child could use some sort of camouflage. And if that were the case, it would be nearly impossible to find him.

He toggled between various camera modes as he scanned the area. His highly sensitive microphones were tuned in for picking up any sounds that might give away the child's position. His senses were on high alert. It was just a matter of time before he would find the child.

· · ·

Myra, Barry, and Frank stood near the *Whale* as they noticed Zeus marching towards them. He was alone. Zeus came closer and looked at Myra.

"Well, that was a big mistake. That creature was our only leverage. Now, its gonna go back and bring the rest of the party here," Frank said.

"And we don't know how many or what kinds we'll be dealing with," Myra said.

"Exactly! We should have gotten outta here when we had the chance. Now, this damn thing won't even fly," Frank said as he kicked the *Whale*.

Myra realized the gravity of their situation. She had wanted to stay and finish every single one of those creatures off, but now she realized there was no way for them to fly out of Chisil. The *Whale* had been rendered inoperable. After all the damage the alien child did in the cockpit, there was no way the lead engineer would be able to fly it, or the autopilot would work. She realized they were stranded, with no communication capabilities with the rest of the world.

"It's a sign," Myra said.

"Huh?" Frank said.

Myra took a deep breath as she hesitated for a moment before speaking. "It's a sign... We were destined to stay here and finish what is needed from us. Chisil chose us to stay."

"Whatever, Myra... you can indulge all you want in your hoo-ha stuff or signs and bullshit theories. All I know is when the time comes, there's only one thing that's gonna determine who walks away and who gets buried. And, as I see it right now, we are losing," Frank said.

Myra turned and looked at Frank. She wanted to say something but exercised restraint. The concern she noticed in Frank's eyes stoked her own worries, but then she rested all her hope on what she was about to do next.

47

THE PLUNGE

Zeus steered the RUV towards the shore as Myra sat shotgun and the rest of the squad huddled in the back. It was a tight squeeze and the gear they had onboard spared no comfort room. Zeus slammed the brakes and stood up. He scanned the horizon then continued driving. They were getting close. It was only a matter of remembering the exact location. There was no extra time for them to fool around. Each one of them was aware of the looming danger. Once again, the lead engineer chose to stay behind. That decision wasn't hard as there was hardly any room in the RUV. Besides, someone had to protect the *Whale*. Even if inoperable, it was still their basecamp and storage. Frank had left his 9mm with the lead engineer.

The RUV came to an abrupt stop as Zeus found the spot he had been looking for. He pointed straight ahead. Myra saw the little cove that led a part of the north Pacific into Chisil. It was as if a small chunk of water had broken free from the ocean and weaved its way into the island.

Myra stood up and looked straight ahead. "Let's do this!"

. . .

Myra walked over to the edge of the cliff that rose some fifteen feet above the water. The channel was to her left. As she scanned the horizon, she searched for Zeus's dinghy that should have survived. She hoped the boat was somewhere close, but she couldn't spot it anywhere, probably sunken if its air tubes had hit one of the sharp rocks that lined the cove. *I'm not sure about this.* Before her doubt could grow any bigger, she heard a voice from behind.

"I'm with you, Myra," Barry said.

For a brief moment, his words sounded cheesy to her, but immediately the feeling went away, and she realized how powerful those words actually were. She knew those simple words meant a lot. She was at the edge, and there was someone who believed in what she was doing and was with her. She knew it was priceless. She gave Barry a smile and nodded. She noticed he was already in his wetsuit and was holding another one, which he extended out to her.

Frank and Zeus backed up the RUV and set the ropes as Myra suited up.

"You think this is gonna work?" Barry asked.

She pursed her lips and let out a sigh. "Well, we are not as strong as Zeus, but he sure can't swim. So, I see no choice but to *make* it work. Once we are in the water, we just gonna have to work fast and use every minute." Myra tried to reach for the long zipper in the back of her suit. She almost got a hold of it when Barry stepped in and zipped it for her.

"Can you swim as fast as you type?" Myra asked.

Barry took a moment before answering. "We'll find out."

The RUV was parked at the edge of the cliff, its back towards the ocean. Both Myra and Barry stood at the cove shore, all suited up. They did the final air check and pulled their goggles over their heads.

Near the RUV, Frank prepped the drone they had fetched from the *Whale*.

Myra and Barry began walking down into the channel as Frank and Zeus watched from the cliff above.

"Be safe," Zeus yelled.

Myra nodded and gave him a thumbs up.

Myra and Barry treaded deeper into the channel, trying not to let the subsurface rocks puncture their suits or damage their portable water scooters. Slow and steady was their approach. There was no reason to hurry and fall and get hurt. As Myra almost tripped over a rock, she leaned towards Barry and grabbed his hand. A few minutes later, the water was up to their chest. They knew they would be under any moment now as they had reached the end of the small channel.

Myra waved to Zeus and Frank in the distance. She put on her mask, stuffed the regulator in her mouth and both of them took a big leap forward as they plunged into the chilly north Pacific.

48

RECOVERY

Both Myra and Barry hadn't prepared for what they faced. The plunge was cold, and the initial splash left them with very little visibility. They could see rocks lined up around them. A narrow path, flanked by some lava deposits, seemed to lead to the ocean in front. Myra checked the GPS watch on her wrist and pointed straight ahead. They were sure it wasn't going to work underwater, but it couldn't hurt to bring it along. Although there was no way Zeus would have known the exact location, he had done the best he could in making an educated guess. All they had to do was go to the site and explore. As they glided ahead, Barry set the timer on his watch. They had roughly sixty minutes.

Myra had been afraid of the water pretty much all of her life. Being in and around water was one of the cardinal fears she harbored as a child and retained through adulthood. It was this same fear that had prompted Eustace to make sure she was never again afraid of water. From swimming lessons to scuba diving to exploring the subsurface in submersibles, he had done everything he could to drill that fear out of her. But just as old habits die hard, all that training did was help Myra manage her fear. The seeds of that anxiety were sown so deep that even after all that effort, there was no way she was ever going to be at home in water. All she had to do was manage her emotions and just take it minute by minute.

They both started the small scuba scooters that propelled them forward at a rapid rate. Barry noticed Myra kept looking around frequently. It wasn't that he was not anxious or afraid himself, he just knew Myra was more uncomfortable than he was. As he saw himself drifting away from her, he adjusted his angle and closed in the distance.

"How far?" Barry asked.

He noticed Myra didn't react. He talked again in his mouthpiece. This time she turned towards him.

She glanced at her watch, trying to guess. "Maybe a mile... or ten... it's not like we know the exact address."

Barry pointed his hand straight, signaling to keep marching on. He tried to keep a positive attitude.

As they moved a few meters in, they suddenly felt a wave of pressure. Myra squinted, but the visibility was low. She turned towards Barry. He pointed forward, indicating her to look ahead.

Myra's eyes widened as she saw a group of penguins charging towards them. *Penguins?* Almost exclusively restricted to the southern hemisphere, she was shocked to find them this far north. Did someone bring them here? Did some of them come on a fishing boat? There was no time to solve the puzzle. Myra angled her scooter to avoid colliding with them, and so did Barry. The wall of penguins was both long and wide. As the portly birds crossed, Myra and Barry managed to dodge each one of them. It wasn't clear who avoided who.

Myra tilted her scooter down as the last ones swam above her. The trail of bubbles left dazzling white streaks all around and gave them a big smile. Myra couldn't help it. The encounter had lifted her spirit.

· · ·

They powered off their scooters and just hovered at a spot that felt right.

"I'm gonna go down and have a look," Barry said.

Myra nodded.

Barry pointed his scooter south and within seconds disappeared from Myra's view. The moment he was out of sight, Myra felt the weight of the whole ocean that surrounded her. She kept looking to her left and right and turned around a few times. The sound of her regulator and oxygen were deafening. She wondered why didn't she go down with him.

"Did you find anything?" She spoke into her mouthpiece and waited for the answer, which never came.

"Barry. You copy?"

She waited a little more. The moments were brief, but their intensity was cosmic. It hadn't been more than a minute that Barry was gone, but she was already beginning to slip into a mild panic.

If there was one fear she had had that was greater than merely being in the water, it was sharks. It wasn't that she hated them; as a matter of fact, sharks were some of her favorite animals. Enigmatic, graceful and, when the time called for it, devastatingly lethal. As she kicked her legs in the water, bobbing with the current, she wished she hadn't seen all the silly shark films growing up. The ones where people labeled sharks to be man-eaters and dragged themselves in droves to go out and hunt them. She always found those films mediocre and unfair as she knew very well sharks maybe killed five people a year across the globe, while humans slaughtered more than a hundred million. She was sympathetic towards sharks, but that didn't help calm her fears. She just couldn't shake off the feeling. Random thoughts of sharks and other underwater creatures kept coming in, uninvited.

A moment later, she felt a faint movement and

wondered if it was another group of animals, or worse, a shark. Myra looked to her left and down and could make out a faint silhouette that was growing in size. The gray shape from a distance did resemble that of a shark. She powered her vehicle and was ready to head the other way when she noticed it was not the shark that she feared but Barry's scooter. The empty machine shocked her even more than a shark would have. At least she could anticipate some possible things to do when the shark would have been closing in, but she never expected a lone scooter. "Barry! Where are you?" she yelled into her mouthpiece as she moved in and grabbed his scooter. If she were on the ground, she would have jumped high after what happened next, but being underwater, she just felt her heart sink as Barry tapped her shoulder from behind. Myra turned around and gave him a shocked look. Barry touched the mouth part of his helmet and made a cutting gesture around his neck.

"Can *you* still hear me?" Myra asked.

Barry nodded. Myra kept kicking her legs gently as she took a few moments to wonder.

"Let's search there," she said as she pointed to their left and continued, "It must be here somewhere."

Barry nodded.

"Just stick close to me. I don't wanna lose you."

Barry wished his mouthpiece hadn't stopped working. Not being able to talk back was annoying, especially when he was underwater, against the clock. He followed Myra closely. They kept an eye on the watch as they descended. She figured they still had about another thirty minutes. There was still time, but not as much as they would have liked. Each passing minute ratcheted the tension.

The new zone granted even lesser visibility. Myra navigated

her scooter, carefully dodging the floating strands of kelp. With their air-filled bulbs, the brown plants stretched long and tall. Barry was just a few feet behind, hoping to stay on the trail that Myra was breaking, wading her way through the kelp mess. The cliff and rock faces behind the plants made it even more difficult to predict and plot a clear route. Myra couldn't wait to get out to a clearer area and just hoped what she was after wasn't buried, entangled in a pile of plants.

Barry caught a glimpse of something in his peripheral vision. He thought it was some big fish, but when he strained harder, he could remember seeing feet. As soon as Barry turned, the thing vanished in the kelp fog. Myra turned back to check on Barry and noticed he was moving away from her.

"Did you find it?" Myra asked.

Barry shook his head and indicated she should follow him.

"Where you going?"

Barry's scooter propelled him through the dense kelp in pursuit of what he had seen. Myra turned around and followed.

Barry slowed down his scooter as he neared the end of the forest. A few seconds later, Myra approached and floated near him. He looked at her and shook his head.

"What is it?"

Barry rolled his eyes and pointed once again to his mouthpiece. He was dying to explain it to her, while she was dying to have it told. Myra realized they were out of the kelp mess and as she was scanning the area, she noticed something substantial under them. She immediately looked at Barry and then throttled her scooter in the direction. He followed.

Just a few seconds later, they reached it. The case was huge. Several feet wide and tall. There was an almost algae-like growth on it already. A very faint film but still very visible. They went deeper and stood at the sea bed. They were some thousand or so feet from the shore and were glad that the floor didn't sink into the abyss where they were. The pressure was still manageable. The case had fallen on a big rock, and the impact tilted it to one side. Myra swam around it and checked the various latches. They were all still intact.

"Stay here. I'll go up and come back down."

Barry gave Myra a thumbs up as he saw her rising from behind the case and heading up.

With one big splash, Myra broke through the surface. She looked straight ahead and saw the horizon, a vast sea of blue stretched in front of her. Myra turned around and saw Chisil behind her. She removed her goggles and could barely make out Frank and Zeus standing on the edge of the cliff with the RUV. She waved instinctively. That didn't do much.

"Guys, can you see me?" she spoke into her mouthpiece while waving her hand.

"We see you," Frank's voice came from the other end.

"Alright! Send it in."

"Copy," Frank said.

Myra waited as she noticed the small figures in the distance moving around. She couldn't believe she was in the middle of the northern Pacific, bobbing up and down. Myra tried not to overthink about it. She knew she was halfway done when she checked her watch. They still had twenty more minutes.

A distant whine filled the air as the drone became airborne. Myra saw the big bird rising high in the sky, carrying a long tail. She found it fascinating as well as somewhat unbelievable about what they were doing. She didn't have much time to ponder as the drone neared her pretty fast. As it came closer and hovered above her, the downward draft sent ripples of water away from her. She could feel the coldness of the air on the parts of her face that were still exposed. The drone lowered further to within inches above her. She could now really feel the cold slaps. Then, with a *snap*, it released its cargo. The rope's end fell on water but a few feet away from Myra as the tension in the line made it retract.

Myra quickly swam and grabbed it as the hooks at the end of the rope were making it sink and if she hadn't reacted fast enough, a lot of it would have gone under. Once she got a hold of the line, she studied the three attachment hooks for a moment. It was a single thick rope split into three at the end, and each end capped with a hook. She thought it looked very professional and as if it had been made for just this rescue mission.

She turned around and plunged back into the water. She wanted to give a thumbs up, but her hands had work to do. Once she was gone, the drone tilted and raced back towards Frank.

Myra attached the last of the three hooks to the latches on the side of the case. She swam up and yanked on the line a few times. Myra and Barry pulled back as they waited. Seconds passed. Barry gestured to try again. Myra swam to the line and this time yanked harder. She pulled back again. Soon, the line tensed and stopped. Finally, the case started tilting upright. It was moving. Barry gave Myra a high five.

"Good work. Let's go," Myra spoke into her mouthpiece.

Barry nodded and moved towards her. Myra had already aimed her scooter in the direction of the line and was gunning it full speed. A few meters in, she turned back, once again wanting to check on Barry. She noticed him making big gestures with his arms, pointing in a particular direction. Myra looked and saw the same creature that Barry had seen a few minutes earlier. The four-foot-long lizard swam as gracefully as the floating kelp that surrounded it. Barry wondered if the animal was a giant salamander, but it was unlike anything he had ever seen. Unlike anything, anyone had ever seen. The dull brown coloring camouflaged the animal perfectly to be around kelp and underwater caves.

Suddenly, a thought entered Myra's mind. *We found them! The Amphibian!*

"Barry, its the *bian*!"

He gave her a big smile.

"We found them! They're real," Myra said.

They couldn't believe they had finally found the creatures which had pulled Eustace and all of them to this corner of the world. They were finally just a few feet away from the bian of their fascination. The Aleutian island native Aleuts had narrated Eustace ancient stories about such rare lizard-like creatures that lived both on land and water, but nobody had ever documented one. Dwelling in caves both above and under water, it had been impossible for people to encounter them in regular expeditions. But Eustace had had a hunch that these creatures existed and were real. And, that fascination had made it all that more important for him to discover and protect them before their home would get sold off.

Myra couldn't control her tears.

Barry raced after the salamander, Myra followed.

As they continued, they neared a towering rock wall, standing some twenty feet high. Around the wall was the beginning of the channel that lead back to Chisil. Suddenly, Barry stopped and so did Myra next to him. They both stared ahead. The salamander was swimming towards the wall, the swaying of its tail propelling the animal forward with grace and beauty.

Barry looked at the wall and noticed a small hole. He kept his gaze fixed at the opening when soon after, the creature entered the opening, and within a few seconds, it was gone. Barry stood there for a few moments as Myra broke his trance, swimming forward.

"Time to go," Myra said as she pointed at her watch. No matter how much she had wanted to stay in those waters, she knew it was time. She looked once again in the direction where the salamander had disappeared, then aimed her scooter towards Chisil.

Myra twisted the throttle all the way back, Barry followed suit.

49

MISSING

The ground shook as both the alien mother and the red soldier charged towards the cave entrance. Their visual system quickly adjusted to the change in light from outside to inside. The mother started searching, frantically. She moved in and sought in various pathways. The mother noticed that the bodies of the moose and the human that they had destroyed were gone. But she didn't care and neither did she had the time to care. There were more urgent matters at hand. The glow in the mother's dome was flickering like a disco full of youths high on life. The colors twitched and dazzled with speed and intensity. The mother emitted a *whoc whoc* sound as she searched the cave, hoping that her child would hear her and come out of hiding.

The red soldier also kept himself occupied searching the areas where the mother wasn't. He made sure to keep his distance. He was all too familiar with what she was capable of, and this would have been a terrible time to get on her nerves. Besides hiding from her in her enraged state, Red wondered what had happened to his brother and the child. When the sounds the mother produced grew both in intensity and power, it really aroused a deep-seated fear in the soldier. It was an unpredictable time for him. He feared the mother might kill him in her rage. The soldier noticed the mother was searching the places she had already combed. He knew the child wasn't there, but for whatever reason, the mother didn't want to believe it. He was watching her go in and out of the sections of the cave in front of him when suddenly he noticed she made a U-turn and charged straight towards him.

The force of the mother's charge sent the soldier back, and she pinned him against the wall. Her tentacles grabbed his neck and began squeezing. Red felt the intensity of the pain. Then just as fast as the charge had come, she released him instantly and bolted towards the cave wall. The mother rammed with full force, and sections of the wall broke in front of her. The soldier knew how strong she was and the charge wasn't going to hurt her much. In any case, in that situation with all that energy and rage in the mother's body, she could have done anything.

The soldier saw her ram into walls, again and again, smashing pieces of rocks, venting her anger. He was glad it was the rocks and not him. Then he saw the mother dash towards the cave exit and stand tall, scanning the horizon. The soldier wondered if she cared at all about his brother. He knew it was necessary for the mother to find her child, but he also wanted to know what had happened to *his* family.

50

POWER UP

The case was hauled in with great effort. Once Zeus had dragged it as close to the shore as possible, he had gone down to the water, tugged the rope and hauled it to the beach. The rest of the journey wasn't easy either, but together, they had managed to bring it to the new basecamp.

Zeus undid the last latch and with some effort opened it. Myra felt relieved, instantly. No water had gotten inside the case, and the machine was still in one piece.

Its design was both complicated and simple at the same time. In the center, there was a long arm attached to tubes. At the end of which were attachment spots for nozzles. The whole assembly was customizable, and the injectors could be swapped with other kinds for custom results. Stacked neatly around the arm were rail-type tracks, which could be rearranged with ease based on the type of job. The tracks fit just like Lego blocks to provide a path for the center arm to move on. But, that was reserved for large-scale operations, what the team had in mind was much smaller.

Barry dragged the power cable closer, the other end of which stretched all the way to the *Whale*, standing dead some ten feet away. He connected it to a socket inside the case, and with that, the machine sprung into action. Myra smiled as she saw the center arm move up and extend several feet high in the air. For a brief moment, there was a purity in Myra's expression. No weight of her father's death or what they had to do next bothered her, at least in that moment. The excitement stoked the fire of her hope. This might just really work.

More sounds of various motors and hydraulics filled the air, and it was then they knew their 3D printer was coming back to life.

"It works," Myra sighed in relief.

"Well, it powers up for sure. We'll see if we can make it work," Barry said.

"Why wouldn't it work?"

"I dunno. Many things could go wrong. The weather, too much moisture in the air, not the right materials, too many variables..."

"We should start soon then," Myra said.

"Well, there ain't nothing quick about these machines."

"How long do you think it'll take?"

"Too long. Too long for how soon we want. Honestly, I'm not even sure if this is even a good idea. We might just end up wasting more time and resources."

"It's our best chance, Barry," Frank said.

"Barry is right – this might just not work." Zeus took a brief pause then continued, "We must secure our other chance, too."

51

RECAPTURE

Z eus steered the RUV hard as it bounced over the uneven terrain at high speed. There was no time to spare. Time wasn't on their side that day. He knew each passing minute could bring their mission closer to failure. In the back, Artemis, Tori, and Mimi bounced up and down with each obstacle that the vehicle crossed.

Suddenly, the RUV came to an abrupt stop as Zeus slammed the brakes into the floor. They stepped out and inspected the ground. The footprints resembled those of a part three-legged bird and part flat-footed animal. But they were in pairs of fours, and Zeus knew what they meant.

"Is that him?" Tori asked.

Zeus didn't answer. There was too much on his mind. He scanned the area as Tori stood, waiting for her answer.

"Artemis, you and Tori cover that butte and the surrounding area. Me and Mimi will stay this side," Zeus said as he pointed.

"Aye aye, Captain," Artemis said, a touch of sarcasm in his words.

Zeus turned around and stared at him briefly. That stare

was enough for Artemis to drop his humor. He knew he was only trying to make the situation a little lighter.

"And don't forget the net canisters," Zeus said.

Artemis nodded as he picked up a rocket launcher gun from the back of the RUV, and a second later he grabbed the canisters that Zeus was talking about.

Tori followed Artemis to the butte they were assigned. The occasional footstep they found kept guiding them. They knew either they were getting closer or the target had moved. Tori tilted her head as she studied the footprints. She wondered if their target had run in circles deliberately to confuse them.

"I don't think he is here," Artemis said.

"You never know, baby. We should search a little more," Tori said.

"Oh, I didn't hear what you said."

"I said we should try a little longer."

"No, I heard that. What did you say before that?"

Tori giggled. Her speakers made it sound a bit tinny, but Artemis loved it.

"Come on! Say it."

Tori looked at him and stared for a few seconds.

"Baby!"

Artemis felt a sudden wave of energy. For some reason, he was dying to hear that from her. He just wanted her to say it again and again. There was no particular reason. And if there was a reason, he didn't care. He was immersed in joy. He touched her arm, instantly transmitting the charged up energy into her body. She felt the sudden jolt as she readied her sensors for his touch. Not shocking but strong enough to take her guard off. She wasn't expecting him to be so charged up, especially when they were on a mission.

Artemis moved even closer and rubbed his face against

hers. His cameras readjusted focus and peered deep into her eyes. She stared back, and the soft glow reflecting in the camera lenses communicated the unspoken.

A movement in the distance broke Tori's attention. She looked over Artemis's shoulder at something behind him. "There!"

Artemis turned immediately and zoomed in. He didn't see anything, just the cliff opening of the Chisil volcano.

"I saw him go in."

"You sure?"

"Of course!"

Artemis stared at her for a few seconds.

"I'm a hundred percent sure. Baby."

Artemis felt another surge of that same energy.

The foursome gathered near the base. With the bot squad's backs against the volcano, they tried their best to not get seen from above.

"I'm going first. Artemis, you take the position there and Tori, you stay here," Zeus said as he pointed. "Mimi, you are coming with me," he continued instructing. The bots nodded like serious little children, in full compliance.

Zeus and Mimi started climbing the rocky path up that led to the cliff opening as Artemis moved towards his assigned position at the base of the volcano.

"Be as quiet as possible," Zeus whispered to Mimi.

The sun was dropping down and getting closer to the horizon by the minute. The warmer hue cast an ominous look over the surrounding area. Zeus looked up at the cliff opening. From his angle, he saw nothing. They continued climbing up. Several layers of lava had caked the side of Chisil unevenly over the years. The deposits served as an excellent pathway to climb up if one was careful enough and had a firm grip. Some of the surfaces were slippery while the rest rough. With each step and touch of a hand, both Zeus and Mimi could feel the heat that transferred from Chisil's inner core to the outer layers. But each step they climbed higher, the temperature of the rocks got just a bit cooler. For a moment, Zeus began to wonder how the alien child was comfortable sitting in a supposedly heated opening that had more chance of being baked from various sides, but the chilly wind gave him his answer.

Zeus handed his gun to Mimi as he navigated a ledge and managed to climb up as quietly as he could. Once there, he lifted her up. It was a sight to see: a hanging Mimi moving up as Zeus pulled her straight up without any strain. They were now only a few feet below the cliff opening. Zeus looked down, and Artemis gave him a thumbs up while Tori stood just a few feet away. Zeus nodded to Artemis. It seemed strange for him that only a few days ago, they were smashing each other's faces, establishing dominance and trying to command respect. Now, they were almost buddies. Artemis was kind of his younger brother now. His thumbs up meant a lot in that moment. But Zeus couldn't afford to miss his opportunity. It was time.

Zeus looked up and noticed the alien child had come out all the way to the edge. He pulled Mimi back as they rested their backs against the volcanic slope. The contact of large parts of their bodies with the warm rock wasn't pleasant. Both of them immediately felt a slight increase in warmth. Zeus looked down and noticed Artemis and Tori were gone. He looked back up again and now the child was gone.

"Are you ready?" Zeus whispered to Mimi.

Mimi took a second, then nodded.

In one final calculated pull, Zeus climbed the last ledge, and his head was now only a few inches below the cliff opening. He lifted himself and peeked inside. The alien child had his back towards Zeus and was sniffing different corners of the area. Zeus wondered what he was sniffing at. Perhaps another animal had been there, he thought. The alien child was honed in on the smell that continued to hold his attention.

Zeus motioned to Mimi, and she inched her way up quietly. The alien child was still facing away. Zeus moved up and climbed into the cliff opening, cautiously. The setting sun cast a large shadow that grew bigger as he moved closer to the child. When his shadow was a mere foot or two from the alien, he knew it was really time.

With one strong stride, Zeus lunged towards the child, who was taken by surprise. They both rolled and moved to one side of the shallow cliff opening. When they stopped rolling, the child came on top. He hissed and punched Zeus while trying to bite his metal skeleton. The child quickly realized biting was futile, so he started hitting again. At first, Zeus decided to block, but as soon as he saw an opening, he landed a sharp uppercut to the child's jaw. The child fell back a few feet. They got up, and the child tried to make himself bigger. He growled and hissed and did a few short mock charges. Zeus stood his ground, waiting to see what the alien would do next. As the child circled in a small arc, still growling, he started a charge towards Zeus but midway, he changed directions and headed straight for the exit.

"Mimi!" Zeus shouted.

The alien child was only a few feet away from the cliff's edge when he started his lunge. As soon as his body was about to go over the edge, Mimi rose up from under and fired her gun straight at the child. A big net darted from the canister and caught the alien off-guard. He lost balance and tumbled to the side in the cliff opening. Zeus rushed in and held the ends as the child struggled. Kicking, moving, punching – whatever he did wasn't really creating any tear in the mesh. Loud wailing and deep stress calls filled the area. Zeus hooked the ends and closed the net off. There was no escaping now.

As Zeus and Mimi stood in the little cliff opening, the alien child kept crying in distress. His low rumbling staccato calls permeated out of the cliff and spread far and wide in all directions as far as the eye could see.

52

RELOCATION

Inch by inch, the rear starboard side rotor tilted down from its vertical position into a full horizontal mode. The blades were static, but the rotor was still able to tilt. After a long and slow minute or two, the rotor was close to parallel to the ground. It was then that the blades started churning and gradually picked up speed.

A few moments later, they whipped even harder, and the *Whale* started shaking. The vibrations turned into a forward thrust as the lead engineer pushed the power to its limit. There was nobody on the ground. Myra, the lead engineer, Frank and Barry were all inside as the *Whale* struggled alone.

Ever since the cockpit was damaged, the lead engineer had been busy figuring out how to salvage the vehicle and make it operable. The full restoration of all the functions was beyond hope, and he knew that very well. It wasn't that he was looking to restore everything, just whatever he could. After hours and hours of tinkering and consulting manuals, he was able to re-route the control modules for power that gave him access to the rear starboard engine. He knew that if he had more time, he could possibly rewire the power to another rotor or two. But time was what they all didn't have, and the mounting pressure compelled him to go ahead with what was available to him then. It was a matter of doing what he could with what he had at the time.

As more power was transmitted to the rotor, the blades churned at their max safe speed. The engineer knew there was room to over-crank, but that was quite risky. That was the only engine he was able to restore, and he wasn't too excited about the prospect of blowing up his chances. Slowly and steadily, the *Whale* inched forward. And slow was apt in this case. The landscape was rocky, with uneven patches of mixed soil and grass. Another piece of machinery that he was still able to work with was the control of the front wheels. Unlike traditional helicopters, the wheels on this bird were steerable. Had the joystick also been damaged, it would have been impossible to turn the *Whale* even an inch. He was grateful that luck was on their side, albeit in a small amount.

The big body of the *Whale* continued inching forward, bouncing up and down every now and then as it navigated the terrain. The strong draft of air that it created rustled the grass and sent small stones flying up in the air.

The behemoth was en route to its new home.

53

HIDDEN

The loud screams and *whoc whoc* sound had calmed down. The alien child's mouth had to be shut. It needed to be gagged; otherwise, the high decibel energy that emanated would have been too much for the bots to take in on their way to the new basecamp. Zeus drove the RUV roughly, and the other bots felt each and every noticeable bump.

It wasn't that Zeus was all callous and hard. Inside that tough exoskeleton was a brain as sensitive and in tune as a human's. A brain and mind capable of empathy, feelings and experiencing a whole plethora of human-like emotions. But there was a time and place for controlling those emotions. Deep down, Zeus knew the alien child most likely didn't do any harm. Even though he had seen him destroy the cockpit, he still knew he was innocent. He must have been just scared. Who *wouldn't* be afraid if they were to be captured by an alien race? Zeus knew that all the child was trying to do was escape and go back to his kind. He hoped that happened, but he still wasn't sure if others of his kind would be as friendly as the humans and the bots had been to the child. Apart from restraining him and binding his mouth, they inherently had done no harm.

The bots were taking a slightly different route than the one they had taken on their way in when they went searching for the child. This route snaked around much flatter areas and seemed to have promised a smoother and faster ride. They were heading straight and knew exactly which direction it was in. Their GPS was still working, still fetching data, detailing the geography of the land.

As the RUV raced forward, the ride got less bumpy as they saw more and more grass. Sometime later, they came upon an area littered with dense brush. *Maybe this route wasn't such a good idea, after all,* Zeus wondered. But they were too far in; turning around and going the other way was not an option. They had to keep marching on.

It was only time before trees began to emerge. Zeus knew if he had been given life just a few decades earlier and they had visited Chisil then, there would have been no trees. A warming climate facilitated the growth of trees in a traditionally barren Chisil. The animal relocation initiative began with planting hundreds, if not thousands, of trees to create a new home for the species that were to be relocated. The trees were planted in areas where it would not affect the population of the millions of migratory birds that nested in Chisil and the neighboring islands every year, the number of which were declining steadily just like every other species on the planet. The bots were navigating through one such man-made tree corridor.

As they drove deeper, Zeus couldn't help but be taken aback by the beauty of the new trees. It was as if he was watching a hopeful new patch of nature growing in a part of Earth that was still magically left unharmed by humans. The scenery filled him with a lot of hope. He was looking everywhere, taking in the view. Each tree was different, and some of them even had birds. In those moments, it was easy for him to forget where they were, what they were doing and what was the next task they were supposed to do.

The alien child's muffled sounds from the back pulled his attention into the present. Zeus looked to his side, and it was then he noticed something substantial, far into the distance. The object of his fascination was big. Big enough to draw attention to itself even though hidden behind the trees. Zeus pressed on the brakes, and the RUV came to a gradual stop as he kept his gaze fixated at the thing in the distance. He stared at it for a moment as the bots sat quietly in the back.

"Hang tight. I'll return soon," Zeus pushed a button to engage the handbrake and stepped out.

Each step Zeus took brought him closer to the thing. As more and more of it became visible through the thick of the trees, he knew what it was. His mind put the pieces of the puzzle together. Suddenly, his foot hit something. He looked down and quickly realized what lay in the grass. Zeus took a step back, instinctively, and stared. Once the initial shock was over, he moved in. The body was too close to him now. Just a foot away. Zeus's odor sensors told him it was several days old. There was no way for him to know how it had happened.

The maggots and flies that covered the body were indifferent. They paid equal attention to the face as much as other parts. Next to the body, Zeus found three rifles. The same guns they had retrieved from the small wood cabin several days earlier. Everything made sense to him now. A few minutes ago, Zeus was on cloud nine, soaking in all the beauty nature had to offer, and now these visuals brought him back to reality. Seeing the maggots crawl all over the human body filled him with feelings of rage as well as a sense of mission. It reminded Zeus of the shortness of time.

He grabbed the guns and the ammunition bag next to the corpse, gave the body one last look and then shifted his view to the big thing in the distance. Then, he got up, turned his back to the body and started walking back towards the idling RUV.

54

TAR

T he water was as murky as he remembered the last time he had taken the plunge. But not everything was the same; this dive was different. Red was alone and each passing moment reminded him of that fact explicitly. There was no one to look at, nobody to watch his back or converse with. Just a few minutes earlier, when he was on the shore, before taking the plunge, that solitude had hit him even more. He was reluctant to go back in, just by himself. Not because he was afraid but because he didn't feel the same. He wondered if he would hear his brother's voice again. But there was another emotion ingrained as deep in him as the bond with his brother. The feeling of duty and servitude, which had compelled Red to take the plunge, whether he felt like it or not.

The red soldier came upon the same areas of the ship that he had with his brother. He was on the first floor and found the hole that led to the bottom. Once through, he was once again in that dark area where he had to use the bright pigments of his body to illuminate his surroundings. In the dark region of the bottom level, he kicked his legs and propelled forward towards one of the walls. His pigment illuminated the chamber, and he noticed the coating on the wall was still intact. He looked around and saw lots of the same sticky substance. He wondered how he would be able to do it. He decided not to think more and just get to work.

The soldier scraped hard against the chamber walls, and some of the black tar-like substance came off. He knew the coating was wet, he would deal with that later. At this time his problem was how to take most, if not all of it back. He scraped more and soon his hands were full. He realized he was getting short of breath and rushed back through the hole he had come from.

Red broke through the surface with a big splash and quickly rushed towards the shore, keeping both of his hands above the water. He looked like an ape crossing a stream, holding pieces of fruit. It wasn't long before he reached the lake's edge and stood on one leg, using his other to flip open the big moose hide that he had left back on the beach.

Once open, he stuffed the coating inside. There was still some stuck to his hands, he tried to scrape it with one of the rocks from the beach. Once enough of it was off, he looked back at the water. He noticed the tiny waves and ripples the wind created. Without much more thought, Red walked back, deeper into the waves.

He scraped more of the same coating and realized it would take him days to get all of it this way. He looked around but found nothing to help, just a dark wall covered in tar. Red stared at the substance for a moment then rubbed it on his arms, like a lotion. He moved back to the wall and scraped some more and rubbed it all over his body. More and more of his body started getting covered in the black gel. When he was almost out of breath, he decided it was enough and headed for the surface.

He stuffed the moose hide with all of the tar he could get off his body. It was still wet and felt like a thick cream that didn't lose its texture or strength in spite of being wet. Many more scrapes later, he managed to get most of it off. He dropped the stone to the side and looked back at the water. As Red stood there, wind hitting his face, he wondered how many times he would have to go back in.

As the body bag dragged over different terrains, it made a variety of muffled sounds. Grass, gravel, soil, and rocks all had their own unique melodies. All the extra weight had made the hide bag quite heavy, and the soldier felt every bit of it, especially towards the end of his journey. Even though Red was tired, he remained determined. The bond with his brother and the duty towards his master compelled him to keep moving, no matter the pain. It was like the last yard in a marathon. He was almost there. But that almost was a big test of his will.

With one last pull, he managed to drag the bag into the cave opening that he and the alien mother had been using to go in and out. As soon as the bag was inside, he dropped its ends and breathed heavily. His four nostrils helped rush fresh oxygen into his tired body. He looked inside the cave; it was quiet as a sleeping baby. A baby that could wake up at any time. But for now, it was silent, and he liked that.

The red soldier walked further in and reached a bend in the long stretch. When he turned the corner, he saw the alien mother sleeping, just as he had left her. There was no other choice. He had to do this, even though he had felt bad about it. There was no way to control her aggression when she was enraged. If he hadn't sedated her, her rage and anger would undoubtedly have killed him. Now that she was sleeping, he could do his work, in peace. He could plan the next steps without having to deal with her unpredictability. Half of his work was already done. But there was still the other half. He looked back at the entrance. The setting sun had wiped off a large portion of the light, but he could still see the giant inflated bag laying in the distance. The thought of his brother came to his mind again and filled him with a renewed energy. He began moving towards the bag.

The laws of the universe are so universal that one can easily take them for granted. When the red soldier began striking two pieces of stones and sending the sparks on some dry kindling he had collected on his way, the process was remarkably similar to what a human would do to start a fire, even though the practitioner was someone from billions of miles away. Strike after strike as the two stones struck, more and more sparks landed on the kindling, and soon some smoke began rising. When the smoke grew, he started throwing more crushed wood powder on it, which began to spark and burn almost like gunpowder. It was then that he added small pieces of wood and then a few bigger ones. Within minutes the little flames began rising and maturing to a size he wanted them to be. He had done it.

The flames illuminated the cave walls, enabling him to see far and deep. If the mother were to suddenly wake up, he would have plenty of opportunity to see her coming, something he wished wouldn't happen. He needed more time. He knew what he was doing would help calm her fears. He knew tomorrow they would be able to start their search over vast areas. He was always the one who had controlled his emotions better than the mother. He knew that in the shock of not finding her child, the mother had

had an emotional overload and was not able to think straight. Red was just glad that he had had the foresight to think about doing what he was about to.

He dragged the moose bag closer to the fire, which was raging by this time. Even though the new warmth gave him comfort, he was careful to keep his distance. He knew all too well what fire could do, and the scars on his lower back served as a reminder of a past encounter with this force back in his homeland. He flipped the hide open, exposing the massive load of the black coating. The dancing flames shined on the tar surface, which still carried a large amount of water weight. He dragged the bag even closer and within minutes noticed the water that had started collecting. He knew the fire would do the work. All he had to do was wait.

Red woke up with a start. The last thing he remembered was watching the reflection of the dancing flames on the black coating and the small pool of water that had started collecting in the bag. That little pool was much bigger now. There was water everywhere around the bag, and the flames didn't reflect that well. He dug his hand into the coating and noticed it was now much harder. The rigid whipped cream-like earlier consistency had turned more into the density of clay. As he molded and squeezed it, the pigments on his body began flickering in excitement. *Finally, it could work,* he thought.

He scooped out a big chunk and flattened it out into a brick that he put between his hands. After a few seconds, he pulled his hands away. The tar brick never fell down. It stayed mid-air, right where he had left it.

The red soldier took a deep, satisfying breath as the pigments on his body danced in excitement.

55

BAIT

The kite flew higher and higher as the gust of wind pushed against it. It was for the better that the wind took it higher as the morning sun was still beginning to rise and it hadn't warmed up enough yet. The kite was desperate to soak any warmth to kick its cells into gear and generate the power the team so needed at this time.

The group had been using all the leftover reserve in the *Whale*. The whole day before and the night, they mostly relied on the juice in the batteries in the belly of the *Whale*. Nobody had thought about recharging them. It was something that just didn't cross their minds, and even if it had, it would have only been useful if the idea had come during the day. It also didn't help that the 3D printers were now running at full speed, sucking up all the available juice. In fact, it was the printers that had resulted in depleting the reserves so rapidly. They may have gotten the job done, but they were undoubtedly bulky and power-hungry.

Once Myra saw the kites climbing higher, she walked alongside the *Whale* towards Barry, who tinkered with the printer. They had parked the *Whale* in such a way that it blocked one of the entrances to the opening between two adjacent buttes, leaving only one way to enter the area between the buttes and the copter.

"Working?" Myra asked.

Barry let out a big sigh. "Working, but too slow. I'm not even sure if it'll be worth it. We might as well save our power."

"Let's finish this one and then we'll test it."

They both knew there was a high chance of their strategy not working. They never had the perfect blueprints and materials to print what they had intended to. When Eustace had conceived the mission, his prime objective was peaceful observation and the discovery of new species. There wasn't even a remote hint of printing objects that would be deadly in nature. There was no extensive library of stored blueprints or models and materials for printing things other than robotic parts or small accessories that could be used for repair and replacement. Any custom design would require generating new models on the fly or modifying existing ones. Myra was too optimistic about the process, while Barry had always maintained his jaded stance. He made sure to paint a more realistic picture for her, as he knew most of the time complex technology failed in unexpected ways.

Myra stood and watched the nozzle of the printer pour more and more plastic material intricately over the chassis that it was now working on. Inch by inch, the shape of the object was becoming more prominent. She could see it was almost done.

"How much longer?"

"Oh... maybe another thirty minutes. It might still need some drying. So, I dunno. But let's see what happens in about half an hour."

Myra looked up at the rising sun as it began warming her cold face. "It's time."

Barry looked up at her from behind the printer. He let out a sigh, then nodded.

They both walked away and towards the *Whale*. The team had nestled the printer in an area behind the big bird and closer to one of the buttes. It was well-hidden. Someone would have to make an effort before they would find their small operation. The camouflage tent over the machine served as another layer of protection from the elements.

The sun baked the landscape with whatever heat the clouds let through. By this time the kites had been flying for hours and sending the juice back to recharge the batteries. Barry held the newly printed object in his hand as he inspected it. The weapon resembled one of the US military sub-machine guns in design. The thick plastic along with composite materials rendered it a bulky look and feel.

The printing process was separated into various stages. First, they had to print the chassis, then augmented parts like metal enclosures and plates. With all the pieces fitting together, Barry couldn't believe what he was holding. It was a real gun that they had printed thousands of miles away from home. He realized how lucky they were to have had the few blueprints and 3D models on hand to feed to the printer with minor tweaks to suit what they were going for. However, there was one thing left that would cement his celebration. He had to actually test it to see if it worked.

Barry was about to put the gun down when a huge shadow fell over him. He instinctively aimed the weapon towards the object in the sky only to notice it was one of the kites. He let out a breath of relief then put the gun down and moved over to the printing station. He walked over, and the sounds of bullet-like pellets falling from the printer drew his attention. The bullets were like little gum balls but made out of composite material.

A unique blend of hard plastic with a slight percentage of metal powder mixed in. The end result was a solid-as-stone round bullet. As Barry scooped up a few, he felt the weight and smiled. He loaded one into the large bullet chamber of the new gun and connected the pump tube. The pump began sucking out all the air from the chamber and created a strong vacuum.

Barry's hands shook a little as he wielded the loaded weapon. He took a deep breath and pointed at one of the rock pieces that he had propped earlier for target practice. About the size of a loaf of bread, the rock weighed enough to test and see if the pellet would be able to do any damage. He pointed the gun, took aim and a moment of hesitation later pulled the trigger. In that brief moment, he realized the uncertainty wasn't because he doubted the weapon, he just wasn't sure what would happen. Would the gun implode on him? Anything could have happened. When the pellet left the chamber, it struck the rock hard and left a huge white mark on it, but the target had barely moved, hardly the result he was expecting. Barry had thought about calling in Myra before the test, but if that was the performance, then there would have been no point. The firepower wasn't impressive, at least not yet.

Barry loaded a new pellet and re-primed the gun. He took aim and was just about to fire when he noticed the rock piece move and fall over. A strong force had hit it. He looked behind him and noticed Myra re-loading her bowgun. "This one still works."

"This works too, just need some tweaks," Barry said pointing the gun at another rock. He fired the bullet, and his eyes widened as he noticed the pellet break through the smaller rock with devastating force. He ran over and grabbed the pieces.

"Wow," Myra said.

"It'll work!"

Myra looked at the pieces and then at Barry. "I told

you so."

The *Whale* had two small rooms. The hull was so large that even after storing the vehicles, all of the crew cargo and gear, there was still room for things like private chambers. Soundproof and not much bigger than a closet, these private spaces were there if needed. The alien child slept in one of them as Myra stood by the door and studied him. She couldn't help but feel pity. Myra wasn't sure if it was true, but the child looked a bit smaller to her than when she had seen him last. Could it be extreme stress and exhaustion that shrunk him? They had tried to offer him food, but the only thing he accepted was water.

Myra noticed the child was curled up in a fetal position. He looked like an innocent sleeping baby. A worry-free baby. A feeling of guilt ran through her mind as she saw how peaceful he was. Myra knew he didn't do anything wrong or was at fault, but she couldn't help shake up the feeling that he belonged to one of the same species who had taken her father from her. The innocence that was spilling from watching the child sleep only made her aware of the power she and her team had over this baby. She just hoped they would use that power wisely.

Frank walked in and stood next to Myra. Close enough that she could feel his breath over her neck. The opening to the chamber was so small he had to be that close to see what she was looking at.

"Let's do this," Frank said.

Myra stood in silence. She knew they had to do it now and wished she had more time. Myra was not comfortable with what they were about to do next but knew it was something that had to be done and was their only chance. She waited a few more moments as if trying to stop time or let her thoughts settle. Then, she turned and started walking away.

"Myra!"

Myra turned back and gave Frank a soft nod. As she walked away from the chamber and towards the cockpit area, she heard loud screams and deafening cries. Myra wished she could shut her ears and block out the calls, but she had already chosen to bear witness to the alien child's pain. To bear witness to this new experience. Somehow, the experience was beginning to make her far stronger than she had been before.

Myra stepped into the cockpit and saw the lead engineer fiddling with panels and cables. "How we doing?"

The engineer looked up. "Oh... you know, getting there. I got another one back. I'll see what I can do."

"At least something."

"It'll be ready. We can fire it up anytime as long as we have juice. We shouldn't be burning all our gas. We don't know how much longer we gonna be here."

"I agree. But the kites are up already. The batteries should be charging, so we have some backup."

"Yeah, but again, I don't trust those batteries as much as the oil in those tanks," the engineer said, leaning to one side and pointing to an array of tanks that were secured at one end inside the hull.

Myra nodded. Suddenly, a distant scream pulled her out of the conversation. "Good luck," she said as she left the cockpit.

The engineer resumed his work. The screwdriver in his hand undid the screw on one of the inner panels that allowed him access to more wiring.

. . .

As Myra walked down the hull, she noticed the bots were lined up close to the side of the *Whale* that faced the buttes, all looking outside into the opening. As she glanced through the window, she could see Frank dragging the alien child away. The screams were louder in that area and somehow seeing the child in distress made Myra particularly uncomfortable. She noticed the goosebumps as the exotic sounds pierced her eardrums.

The bots each wielded the rifles that Zeus acquired when he had stumbled upon Leroy's body. Myra glanced at the ammunition box. Everyone including her knew they only had fifty rounds. Then there was Frank with his 9mm and several clips, but somehow all of that seemed inadequate. She walked further and rested at another window not too far from the bots. The loud hammering sound struck heavily upon her. She saw Frank nailing the post deep into the semi-solid ground. Each hit that drove the piece of pipe in also drove the anxiety deeper into her brain. All this while the screams of the alien child didn't stop. It felt as if the child could sense what was coming. He knew what was going to happen and the anticipation was taking its toll as he bounced and danced, desperately, trying hard to get out of the chain that Frank had secured around one of his legs.

Frank held the chain tightly under his foot as he hammered the pipe one last time. He wiped the sweat off of his forehead and then looked down at the alien child. For a moment, he had the same feeling that Myra had had back at the small chamber inside the *Whale*. A sense of wielding this immense power over someone else. It wasn't crucial whether that power was amoral. The thing that hit him most was that he *did* feel that power over this defenseless alien child.

Frank snapped out of his trance before his thoughts pulled him in deep and secured the other end of the chain around the long pipe. He took a few steps back and watched the alien child struggle, desperately. The child yanked on the restrain hard then bounced back, using all his force to escape. He was still in that state where when an animal encounters a new trap, it thinks it can break free. His effort was still new, and there was no way for the child to know what was possible until he tried further.

As Frank looked back at the *Whale*, he noticed Myra and the bots staring at him. He spat on the ground and turned around. As he walked back, the alien child continued his struggle, tied in the middle of the two buttes as the humans and the robots watched.

Everyone knew how much time had passed. Sitting and waiting was always like watching paint dry. There were no more screams to bother and tear apart Myra. With their guns pointed out, even the bots were getting restless.

"I wonder how long this is gonna last?" Barry asked.

Myra didn't answer. She just kept staring at the alien child then set her bowgun on the floor. She had finally realized it was too heavy to hold for that long, even though she had the barrel propped against the window ledge. A faint but familiar sound drew her attention. She turned around and went towards a deeper part of the *Whale*.

Myra came near the terrarium and saw Titan bouncing up and down, frantically. She wondered how many times he had done so since he was in that prison. She wished to one day release him in the wild but knew that was not possible. He would not survive. She promised herself to build a palatial terrarium for Titan if she ever got back home. A terrarium with a heater, water, and all the food that he could possibly stuff in his tiny mouth. She could even have a section where the natural process would facilitate the growth of flies. She dropped some dry food in the terrarium. Titan didn't even seemed to notice and continued bouncing.

A tear rolled down Myra's face. She didn't know why, it just did.

"This is ridiculous," Frank said in the distance.

Myra turned and saw Frank putting his handgun in the holster strapped to his cargo pants and pushing the button of the rear hatch. She frowned and started closing Titan's food container as the rear hatch began opening.

"Frank!" Myra yelled as she walked towards him, but he had already exited.

Myra walked over to her position on the window near Barry and saw Frank walking outside. He was rushing towards the alien child who at this point had given up all resistance as he no longer tried to break free. He wasn't trying to scream out his pain or throw any tantrums. The child just sat quietly, chained to the pipe, the midday sun baking his colorful skin.

Something about Frank's gait made Myra a bit uneasy. She picked up her bowgun and rested the barrel on the window ledge.

"What's the matter with you?" Frank asked as he looked down at the alien child.

The child growled when Frank kicked him, gently.

"Frank!" Myra yelled from inside the *Whale*.

Frank turned back towards her and then again at the alien child. "You're a lucky little bastard. Look how much she cares for you. But to me, you are a useless piece of shit. A worthless creature. And if I'm not taking you back to sell you, then you are even more worthless." Frank continued as if the child could understand what he was saying, "But looks like it's not you who we want. We want the others who killed Eustace. Where are they? Call them!" He positioned himself between the child and the *Whale* and squatted down. His body blocked the child completely from Myra. "Now scream as loud as you can," Frank said as he made a cut on the child's arm with the knife he had just taken out of his pocket.

The child screamed in agony. The pain was unbearable.

"Oh! Now you're gonna scream?" Frank said as he got up and pulled back. He continued, "Come on! Louder!" all the while walking back towards the *Whale*. He turned as he locked eyes with Myra. The look on her face suspected his malice. But Frank didn't care. He got the job done. The little fucker was screaming again. And the screams were much louder this time, echoing as they bounced off the buttes and the *Whale*, permeating in all directions.

As Frank treaded back, a giant shadow appeared in front of him. For a moment, he stopped dead in his tracks, then instantly he thought it must be from one of the solar kites and relaxed. As the shadow got grew, he instinctively reached for the gun strapped to his thigh and turned back.

It was as if time had slowed. Frank looked up and saw two towering alien figures descending from the sky. They closed in rapidly. Frank was in the process of pulling out his gun when he noticed the mother jump between him and the child and before Frank could even fire a single shot, the mother pointed at him the weapon that was wrapped around her arm.

The force field that ejected drilled a hole straight through Frank's body, and he shot backward. As he went down, the full figure of the alien mother got revealed for the first time to the team inside the *Whale*.

The mother stood up on her hind limbs and roared. It sent chills down Myra's spine and assurance to the alien child's mind. The mother turned around and looked at her child tied to the pipe. She began moving towards him.

Barry grasped the newly printed gun as firmly as he could with his shaking hands and pulled the trigger. The solid pellet launched and bore a hole through the mother's left arm. She jerked back and hissed towards Barry. A moment later, Myra and the bots aimed their guns and opened fire.

Each new hit enraged the mother even further. Then suddenly, the red soldier jumped down from the sky in front of the mother. He quickly moved the tar platform they were hovering on between them and the team as a shield. The humans continued firing. The bots fired the rifle, Barry fired his newly printed gun, and Myra just kept her bowgun cocked, looking for an opportunity.

Behind the alien shield, the mother quickly broke the chain and freed her child. The red soldier stretched the black clay-like substance, and the platform grew in size. Amid the volley of bullets, he quickly angled the platform, and all three of them jumped on it as their ingenious craft began taking them to the sky. Barry held his fire as his mind raced. He rushed out of the *Whale* through a side door and towards the printer.

As the alien craft was taking the extraterrestrials away, Myra saw her opportunity. She steadied her breath, took aim and pulled the trigger of her bowgun. The arrow shot at lightning speed and scraped a large chunk off of the alien mother's thigh. She screamed in pain and aimed her glove weapon straight towards Myra and fired.

Myra jerked back towards the other end as soon as the electrical field reached the *Whale*. The electronics short-circuited and a current ran through the entire body of the chopper. Myra was lucky. The charge dissipated over Whale's large body but the impact rendered her and the lead engineer unconscious as the bots' systems overloaded.

Recon emerged from behind the *Whale* and flew in pursuit of the alien craft. Barry walked around the chopper as he saw Recon follow the aliens in the distance. He paused and stared at Frank's destroyed body in front of him, then rushed inside the *Whale*.

56

PAIN

There was blue blood all over the cave floor. The red soldier thought he didn't get any injuries, but he stained the cave floor red with his as they walked in. The atmosphere inside was hysterical, a wild energy of emotion. An uncontrollable aura that was hard to tame. Even the red soldier didn't try to contain it.

What tore the alien mother's heart most was supporting her child as he limped alongside her. Her own wounds paled in comparison to the pain of the single injury on her child's body. She could not bear the fact that someone had dared hurt him. The glow that emanated from their domes was ferocious, a dazzling display of wild emotions. Although most of the feelings related to what had happened were leaning towards rage and anger, there was another force that helped counterbalance some of those emotions. The brief encounter with the humans had left both the mother and the red soldier in a hyper-energized state, a state akin to an adrenaline-induced trance that humans face. There was both an excitement for having met someone who would fight back as well as the pure raw, rage-filled desire to destroy whatever that had touched her baby.

Even though the mother's focus was on her child's wound, as she walked, every now and then her own injuries commanded attention and waves of pain shot through her body with each new step she took further into the cave. She noticed Red was leading them, confidently. She was sure he had also gotten hit but saw his braveness in not showing his pain and guiding an emotionally charged mother in the right direction.

Whenever her pain called her attention, the mother would remember the face of the girl who had shot that arrow at her. In all their excursions no other animal had managed to wound and challenge her ego. Myra's face refused to leave her consciousness easily. It kept coming back often with each passing minute and with the memory of the face came more pain.

The plant network was dense this deep into the cave. There were no markers, but somehow Red was able to navigate following the growth or using his acute memory from a previous trip. The soldier was stunned for a moment. He wondered how the plants had managed to grow so much so fast. They were everywhere. It both surprised and intimidated him for a brief moment. He knew it was bound to happen. The plants were supposed to take over, but still, the sight took him by surprise, especially knowing about the kind of damage the plants were capable of unleashing. Red just wished they wouldn't turn against their cultivators.

As the red soldier noticed a variety of bulbs that had grown anew since his last visit. He bent down and pried opened the oval shape of one of them. As the lump opened, a thick, yellow, honey-like liquid flowed out of it. Red looked back at the mother and the wounded child as they walked closer. The soldier got up and applied the paste on the child's wound. As soon as the liquid hit his skin, the child let out a roaring scream that echoed all over the cave system. The colors of the mother's head exploded in vibrancy as her emotions raged. It was already too much to see her child in this condition, and now the application of the paste just raised it to another level. The mother wisely chose not to reveal too much, barring the excited colors. Any show of weakness now would make her lose the respect of her offspring, something she wasn't ready to do.

The subsequent application of the paste didn't hurt as much. The soldier had made sure he coated the wound with a thick layer to aid in healing. Once done with the child, he took the same paste to the mother. For a second she was hesitant to let him apply it, but then she gave in. The mother wasn't sure what she wanted in that instant and just chose to go with whatever the soldier did. Her thinking was clouded as her emotions took over.

As the paste hit her own wound, it stung. As if being bitten by a hundred insects of the worst kind from her native planet. She didn't scream like her child, didn't even flinch or move. She took it all in, like the mother she was.

57

SACRIFICE

With each breath, his body rose up and down. Each breath in safety that the child took put the mother at ease. Ever since the healing process had begun, the alien mother hadn't taken her eyes off of her child. In great adversity, the strength of bonds is always tested, and in this time of war, the mother found herself ever closer to her child. As she stared at her sleeping baby, she remembered the importance of his existence. The significance of the idea that her child represented. There was no doubt her maternal instincts were in high gear, but she could also not shake off the feelings and memories that lingered in her mind.

Those memories were mostly good. She remembered the father of her child. Her soulmate. She wondered what he was doing now and whether he was thinking about them. It was a significant risk she and her soulmate had taken when they conceived their child. In their world, not everyone had the privilege of bearing an offspring. Having a child was reserved only for the chosen class, the ones whose genes were considered purer. The ones whose genes were deemed to be critical for the future of their planet were allowed to bear new fruit. Anyone lower in the societal order was barred from procreation. If a low-ranking individual like the alien mother herself were to carry a child, she would have been killed. There was no other way around that. She could not have reasoned with the law of her land, which was fiercely enforced.

If this behavior seemed off-putting and immoral, then one would not have to go too far from their own planet to witness the enormous imbalance in rights granted to humans. For the alien mother, that was the norm. All her life as she was growing up, this idea had been distilled in her that when the mother would be of age, she would not be allowed to conceive a child, unless of course she had wanted the death penalty. It's strange how the emotions play out. She had almost accepted this reality and had never developed the desire to bear one. If there was any desire that arose, her conditioning was able to squash it down quite effortlessly. All that changed when she had met her soulmate.

The child turned over to his other side, and a whistling sound emanated from his nostrils as he struggled to breathe. The mother's attention shifted back to the present, but as soon as the child was comfortable again, she couldn't help but remember the time when everything in her life had changed.

As she dug into her not-too-distant past, she couldn't help but feel a surge of emotions. Her dome began glowing with vivid colors once again. She remembered the rush she felt when she had first met her mate. How exciting things had been for them. It was almost like a dream for her. A trance. A trance that she had never wanted to come out of. She could only wish she had stayed in it forever.

When the result of that trance ended up in her becoming pregnant, everything changed. Once the seed was in her, there was nothing she could have done. The glow on her belly had lit and announced her pregnancy to her world. A flashing death warrant. The regime would have noticed the glow and killed her instantly. What was a desperate mother to do? She had done what she thought was the best.

The decision of sneaking into an extraterrestrial explorer ship and just launching it in a random direction was not the smartest thing she had done. But then again, an emotional mother is seldom wise. Whatever her emotions had dictated, she obeyed. The innate desire to save her child, to see her child's face and hold it in her arms, was too strong to not have left her planet. They had been fortunate to have survived their crash landing on Earth. She just could not believe it all had worked out.

As she stared at her baby, she kept reflecting on her decision and what their future would look like here on this new world. She also missed her soulmate dearly. A soft clicking sound from behind pulled her out of her memories and into the present. She turned back and saw the red soldier standing. He looked ready for something. She could sense that he was prepared. She stared into his eyes, and there was a telepathic exchange. As the message was delivered, the colors in her head glowed even more vividly and in a staccato fashion, with sharp spikes of intensity. The mother stood up and stretched to her full size.

The soldier knew it was only a mock display. It was the denial phase. He was wiser than her in that instant. He knew there was no other option. It had to be done. He understood the mother had taken immense pain to leave her planet, to bear her child, but if her further ambitions had to be realized, she had to do this. There was no other option. With that in mind, he gave her plenty of space to roam or think and come to terms with her emotions.

As minutes passed, she calmed down, as expected. The red soldier had nothing but great sympathy for his master. He knew it would not be an easy decision for her to make, but he also knew that for the greater good and her bigger ambitions, it must be done. When all her rage had vanished, and she became a much milder version of herself, the soldier approached the sleeping child. He looked up at the mother a few feet from him.

The mother kept staring at her baby. The soldier knew it was time. He moved his hands towards the child's legs. As the mother saw his hands approach, a part of her died, but she immediately blocked her emotions and let the soldier continue. The soldier secured the child's limbs tight as the application of force woke him up. He screamed and yelled. Random short and long clicks filled the cave as his struggle ensued. But these sounds were not impacting the mother anymore. Just like how she blocked her emotions when she had left her planet and her mate, she did so once again. In that moment, her child was not hers. He was just a means to her end. She knew she could have hundreds more like him once she was through. After what had happened, there was a high chance her baby could die, and if that were to happen, her dream of ruling this planet would die with him. What's the sacrifice of one when you could have hundreds?

The child struggled as the soldier maintained his firm grip. The mother positioned herself over and grabbed the child's neck with her tentacles before inserting a tiny elec-trode-type bulb and pushed down. As soon as the probe touched the neck, her child's struggle eased. There was a surge of electric waves running through his body, and with each set, his effort weakened. When the waves were at their peak, at the right moment, the mother inserted a small tube just under her child's belly. As the tube penetrated his body, he let out an even louder scream, and his struggle returned. The soldier tightened his grip. The needle kept going deeper until all four inches of it was inside her child's body. Suddenly, the mother retracted the needle and then inserted a narrow tube in the same opening she had created.

The first phase was over. She knew they were almost done and soon her baby would not feel this pain. As the tube penetrated the child's body, the electrode that was near his neck began sending more electrical surges through his body. With each more powerful wave, the child convulsed, and his torso bounced up and down. As the tube sucked the liquid up, the mother arched her back, creating more of a vacuum. It was a synchronized ballet. Sometimes the child's body convulsed, other times the mother arched.

Suddenly, the mother felt something in her body and pulled the electrode off of her child's neck immediately. She retracted the tube and pulled back several steps. The soldier let go of the child too, who now lay motionless. The mother paced back and forth near the child as the colors in her dome danced. The strange hues of magenta and pink reminded her of the memories with her soulmate. She didn't have to wait too long before the pigments near her belly started flickering blue before turning solid. The red soldier moved closer, and for a brief moment, he was ecstatic. The mother didn't bask too long in the glory of her accomplishment. Once the pigments stopped pulsating and stayed solid, she immediately turned towards her child.

All the emotions she had blocked for those brief minutes had come back. She let out a barrage of clicks and sounds as she shook her child's body, violently. She touched his face with her tentacles and tried to sense his energy. There was a new rage in the colors of her dome.

The red soldier was having a hard time discerning what would be going in his master's mind, but he already knew what had happened. It was only a matter of time before the mother would come down from her emotional high and faced the reality of the sacrifice she had committed for her bigger dreams.

58

BLUEPRINTS

Barry stood motionless as the whirring sounds and beeps entered his ears. In the tent, next to the *Whale*, there was no one, just him and the machines. The machines which were working hard to crank out new parts as fast as they could. He leaned against one of the cases, opened his hand and stared at one of the round composite pellets he had printed some ten minutes ago. His dirt-covered hand shook as he studied the projectile. He still couldn't shake off the uncomfortable feeling. What he had witnessed earlier made him realize how emotionally vulnerable he really was. The support brace on his arm wasn't helping much, either. It felt as if the stress had brought back his arthritis. He tried to shake it off, but the pain kept pulling him into the darker regions of his mind.

Barry couldn't decide which image to focus on. Every time he tried to think about Frank, remembering his face when they were burying him, his thoughts would get hijacked by the images of the alien mother and the soldier. The sheer novelty of the experience of witnessing these creatures rescuing their child, the excitement of the moments and the pain of the aftermath – everything was still fresh in his mind. He couldn't decide how affected he was with Frank now gone. Barry tried hard to feel for Frank, but for some reason, he just couldn't muster the emotions. Was his brain shielding him from the trauma? His thoughts also went towards the junior engineer and, of course, Eustace. How could he forget him? After all, it all had started with his being missing. He even thought about Hunter.

Hunter! Suddenly, he remembered something. He set the pellet aside and reached for a hard plastic case behind the printer, which was still busy whirring away. He opened the case and removed his laptop. The wallet was still there, underneath, where Barry had last put it. He stared at the dull steel then removed it from the case and studied it, trying to find a way to open it. He worked both thumbs, but it didn't budge. As he pushed harder, the growing arthritis pain stopped him. He looked around the tent.

Barry wedged a screwdriver in the middle and hammered it down with one of the steel pellets. It still didn't open. He held it firmly and once again hammered the screwdriver, this time with much higher force. The impact drove the metal *in* and with that, Hunter's steel wallet case sprung open.

Barry stared at the flash drive inside. No more than an inch long, the drive was secured with red elastic straps. He pulled it out and studied it carefully. He noticed *Hunter* carved on its one side, barely visible but still there for someone who was looking. He rushed for his laptop and fired it up.

Barry entered his password and then slowly inserted Hunter's flash drive into one of the USB ports.

59

WAVES

The red soldier stepped out of the cave into the wind that tried to disperse the fog with its ever increasing speed. The touch of the wind, the feel of nature, was a welcoming break. It had been a stressful atmosphere inside. Both the mother and the soldier knew the procedure was inherently dangerous. There was a high risk associated with it, and there was absolutely no way of controlling its direction with certainty. But the soldier was not bogged down with any guilt. He had made sure the mother realized it was entirely her decision to extract the liquid or not. If the mother had not agreed, there was no way the soldier would have aided her in experimenting with her child's body.

Red took a few more steps out into the open and stared at the glove gun that was in his hands now. For some reason, it felt heavy. Perhaps it was the weight of all the heavy emotions the weapon experienced since the mother had started wearing it on Chisil. But there was no time to think more about emotions. There comes a time when one has to control their feelings to do what is necessary. It was now one of those times. He knew he would be able to control himself. He just wished the mother would, too. He believed in her abilities. He knew how strong she was. He kicked a stone out of the way as he cleared an area. Red checked the cave opening; there was nobody there. He looked up at the sky. The cloud cover was not overly thick. He hoped for clearer skies when the time came. Although, he knew if the energy was strong enough, clouds or no clouds, it wouldn't matter.

Once he was happy with the exact spot, he pulled and separated three small pieces from one end of the glove weapon. He placed them in a triangular formation close to each other. The black organic material composite parts lay on the short grass that blanketed the area. He looked back at the cave opening again. Still, there was nobody. He waited a few more minutes and saw the tentacles of the alien mother emerge. Soon, the rest of her followed. He noticed how tenderly she was carrying her child's body. Limp and lifeless, but the mother still held the body as if that wasn't true. She gave it the same care as she would have, had the body been alive.

The mother moved closer and looked down at the composite pieces on the ground. She then noticed the cloud cover had stationed right over them, painting them dark in its shadow as it inched forward at a snail's pace. She moved right at the center of the pieces. As she took her place, the soldier instinctively stepped back a few. He knew all too well the power of the procedure, and it was in his best interest to give them some space. Not everything goes as planned as he had seen earlier.

The mother lay her lifeless child on the ground and then stood there on all fours right in the center of the triangular formation. The soldier knew the procedure was starting as he saw a shift in the pattern of the colors in her dome. Shortly after, the three pieces began floating in the air. The soldier took another few steps back, instinctively.

The mother continued to concentrate, standing right on top of her child's dead body. The pieces floated at an even height, levitating just a few feet from the ground. The soldier could almost feel the field of energy radiating from the mother's body. Then, shortly after, she tilted her face up towards the sky. The electric probe near her neck pointed up with it. She took a deep breath in and jerked back hard. A shaft of white light emanated from the probe and raced into the sky. She jolted back another two times. Each time, another field of energy shot up and followed the one before. As soon as she finished the third time, she dropped on the grass next to her child. Soon after, the three weapon pieces fell back to the ground, no longer levitating.

The soldier hurried towards the mother. Her breaths were fast and heavy, she was still alive. He knew she would recover. A procedure like this would have taken *all* the energy from her body. The deepest of the deepest reserves had to be tapped, and this could be performed only once every month. If she had wanted to shoot more of those waves into the sky, she would have to wait another month for her system to rebuild the stores. The soldier kept staring at her, then he looked up at the sky.

The cloud cover above them had passed.

60

CHARGES

The added weight of extra gear taxed his engines as Recon penetrated the low altitude fog at a bee's pace, guiding the way for Myra and the team below. Zeus steered the RUV at a comfortable speed as Myra looked up from the passenger seat and wondered how much longer before they reached their destination. As she noticed Recon's louder-than-normal engine whine, she understood they weren't going to get there any faster. Even though all the added gear had slowed Recon down, Myra was glad that Barry had sent him behind the aliens. She tightened the grip on her bowgun as the images of the aliens flashed in her mind.

Myra remembered the moment she had made eye contact with the alien mother. Her penetrating eyes and glossy skin, the flickering glow and the excited tentacles: every detail was still fresh in her mind. Myra knew the alien mother was the one who had robbed her of her father. The way Frank's body was destroyed with a big hole through his torso; there was no doubt. She tried not to picture her father's body in that mutilated form. A few moments later she remembered watching Barry when they were burying Frank. The way he was shaking... it had surprised her. She had not liked seeing her otherwise bold and snappy friend in that vulnerable position. Did the fear of a formidable enemy scare her brave friend?

Myra herself felt free. Now that she had seen what she was up against, a significant portion of her fear had vanished. What she didn't know back then was more frightening than what she knew now. Best of all, if anything, her arrow had told her was that the alien mother wasn't indestructible. "Barry, come in," she spoke into her radio and waited. She just hoped Barry was still OK back in the tent by the *Whale*. No matter how much she had tried to convince him to come along, he refused. She hated leaving him there, alone, but she also knew she didn't want to force him. She wondered if Barry felt safer next to the printer, among the machines. Things that he could understand, trust and control.

"Don't worry, he'll be OK," the lead engineer assured her from the back of the RUV.

"We can check on him on our way back if you want," Artemis said, also from the back of the RUV, looking at Tori and Mimi.

"That's a good idea," Zeus said.

"But, we'll need those batteries ASAP. Every last one of them. The dead ones will force the remaining good ones to work harder. The *Whale* will shut down fast," the engineer said referencing the batteries which were now unusable due to re-routing of power throughout the copter. The engineer hadn't been able to get into a large block of them, and the *Whale* was running on the ones which were easily accessible. He looked at Artemis and continued, "Try to get him on the walkie first, time is short."

"Aye, aye, engineer!" Artemis replied.

Recon dodged the branches among the thin tree line in front as his engines whined.

Zeus continued steering the RUV, following behind Recon as the humans and the bots drove in silence.

"This is the one?" Myra asked as she stared at the large cave entrance in front of them.

Recon continued hovering in the same spot near the entrance that he had led them to.

"Are you sure?" Myra asked, looking up at Recon.

Recon looked tiny against the towering Chisil Volcano a mile behind him. He just hovered without any confirmation or denial. A moment later, his engines whined, and he began descending. He knew he wouldn't be able to carry on much longer. Either he gave his pistons some rest or risk burning all the fuel, rendering him useless for what he had been brought along for in the first place.

Myra stared at the familiar cave entrance with dread. "We've been here before. This is where we took dad out o-" she stopped midway as tears started welling in her eyes.

"This is it, guys. Let's get this over with. We must get as close to the core as we can!" the engineer said as he stepped out of the RUV towards the cave entrance, hoping to distract Myra. He looked behind and noticed she was still in the rear passenger seat. He sensed her hesitation.

"You guys can go. I'll wait here." Myra said.

Zeus and the other bots stared at Myra and then at the engineer.

The engineer came up to Myra and tried to make eye contact, which she skillfully avoided. Once he was close enough, she finally lifted her head and looked him in the eye. He put his hand on her shoulder and said, "It's OK, Myra, you are a strong girl... strong like your father." He noticed soft tears rolling down her face. He took a moment and then continued, "There is nothing I can say that'll make you feel any better but having known you for as long as I have, I'll say one thing. Save your emotions, Myra. Save them for when we reach home. Make them your strength, your weapon. You can be the girl who lost her father later – right now you are a warrior. Don't let emotions cripple you. Be a machine. A *war machine*."

Myra took in each and every word with the most amount of patience she could muster. She struggled to balance the two battles being fought within her. The first one dragging down and painting her in colorful emotions, making her stay where she was, the other forcing her to get up and take action. She knew what the right choice was, she just had to make that decision herself.

Myra nodded gently at the engineer's words. Her tears already seemed to have been drying.

"We're going in. Artemis, you take Mimi and Tori and fetch me those damn batteries," the engineer said.

Artemis didn't respond, he just looked at the engineer from the corner of his lens.

"Am I clear?" the engineer asked.

Artemis got in the driver's seat with Tori riding shotgun and Mimi in the back. He put the RUV in gear and said, "Aye aye, Captain." As the words emanated out of his speakers, he revved the RUV away, leaving a trail of dirt and gravel behind.

Myra, Zeus and the engineer stared at the cave entrance with their rucksacks on their backs and Recon hovering in front of them.

Each step that Myra took further into the cave brought back memories from her recent past. She knew they were getting closer and even after the engineer's speech, she didn't feel she was ready. Her anxiety grew by the minute. She wondered if she would see more of her father's body parts that they might have missed earlier. She hoped they wouldn't find any. Myra wondered if she was underestimating herself. She had already faced the loss of her father – would going again to the spot where her father was murdered shatter her beyond repair? *A war machine...* the engineer's words echoed in her mind. She continued marching deeper, tightening the grip on her bowgun.

Each new step was more cumbersome now. All thirty pounds of their rucksack and suits tried to hold Myra and the engineer in place as the trio ventured deeper. Zeus kept his senses on high alert as he continued scanning the area, his gun always facing forward. The weighty proximity suits they wore shielded them from the heat fine but inside, sweat and strain made their steps labored as they inched their way closer to the core of the volcano. Their lights bounced off the shiny silver of the suits in an otherwise dark cave. As if the suits weren't enough, they also had to navigate through the now denser plant vegetation that was prominent this far deep into the cave. It seemed as if every few feet these alien plants were conspiring to entangle them. Even at his quietest, Recon was still loud enough to stir things in motion.

"These look like they've been here for decades," Myra said as she stepped over a bed of branches on the cave floor. They didn't snap. Their soft structure let them handle her weight easily.

The engineer shone his flashlight onto some of the vines littered across the cave wall. He noticed minimal color variation among the branches. To him, everything appeared to be of uniform hue. "I don't think they've been here for decades," he said.

"True, the last eruption would have burned these all," Myra said.

"That, plus those creatures haven't been here for

decades. These plants came with them," the engineer lifted a vine with his flashlight and continued, "I'm sure they can grow fast."

Myra came closer and stared at the branch the engineer was studying.

They stood still some 100 feet away and observed the wall in front of them. Even in silent mode, Recon was still loud enough to be uncomfortable, especially with the sound echoing. Myra was glad they had brought the proximity suits, without which it would have been impossible for her and the engineer to venture this far into the caves. Even with the protection of the suit, she could still feel the wave of heat emanating from the wall in front of them. All around, there were layers of deposit of solidified lava, each band a time capsule telling a story from the time the old lava flow must have left its mark.

Suddenly, Recon dropped from his hover and landed straight onto the ground. Myra and the engineer rushed and started checking.

"His engines are almost done. Certainly low fuel but could be debris and dust... also heat," the engineer explained.

Myra touched one of Recon's arms where he tried to restart his blades, but they kept stalling.

"We gotta do this now, or we'll lose him," the engineer said.

The trio lifted Recon and held him midair; all the while he kept trying to restart his engines.

"Hang on," the engineer said, motioning Zeus and Myra to continue holding Recon while he opened an underside panel and reached for Recon's control box.

"What are you doing?" Myra asked.

The engineer took his time then stepped back. "Let him go."

Zeus and Myra looked at him.

"Just let him go."

As soon as they let him go, Recon fired up four of his eight rotors and once again hovered perfectly.

"I cut off a few rotors," the engineer said. He took a pause then continued, "We gotta leave. We can't stay here for long. Let him do his thing."

Myra knew the engineer was right. Now that they were close to Chisil's core wall, they had to leave and let Recon do his work. She knew when Recon would start drilling there was no telling how many gases would escape through and suffocate them. She was glad they came along and didn't have to send Recon all by himself. But now it was their time to leave, as Recon's fuel supply was low and he had a job to finish. She kept staring at Recon as he once again started swaying left and right, unable to maintain a perfect hover.

"Now, Myra!" the engineer said as he led them back the way they had come in.

Myra followed Zeus and the engineer on their way out. She turned around to face Recon. "We'll see you soon!" she said but wasn't sure if Recon heard her.

Recon began the first phase of his mission. The laser discs from his underside opened up, and he started cutting the core wall in several places. With each burst, the lasers burned their way through more of the solidified surface. Once deep enough, he stepped back and aimed at the center of the cut area. He fired a canister, but his sway made him miss. The cartridge fell on the ground. Recon stabilized himself and tried again. This time the canister landed in the intended hole. One by one he fired more shells, filling all six cavities he had cut into the core wall.

He swayed left and right as he tried to move away from the core. He noticed his speed was no longer as it had been just a few minutes ago. There was a pronounced shake and sway in his movement now. He was glad he had fired the canisters when he was still fully functional.

He continued moving away from the core, tracking his way back through the cave system. His only hope was to get as far away from the canisters as possible and to be able to see his *humans* once more. As he struggled his way out, the memories of his brother Scout flashed in front of him. Now he understood how Scout must have felt when he had entered into the cave system.

The darkness that surrounded Recon made him nervous. The memory of when he and Scout had said their final goodbye flashed in front of him as he struggled to maintain a steady hover.

61

RED

A rtemis, Mimi, and Tori all pushed and flipped the rolled over AUV right side up. The day was still young, and there was a new level of energy in the bots. Artemis adjusted the gun on his shoulder as he moved closer to the vehicle. It was the same kind that Barry was able to print in a short time using the available materials after some experimentation. Artemis tried the AUV's broken door, but it was stuck. He gave the handle another hard tug, but it didn't budge. "Stand back." He punched a hole through the window glass. Once in, he grabbed the frame and gave it a strong pull. The door budged a little but not enough. He needed to reassess the amount of force. He readjusted his position and tried one more time. This time with a lot more power. The hinges gave in, and the door came out in a snap.

Artemis slid into the driver's seat, kicked open the passenger side door and exited from that side.

"Me and Tori will start gutting it. Just hang tight," Artemis told Mimi.

She saw him go back in and Tori entered the AUV from the other side. Mimi stood there, scanning the horizon for any possible threat. For some reason, she found herself vulnerable. Her friends were just a few feet away, but she couldn't shake up the feeble feeling. It was one of those moments when you feel something whether your logical brain gives you contrary evidence. Mimi moved over and grabbed Artemis's gun that he had propped on the AUV's side. With a gun in hand, calmness returned to her circuits.

Inside the vehicle, the bots were busy undoing the floor panels. They began removing the latches one by one. Artemis took off a big tile and set it aside. As soon as he saw what was underneath, he froze for a moment. "Oh boy."

"Well, let's get to it," Tori said.

Artemis wasn't very fond of spilled chemicals. It was one of those things that made him nervous. Having a metal body made him vulnerable to very few things, but electrical interference and chemicals were still fair game. If someone swung a baseball bat at him, he could have taken the hit with no problem, even breaking the bat in the process -- but chemicals were the stuff of nightmares. Tori grabbed some rugs from the back of the vehicle and started dabbing the acid that had spilled from one of the batteries under the panel. She took great care to cover her hands and made sure the bundle of cloth was not saturated enough to start burning her skeleton. Once satisfied with the cleanup, she threw the rug in the back and looked at Artemis. "Come on big man... you can do it." It always baffled her how this monstrous metal machine could break through stones and kill pretty much anything and yet was so scared of small things.

Artemis didn't respond. He just took his own sweet time then looked up at Tori and began unplugging the batteries that were still intact. The network of connections was straightforward. A bank of cells arranged in bays with each containing four cinder block sized juice boxes. There were more than they needed. There was no way they were going to use all twenty of them. They just needed about a dozen, the ones that hopefully still worked.

As Artemis pulled out the first battery, he realized it was damaged and saw a pool of acid underneath. He immediately tossed it towards the back of the vehicle. He was fortunate it landed on one of the seats and not on the floor. He reached for another one under the panel.

Mimi was moving away from the vehicle. Something had caught her attention and was pulling her towards it. She took a few more steps then bent down and came face to face with it. The newly sprouted weed was face to face with *her*. It was the most fascinating thing she had seen in a long time. She couldn't understand why this single weed had suddenly captivated all her attention. She leaned and smelled it. Her sensors with a stored database of fragrances and how they were perceived by humans didn't spit out anything that would tell her how the weed should smell. The disappointment was short lived as she fantasized how it should have felt. So what if she didn't know how it was supposed to smell. Her vivid imagination was enough to make up her own fragrance.

It was one of the purest moment she had felt in a long time. She realized, ever since the mission had started, there had been a certain tension and energy in the team and the whole operation. The cascading events all had led to increasing violence. But she could leave all that behind for this moment. She was so captivated by the tiny yellow weed flower that it healed all her dark memories. It was as if she was getting her Post Traumatic Stress Disorder fix. If her facial construction had allowed her to express a smile, she would have done that by now. She shut off her cameras for a moment to just feel the touch of the wind and imagine whatever image of flowers or bloom she wanted.

It was as if time had slowed and Mimi was inside a sequence of fantasizing a fairy wonderland. After several of those private moments, she slowly let her cameras come back to life. There was a very brief readjustment period as they compensated for the light difference. But she noticed something dark. It was as if there was a dark area around her and it was getting bigger.

She lifted her head and looked up, slowly. A thundering bolt of electrical energy descended from the sky towards her. A power so intense that it burned right through her body. Her arm that held the gun severed and landed several feet away. There was a long gash in her body where the bolt had penetrated. Her separated head kept rolling several times before it came to an abrupt halt as it hit a rock many feet away from where she had tried to smell the weed.

The impact commanded attention. Artemis stepped out of the AUV and locked eyes with the red soldier flying towards him. Artemis immediately went for the gun that he had propped against the vehicle. It wasn't there. He looked around and a few dozen feet away he could see Mimi's body separated by parts and the gun that he so needed now. Just a moment later he saw Tori get out.

"Get back in the car!" He yelled.

As he turned around, he felt the same bolt of energy that had destroyed Mimi. The red soldier had aimed the glove gun and fired with the same vengeance. It hit Artemis straight in the face. The impact severed his head off and flung it what seemed like dozens of feet away from the AUV.

"Arti!!!" Tori yelled.

She hadn't even gotten the chance to get back in the car. Everything happened in a few fast seconds, there just was no time for anything. Tori stood there, still as a tree while the red soldier hovered over the AUV and was banking around her. Tori turned as Red made the landing.

They both stared at each other for the longest few

moments. When Red was done thinking, when he was ready, he stood erect and revealed his full size.

His gun had already taken aim.

As Tori stared at the alien soldier, right in the eye, over his shoulder, she could still see smoke coming out of Artemis's severed head. She closed her eyes and whispered to herself.

I love you Arti!

62

THE RIDE

"Art, come in," Myra spoke into her walkie. Heavy breathing intermixed with her words as the team continued walking at a brisk pace. She waited a few moments for the reply from the other end before speaking again. "Mimi, Tori, you guys there?"

"I have a bad feeling about this," the senior engineer said.

Myra looked at him. "What do you mean? About the bots?"

The engineer shook his head and continued, "No, not about the bots. About us walking all the way back."

"What can we do? I'm trying," Myra said as she tried again on her radio.

"They won't reply... If they were gonna, they would have by now," Zeus said.

Myra just looked at him and tried the walkie once more, hanging onto her last sliver of hope. "I hope Recon will know when to do it," Myra said as she looked back at the cave entrance in the distance. It hadn't been easy for her to leave Recon behind, but the engineer's words earlier had given her some courage to face those tough decisions.

"I hope so, too," the engineer agreed as the trio continued jogging their way back.

Myra's pace quickened as she saw the *Whale* now only some twenty feet in front of her. Her hungry eyes scanned the area meticulously. "Barry!" She shouted as she looked around.

Zeus and the engineer stood near the rear hatch as Myra circled around the *Whale* towards the small tent and around.

"He's not here," the engineer confirmed as Myra came back to where they were standing.

She walked past them and scanned the horizon as if she could figure out which way Barry might have gone. "Barry, come in," she spoke into her radio.

"He's dead," the engineer said.

Myra turned back and offered him a sharp look.

"Why else would he not respond? Barry isn't among the irresponsible ones," the engineer said.

"You don't know if he's dead, so please don't say such things."

The engineer tightened his grip on his gun, "Let's go."

"Where?" Myra asked.

"To the AUV crash site. The only thing left is to check on the bots. Maybe their radios are dead or something."

"Let's go," Myra said as she began walking past the engineer and Zeus in the direction of the old AUV dirt tracks. Suddenly, she turned around. "Just a second."

Zeus and the engineer watched her go back into the *Whale*.

Myra searched the interior. She scanned to her left and then to her right. Several cases were opened, equipment on the floor, cables jumbled up. *Barry, what did you do?* She suspected it must have been him, as he had been the only one left behind. She scanned the area, hoping that Barry hadn't damaged the terrarium in his escapade. In one of the far corners, tucked behind some rain gear, she saw what she longed for. Titan was bouncing in his terrarium, still trying to make an escape.

Myra navigated the maze of clutter, put her bowgun down and reached for him. Titan calmed down for a minute as she picked up the terrarium and looked closely inside. Myra was glad the frog was precisely how she had left him. She watched him as he now sat in silence. Out of nowhere, suddenly images flashed in her mind. Images of her father. One particular one was strikingly clear. It was clear because it had some memorable words attached to it.

Myra jolted forward as Eustace slammed the brakes when the car in front of them stopped without notice. "Watch it, Dad!" Myra looked at Eustace, but he didn't look back. She peered around at the slow-moving traffic, shook her head and continued reading the romance novel she had been devouring for the last two days. The book had a magical attraction for her. The way idealistic fantasy romance novels are constructed, they are clearly designed to make the right kind of reader keep their eyes glued, page after page. Spending the first five years of her life in an orphanage in India had given Myra enough pain in the beginning hours of her life to relate to the ups and downs of the protagonist's life. The protagonist's struggle to have who she had wanted as her soulmate, her battle to challenge societal conventions and her goal to never give up hope – it was pure crack for Myra's teenage mind.

It was hardly any trouble for Myra to find sections of memorable lines in the book. The small Post-it bookmarks were her trusty navigation markers, each taking her precisely where she had wanted to go, each taking her precisely to a place that would have made her experience a particular emotion once again.

The sound of the large horn from the pickup behind them startled Myra and immediately yanked her out of the chapter she had wanted to finish so badly, albeit slowly. She turned back and gave the truck's tinted windows a mean cold stare. "Assholes."

Eustace chuckled. Something about hearing it from his fourteen-year-old daughter made him laugh. Maybe it was the tone, perhaps the slight accent or maybe her fierce intensity; He found something amusing.

Myra looked around at the long line of traffic in front of them. The 105-degree southern California weather didn't help, either. The full blasting AC seemed not to be able to prevent the hot windows from radiating heat. She craned her neck up and looked in front.

"Dad, you can squeeze through here," she pointed at the narrow gap between the cars in the next lane. Eustace just nodded. He knew needling through such slow traffic wasn't going to save him any more than five minutes. He would instead enjoy those extra minutes next to his daughter. Myra stuck her hand out the window and pleaded for the car in the next lane to let them pass. Eustace obliged when the courteous driver gave them the way.

The tires of the car in front of them screeched as it raced to make the left turn at the intersection light. Eustace pulled forward also to turn left before the light changed. They both stared at the oncoming traffic as he waited for a gap to turn.

"Now," Myra said with her typical teenage annoyance.

"I'll go when I'm ready," Eustace replied.

Myra sat still as seconds rolled by, and they studied the oncoming traffic. Eustace inched the car forward as he saw a gap after the next car. Somehow, he had misjudged the speed of the following car and just when he was about to make the left turn, he second-guessed and stopped.

"You could have made it, Dad."

"I'll just pull over, and you can drive." Finally, there was a touch of frustration in Eustace's voice.

Myra just sat quietly after that. Her thoughts intermixing reality with the fiction in her hand. She took in deep breaths.

"When I'm gone, you'll remember," Eustace said. He knew those were utterly painful words that he didn't want to say. They just came out of him. As patient as he had been with raising his daughter, in that moment, she somehow made him feel as if he had fallen short. As strong as he had been, he wasn't invulnerable. Words affected him equally, especially her words.

Myra sat in silence. She turned and looked out the passenger window as tears rolled down her cheeks. She breathed slowly, trying hard not to let her breaths reveal her emotions. The words spoken a few seconds ago sliced through her heart like a hot knife through butter. She felt a wave of intense pain, more pain than any event in the book had made her experience. More emotions were stirred than any plot twist or dialogue in the novel could have managed. She wondered why her father had to say such harsh words to her, then a minute later she apologized to her father, internally, making a note to let him know she was sorry at some point in the future.

Myra regretted that chance never came. She had never taken the time to let her father know how she had felt. All she had now was a memory. A memory that was now many folds more painful. An uninvited sound entered between her and the memory of her father and tugged at her attention. A sort of sound that sends chills up a spine. She wasn't entirely sure if it was a scream or a crash. Perhaps a mixture of both?

She clutched the terrarium tight in her arms and rushed out the rear hatch. Myra noticed both Zeus and the engineer looking up at the sky. The engineer pointed his gun at something above that was out of her sight. She stepped out further.

"Get back inside," the engineer yelled as he aimed the crafted rifle up in the air.

Myra stepped out further and tried to look up, the cloud cover blocked her view of what Zeus and the engineer were pointing at.

"Myra, please, get back in," Zeus requested, still looking up.

She waited then stepped out further. A faint red color peeked from behind the clouds and grabbed her attention. Her eyes widened as she saw more of *him*. She turned around, and with her heightened senses, it almost felt like she ran back inside in slow motion. Once the moment of hypersensitivity was over, she rushed back inside as fast as she could. She put the terrarium back under the rain gear and secured it by wedging a few things around. She grabbed her bowgun from the corner and loaded in the arrow and chambered a round. The gun felt heavy. Much more substantial than when she had set it aside only a few minutes ago. She took in a deep breath and rushed outside.

The moment she stepped out, a waft of warm wind struck her body. Was it warmer? The air did feel different to her. Whether it was just her imagination or extra sensitivity, she wasn't sure. She looked up and scanned the sky. As she turned to the right, she froze. The red soldier emerged out of the dense fog cover and descended from above. He jumped from his tar platform and lunged straight towards the engineer.

The engineer fired a pellet and tore a chunk of meat off of the soldier's right arm. The soldier jerked back a little and lunged straight for the engineer. The engineer tracked backward and fell. The red soldier stood towering over the downed engineer and took a deep breath as he bared his teeth. A sharp blow knocked him sideways. The soldier dragged across the grassy land and landed a foot away.

Zeus extended his hand and lifted the engineer up.

"You OK?" Myra asked as she rushed and stood next to the engineer. He nodded as he pointed his gun straight at the soldier.

The red soldier recovered faster than Zeus had thought.

"Get in," Zeus motioned Myra and the engineer as he leaped towards the soldier on the ground.

Before the soldier had any chance of getting up, Zeus landed a massive blow to his head. The soldier jerked back again then turned around swiftly and grabbed Zeus from behind. The soldier sat on the ground as his four limbs held Zeus in a choke hold. Zeus struggled. Unable to reach for the soldier's head behind him, he tried to undo the hold, but the soldier was enraged. Those weren't the moments of average strength. As the soldier's grip tightened even further, Zeus felt the pressure on his sensors. His joints quickly started to become weaker to the ever-increasing vice-like grip.

Suddenly, a blast of heat licked the back of the soldier. He squealed, and his body twitched as he let go of Zeus. The soldier danced around, his head bouncing up and down as he tried to fan out the fire.

Myra lifted her bowgun and pulled the trigger. The bullet ripped through the upper part of Red's back as he stumbled and rolled on the ground. It was as if the fire was leaving his body on its own. His skin no longer appeared to be flammable. Did he change the composition of his exoskeleton? Red blood and acid leeched from where Myra had torn a new hole in the soldier's body. He regained his balance as he tried to get back up. The soldier turned and noticed the pilot flame still sizzling on the thrower that the engineer held in his hands.

They stared into each other's eyes as the engineer tightened his grip on the thrower once again and the soldier lifted his glove gun. The engineer pulled the trigger, and as soon as the hot streak escaped the nozzle, he felt a wall of energy rushing towards him. The bolt pushed all the flames back onto the engineer, and as soon as the charge hit his body, it tore a hole few feet wide right in his midsection. The rest of the engineer's body burned as Myra and Zeus watched.

Myra noticed the soldier pointing his glove gun towards Zeus, who was still recovering from the choke hold. His sensors were still adjusting from the overloaded distribution of pressure and were frantically restarting in an attempt to restore full functionality as soon as they were able to.

Still unable to move, Zeus awaited his fate as the red soldier lifted his gun. Myra took a deep breath and stared down her bowgun's scope. She once again hoped she would be able to take advantage of the heightened state of the moment. She saw the soldier's arm rise up and aimed at the glove gun as it was moving. As her and the red soldier's arms began lifting, Zeus turned back and stared at Myra. He wanted to make sure she had *his* final goodbye. This life had been precious, and he was ever so grateful to have had it through X-corp. He would have hated it to not have said his final goodbye to the girl he loved.

Myra maintained her focus and gently turned her aim. Before the soldier had a chance to level off, her bullet escaped the barrel straight for her intended target. The bullet penetrated straight into Red's shoulder joint. He squealed in pain as blood shot out like water from a busted fire hydrant and painted Zeus red.

The soldier jerked back as he watched his flailing arm just dangling from the joint. Mere strands were holding the rest of it as it swung back and forth with every move he made. The soldier started in Myra's direction with a new rage, teeth bared, acid dripping and blood still oozing from the fresh wound. Myra loaded another round into the chamber and took careful aim, this time straight for the head.

The soldier raised his good arm and expanded the skin around it, which acted as a flexible shield, covering his face. The skin continued expanding as the soldier pumped more air into it. Myra shot the inflating arm, but the impact only made him jerk a little and further fueled his determination. *Does he not feel pain?* Myra wondered. She tightened the grip and peeked down the scope one more time, trying to catch the small gap under Red's arm which would have given her a clear shot at his neck. The opening was narrow and with Red's fast-moving body and her last bullet, she only had this one chance. She took a deep breath, much deeper than the ones before. *You won't get me. I'm not scared of you. You can do this, Myra... you can do this.*

With those thoughts, she pulled the trigger. Right when the bullet left the barrel, she closed her eyes. Either way, she didn't want to see what happened next.

Her bullet grazed against the soldier's skin. Then another shot hit him. And another... one after another, dozens of bullets drilled new holes into the soldier's body. His momentum continued carrying him a little further before he finally collapsed just inches away from Myra's feet.

Myra opened her eyes and saw the lifeless quadruped body at her feet in a pool of red alien blood. She turned around.

"Barry!!" She started towards him with the same urgency one meets a lost lover with, only she knew it was just sheer excitement. As she ran, her eyes widened seeing Barry on top of Falkor. Riding on the X-corp quadruped bot horse, Barry looked nothing short of a knight riding his mount.

"Where have you been?" Myra asked as she couldn't contain her excitement and tears rolled down her cheeks.

"You are welcome..." Barry gestured with his hand as if presenting Falkor as a gift to Myra.

Myra stared at the horse bot as Barry began climbing

down. She noticed the heavy Gatling-style gun that Barry had mounted on Falkor's underside right between his legs. She took a step in and touched Falkor's leg. When he sensed her touch, Falkor lowered his face, and his eyes met with Myra's.

"You like what you see?" Barry asked.

Myra rushed in and hugged him tighter than she ever had. Barry wondered why the previous hugs paled in comparison. But the rush of chemicals filled him with happiness. He couldn't remember the last time someone hugged him with such genuineness. He felt as if he had waited all his life for a connection like that. He could only wish the moment lasted forever. It didn't.

"How did you do it?" Myra asked as she released Barry from her embrace.

Barry struggled to take it out of his pocket, but finally, he managed. He gave a big smile and waved Hunter's wallet in front of her. "We have Hunter to thank for it."

Myra tilted her head to one side. A moment of sadness reflected on her face as her thoughts went towards Hunter.

"Did you steal it?" She asked.

"I-... Zeus!" Barry shouted as he walked past Myra.

Myra followed. "What about the gun? Did you??"

"Yes," Barry said as he kneeled down next to Zeus. "You OK?"

Zeus nodded.

"He's coming back. Just a few more minutes," Myra said.

She stared over Barry's shoulder at Falkor back in the distance. It was hard for her to come to terms that Falkor was there, actually with them. The eight-foot-tall quadruped gave her the assurance she craved. It was her dream to see Falkor move again and knowing all too well how much she had wanted it, she remembered Hunter deliberating pushing the Falkor project on the back burner. She had already learned that some people just enjoyed annoying others even for no particular reason. She was just glad Barry wasn't like Hunter.

Barry looked over Myra's shoulder at the body in the distance. He stood and rushed. The backlit sun cast Barry's shadow over the engineer's remains.

"Morgan..." Barry whispered as Myra came and stood next to her. She put a hand on his shoulder, but that didn't seem to do much. It was as if they both had lost the capacity to mourn. Immense pain in rapid succession tends to do that.

Myra, Barry, and Zeus jostled back and forth as Falkor strode on the uneven grassy terrain. Sitting in the three seats on Falkor, the trio could not have wanted the comfort more. They cherished the fleeting moments, taking it all in when they had the chance. They knew all too well that this could end, anytime. They sat in silence for a long time as Falkor continued.

"Morgan was a brilliant man," Myra said as she removed fresh dirt from her nails.

"And pilot," Barry said after a moment of silence.

"I remember when Dad commissioned the *Whale*, it was Morgan who test-piloted it, fearlessly... so brave," Myra said as her thoughts wandered and she clutched the terrarium tighter in her arms.

"He lusted for thrill and adventure... He never told me if he had a girlfriend," Barry said.

Hope he was single, Myra thought as she sat silently watching Titan being bounced around in the terrarium as Falkor tried to close in the distance.

"Artemis, come in," Barry spoke into his radio then shook his head.

Myra looked straight ahead in the direction Falkor was taking them.

63

WAR MACHINES

F alkor dug his hind legs into the ground as he pushed from his side. It was heavy, but Falkor was strong, and he had something to prove. Even with his limited brain, he could sense the emotions of the humans around him and wanted to do everything he could to ease their pain. He wanted to show his loyalty to Myra and Barry. That was the nature of machines with intelligence. There was no telling who they would favor. One could design and bring a sentient robot to life, but still, it doesn't guarantee loyalty. Although there was a deep admiration towards his creator, Hunter, Falkor knew he enjoyed Myra and Barry's company more. It was his chance to gain some points, and he sure wasn't going to let it slip by.

The AUV was on its side once again with a two-foot-wide hole on its passenger side. Falkor pushed against the vehicle with the side of his body as he inserted one of his front feet underneath. He began lifting, and with it, the six-ton AUV started moving. As he raised the vehicle's side a few feet in the air, he dropped it back down. He tried again, and this time Zeus helped him with the lift. Together, they managed to exert enough force, and in the end, Falkor gave it a strong push. The AUV dropped straight on all fours. Shards of broken glass spilled from its windows as it landed on the ground. Zeus went inside and searched for anything that was salvageable as Falkor stood on watch.

Myra cradled Tori's head as she mourned once again. Her dry face was expressionless. The memories of time spend with Tori flashed in front of her. Even though they were at odds with each other many times, she realized how much she missed her now. Tori had been the spark in any conversation. At times bitter and spicy but still flavorful. Myra knew she would miss Tori as much as the other fallen ones.

"Time to go," Barry said as he put his hand on Myra's shoulder. She just sat there, motionless. Myra knew once they left, she would never see the remains of the bots again. She wished she could have spent more time with each and every one of them. Artemis, Mimi, and Tori – their memories were still fresh in her mind. She also wished that all of this didn't happen. A dark cloud of guilt hovered in her mind. Was she responsible for all that had happened? If she hadn't insisted on burying Eustace's body right here on Chisil, none of this would have occurred. Then, the pain would have just been hers. Now, so many others made the ultimate sacrifice. She felt sorry and hated herself. Would she be able to live with all that guilt?

Zeus stepped out of the AUV and moved towards Myra and Barry. "Nothing."

"Myra, let's go," Barry said as he tried to lift her up.

Myra got up, slung her bowgun over her shoulder and held the terrarium tight.

Falkor crouched, and the trio jumped on top.

"One klick westbound...," Zeus ordered as he pointed in a direction. The humans were aware, and confident Zeus knew where he was taking them.

The trio grabbed onto their seat handlebars as Falkor

turned his head around, trying to orient. He tried to lift his hind leg. It didn't budge. He tried again, but the leg remained motionless.

"What is that?" Myra asked as she heard a scraping sound coming from below.

As she bent over to study the source, another sound from behind commanded attention. She turned around and stared at the moving vines. All around Falkor, vines started emerging from the ground, the same kind that prevented him from moving. By now, the rapidly climbing rope-like vines bound all four of his legs.

"What the..." Barry said as Zeus jumped down and took aim at one cluster. He shot straight at Falkor's foot. The pellet tore through some, but almost immediately more vines snaked up through the soil and tightened their grip even more. Falkor shook his body back and forth as he tried to break free. The more he struggled, the more he got entangled in the web of ever-growing vines.

"Get ready," Barry said as he grabbed his printed gun. Myra instinctively looked up towards the sky, her hungry eyes trying to catch any detail among the perpetual fog. She kept both the printed rifle and her bowgun close. Something caught the corner of her eye. She turned and noticed a giant blade of a leaf with sharp edges spinning at high speed and descending fast towards them. She took aim and shot at it. The disk plant disintegrated into a dozen smaller pieces. Then, there were more.

Myra and Barry jumped down from Falkor as they tried to dodge the rotating disk plant leaves spinning from the sky. Barry disintegrated another one as his pellet shattered it into pieces. Myra ran straight for the AUV as Zeus grabbed one of the fallen blade leaves and smashed it into pieces. Falkor's main gun was pretty much useless now. The constant struggle to break free kept him occupied. It seemed there was nothing on his mind except to break loose first. He was now as useful as he had been all this time before Barry had awakened him.

Myra's breathing escalated as she opened the AUV's rear door and secured the terrarium inside, on the floor. She immediately scanned the back of the vehicle for anything she could make use of. Lots of supplies, a first aid kit, cans of food – a lot of items but nothing she could use against the plants that were coming for them. She bent down and continued her search under the seat. She took a pause and stared at the only moving thing: Titan. She peeked outside through the broken glass and saw Barry shooting into the sky as Zeus grabbed and tore as many as he could into pieces. *Shit...* Beads of sweat rolled down Myra's forehead. A moment later, Titan again caught her attention.

She rushed out of the AUV and aimed the printed rifle towards the sky as her bowgun rested slung behind her. As she looked up, she felt like a soldier landing on the beaches of Normandy. When she had left for the AUV, there were only a handful. Now, the sky was littered as more and more of the rotating discs emerged out of the fog. Once again, in a heightened state, she noticed Falkor's gun now smashing dozens of them into dust. As each one exploded, their remnants rained from the sky. Myra blasted another one of the plants as she raced to join Barry ducking under Falkor.

"You OK?" Myra asked Barry, her words barely coming out. She couldn't remember when was the last she had dashed this quick.

Barry nodded. "And you?"

Myra pushed him to the side as she took aim and blasted another one. Barry shook his head as he recovered from the sound of Myra's gun so close to his ears.

"Sorry," Myra said as she turned and aimed at the sky, searching for a target. If there were more, the fog sure did conceal them.

"Is that it? Did we kill them all?"

"How would I know?" Barry asked as he shook his head, rifle still pointing upwards.

"We have to get outta here, now!" Zeus said as he rushed towards the humans.

Myra and Barry emerged out from under Falkor, and they all stared at the vines that had kept the horse grounded.

"Stand back," Barry said as he slung his thrower forward and aimed at one of Falkor's legs. "I'm sorry, this is gonna sting a little." He pulled the trigger, and a wall of fire shot out straight and licked the vines. The alien plants sizzled and wriggled as they loosened their grip and Falkor yanked out his foot. Barry dashed to the other side and pressed the trigger once again. The vines retracted as Falkor began regaining his freedom.

Barry aimed the thrower at the third foot when a spinning slingshot-like plant landed and clutched his legs. He fell over. He screamed in pain as the plant grip tightened. Zeus rushed towards Barry as Myra pointed her rifle at the sky. Her eyes remained transfixed as an intuition descended upon her. A moment later, a familiar figure began revealing itself from behind the fog. Myra's rifle was ready. Aimed, but with hesitation. Her hands shook as she followed the *alien mother* descending down from the sky. *I shouldn't do this,* Myra thought as she calculated whether to shoot or not. She wasn't sure what would happen. She hoped the alien mother attacked first, which would give her the chance to retaliate instead of firing first.

The alien mother jerked back as the pellet grazed against her torso. She turned and eyed Zeus, his rifle still pointing at her. The mother removed her tar platform and used it as a shield behind which she shoved her hand deep into the soil, and waited.

"What's she doing?" Myra asked.

They didn't have to wait long to find out. The trio tried

to maintain their balance as the ground shook. They rushed and took shelter under Falkor, who still struggled to get out of his remaining binds. The ground shook further as a sinkhole appeared right in front of where the alien mother stood. As the soil caved in, out came rope like arms. Twenty feet long and as thick as a man's thigh, one after another, the tentacles crawled out of the sinkhole. They latched onto the edge of the hole and dragged the *bulb* out of the ground. Myra's eyes stayed transfixed as inch by inch the enormous plant bulb emerged out of its den. More and more soil sunk in as it gave way.

"This is it," Barry said.

The ground didn't shake. For a brief moment, things seemed eerily quiet. Midway in its ascent, the bulb stopped. The portion that was already out wriggled back and forth as if trying to pull the rest of it out. When its wriggling intensified, so did the ground shaking. The bulb stopped once again and then, as if taking in a big breath, the portion that was already out started expanding. The earth trembled as the sinkhole expanded and its edges burst as the rest of the bulb shot out from the hole. The whole bulb shook and rose up. Shaped like a long tube with tentacles coming out from the open end, the bulb rose higher and lifted itself, all thirty feet of it. It looked like a tulip bulb with an octopus attached to the end, and it now faced the trio. The bulb swung back and forth thirty feet up in the air, its tentacles wriggling as more of its ten-foot-wide stem emerged from the ground.

If there were any fears in Myra's mind, this wasn't the time to entertain them. She noticed the bulb and its stem bending down. Myra squinted as she saw the alien mother starting to climb the lowered plant. The mother jumped up the stem and then the bulb. As she rose higher, the bulb straightened up.

Myra smelled something burning, and from the corner of her eye, she noticed Barry freeing Falkor from the last of his bindings. She turned her head and saw the alien mother climbing ever higher until she had reached the top of the bulb. The mother attached herself firmly to the bulb; they were one unit now. The mother now commanded the plant monster with hungry tentacles eager to grab anything that stood in their way.

Myra wasn't sure whether it was all an illusion or something happening in real life. Amid the chaos of watching the bulb and the alien mother, she had failed to notice the tentacle that was swinging towards her. Only when the plant limb was a mere few feet away did she think about dodging it. She moved behind Falkor's leg just in time, and the tentacle lashed out against the horse at full force. An elongated and stretched buzzing sound emanated from Falkor as his sensors registered the impact. Barry came around before burning off the last binding and hid behind Falkor's leg.

"Stay here," Zeus said as he walked in front of the bulb, its limbs still swinging back and forth. Zeus tried to keep all four of them in sight, anticipating which one would attack next. As the tentacles came back from their pendulum-like swing, one of them headed straight for him. He dug his hind foot in the ground and waited. As it closed in, he noticed just how big it was. But he was ready now. Ready to take on whatever that long thing had to throw at him. The tentacle swung with accelerating speed. Zeus held his arms in front, bracing for impact.

Zeus's body rose up as the tentacle grabbed and lifted him up in the air before finally dropping him on the ground. The alien mother watched from the top as one after other, all four tentacles went after a downed Zeus. He punched and kicked. It only helped in delaying their impact as they began wrapping around his body, ever tightening their grip. Like a python choking the life out of its victim, the tentacles wrapped around Zeus's torso and legs, and began tightening. Zeus punched repeatedly, but it only made the limbs constrict more.

The bulb shook back and forth as bullets tore new holes into it. Falkor charged at it in full stride, his Gatling gun in full bore mode. The tension in the tentacles increased as the bulb tried to retract them, but they remained held tight, wrapped around Zeus. Falkor put his foot down on one of them that held Zeus. He aimed his gun and fired round after round. Green liquid oozed out as the tentacle was pulped into pieces from the impact point. Once done, Falkor delivered the same fate to the second tentacle. Zeus was coming out of their grip when suddenly a charge of electricity hit Falkor and knocked him on his side several feet away. The mother up above pointed her glove gun once again at Falkor and delivered another charge. Falkor rolled in time and missed it by only inches. His electrical systems overloaded, he stumbled as he tried to get back up.

Barry delivered a wall of fire to the other tentacles that still held Zeus. The hot fire began climbing up the plant limbs as Myra took aim and fired pellet after pellet into the opening of the bulb where the tentacles originated from. Soon, there was no tension in the plant limbs. One after another, they all fell from the sky as Myra and Barry dodged being squished. The burning tentacles fell on the ground as Zeus untangled himself. It was as if the bulb was discarding its damaged limbs.

The bulb swayed back and forth violently as the loss of tentacles made it keel slight off balance. Was it readjusting its center of gravity? Barry helped Zeus as Myra took aim once again and tried to shoot more pellets into the swaying bulb. The ones that had hit managed to make green liquid rain from the sky. Now out of ammo, Myra discarded the printed rifle. She looked towards the AUV. Maybe there was more ammo there. But she knew it was too risky. She slung forward her bowgun and undid the safety. Once the safety was off, she removed the cloth that she had tied over the arrow in the upper chamber of the bowgun back in the AUV. She knew she had three rifle rounds and that single arrow. In that moment, she wished her bowgun was designed for combat with a larger magazine instead of target practice.

Barry dashed and pulled the trigger of his thrower at the stem of the bulb. Almost instantly, a fire started climbing up. The bulb swayed back and forth as more of its blood spilled from the holes Myra had created. A second later, another type of liquid flowed down the stem. This liquid wasn't green, and it was intentional. The juice ran down its stem, and the flames begin subsiding.

The alien mother tried to take aim at whoever she could, but the rapid swaying made it harder for her to keep her glove gun on target. The same sway also made it almost impossible for the trio to take their aim at her.

Myra pointed her bowgun straight at the mother. *Steady Myra, steady.* She thought as she tried to find a split second that would allow her to take a shot. Her finger ready on the trigger, she took in things as calmly as the moment allowed. Her senses and perception hyped up, she hungrily sought that narrow opening that would send her bullet home.

Myra was about to squeeze the trigger when suddenly an explosion shook their very foundation, and its echo tore through the valley. The trio fell back as the ground rattled. She looked to her left at the volcano at some distance. A hot mess of gasses started rising from the cone. The bulb swayed even harder and began to shake and vibrate. Tiny openings in its stem began bursting, one after another, as the liquid inside boiled. Each burst painted the ground with its green blood.

"Recon! He did it!" Myra said as she rushed close to Barry and Zeus.

The bulb began retracting into the ground as more and

more explosions damaged its stem. Deep underneath the soil, fresh molten lava had started rushing into the tunnels, charring everything it touched – the intricate network of alien plant growth.

The vines covering the cave walls. The bulbs holding the seeds of a new generation of offspring – everything was nothing more than a twig in the path of the 2000-degree lava flowing at thirty miles an hour. Massive amounts of gasses rose up from the sinkhole, engulfing and choking the bulb. It wriggled and swayed as the lava burnt its roots. In a last-ditch effort to save itself, the bulb started retracting back into the hole, perhaps trying to evade the rushing lava. The alien mother jumped down as the bulb hovered few feet above the sinkhole before continuing its descent. Falkor dashed towards the bulb and unloaded more of his bullets. The bulb shook as it took the last bullets without resistance. Falkor turned around and aimed his gun towards the alien mother as the bulb was almost gone. Before he could fire, a new set of tentacles shot out and wrapped around Falkor's hind legs. Falkor shook and struggled as the plant ropes pulled him down into the sinkhole with them.

"Falkor!" Myra screamed as she raced.

"Don't," Zeus said as he stopped her from getting too close. He didn't want her to be dragged along, too.

Myra stood near the hole as she stared into the darkness. She could still hear Falkor's buzzing, but they were fading fast. When she heard pops and metal grinding sounds, it was then she knew it was all over.

Myra didn't get much time to mourn. The alien mother stood up on her hind legs and spread her arms wide as the trio began fanning out. They quickly began surrounding her. Myra thought the mother appeared larger this time. Much much more significant than when they had met her for the first time. Was the alien mother stretching her cells and growing?

. . .

It was much wiser for the squad to flank her from all sides as opposed to just being in front. Guns drawn, the team each step with caution. They knew any misstep or fast movement could trigger her and then there would be no telling what the alien mother would do. If anything, they were just glad the mother hadn't attacked them, yet. Myra wondered what the mother was thinking. Myra was sure the mother had a lot of rage for them.

As she stared deep into the mother's eyes, all Myra could think was about her father. It was this creature who had taken her father away from her. And now, she was right in front of her.

The mother looked back and forth at the trio as they surrounded her. Her glove gun pointed straight, following whoever she stared at.

"We gotta get her gun," Myra yelled.

The mother pointed her gun and stared at Myra. Then she quickly turned to Barry.

"Keep moving. She's a bit confused. Doesn't wanna attack and get backstabbed," Myra said.

Barry and Zeus continued circling, hoping to keep her distracted.

"On the count of three, we fire at her hand," Myra said as Barry and Zeus concurred.

"One... two...," every time Myra opened her mouth, she attracted the mother's full attention. Myra wondered if she was going to get vaporized before her count was over. "Three..."

Myra and Zeus fired at her hand. The mother jerked back as blue blood spilled on the ground. She tended the glove hand with the other. Zeus took the opportunity and lunged straight for her hand as Myra maintained her distance, bowgun still pointed. The alien mother struggled as Zeus clutched her gloved weapon. The mother struggled to move it free from Zeus's grip. Then, suddenly, she wrapped a tentacle around Zeus's neck and pulled him out. He landed a few feet away. Myra aimed straight for the mother's heart and pulled the trigger, but she missed. Her second bullet grazed past one of the ribs as the mother screamed and aimed her weapon at Myra. Before the mother could pull the trigger, a wave of fire hit her from behind. Barry advanced, his finger pulling the trigger as hard as he could. The fire started burning the alien, immediately. Her skin began to darken wherever the flames licked, she started rolling on the ground.

Myra took aim and pulled the trigger one more time. Her third bullet entered the alien mother's stomach. A fountain of blood shot out, painting the ground near the AUV blue.

The alien mother pushed against the vehicle's tire and lifted herself up, drops of blood spilling from her mouth. Before she had the chance to aim her gun, Zeus lunged and delivered a titanium blow straight to her face. She fell again, sideways. Zeus sat on top of her and continued punching. One after another, he pulled with all his might and hit her straight, each blow knocking her system out of order, adding to her concussion.

The alien mother's torso lifted in the air as she turned and reversed the position. Now, she sat on top of Zeus, her head still swinging. It was as if her body had acted separately from her mind. Her brain might have been dealing with the aftermath of Zeus's punches, but her body seemed to have had autonomous properties to separate some functions independent of her mind. Her hands moved autonomously as she punched Zeus and grabbed his neck. While her head recovered, the body continued tugging on Zeus's head with all the strength she could muster. The neck being one of the most sensitive and fragile areas, Zeus's sensors struggled with the added strain and pull. He tried hard to undo the mother's grip, but she was enraged. When this enraged, there was no telling what she would be capable of.

Myra and Barry rushed towards the AUV.

"Zeus," Myra yelled as she raced faster than Barry. *I don't wanna lose you!* "Light her up, Barry," Myra said as she went around the AUV.

Barry stopped within striking distance, pointed his thrower and pulled the trigger. A small burst of flame shot out of the barrel, barely enough to reach more than a few feet from him. Not even close to touching the mother.

"Fuck!" Barry yelled as he tried to shake the canister and try again. Each time he tried, the flame got smaller and smaller. He took the thrower and tossed it at the alien mother. It bounced off of her. In that moment, it was nothing more than a matchstick against a castle wall.

The mother put one foot on Zeus's chest as she tugged harder on his skull. Each increase in pressure further strained Zeus's sensors. They were now getting overloaded and overheated, a deadly combination. Zeus knew it, and he knew time wasn't on his side. He tried punching the mother, but her long arms kept her at bay. The mother took a deep breath in and yelled out a deafening roar. She bent down and with one herculean pull, yanked on Zeus's head. A wave of shock ran through the robot's body. His electrical systems began shutting down. The sensors started turning off to prevent pain. First, it was the touch sensor. Zeus could no longer feel the touch of the alien mother's sandpaper-like skin. He knew it was time.

He heard some faint sounds. It felt like someone was walking on the AUV's roof. He turned his eyes and saw a silhouette emerging from the fog.

Myra dashed the last few steps she had to take on the AUV's roof and once at the edge, she jumped without looking down. In that heightened state of being, she noticed the alien mother's dome beaming a dazzling variety of exotic colors. They were so bright that if it were night, someone would have been able to spot them from perhaps a yard with a clear line of sight. Myra aimed her bowgun down in an instant, faster than she ever had any other time in her life. In that tiny fraction of time, she peeked down her scope, lined up the crosshair and took aim for the mother's dome. Even in that brief moment, thoughts managed to enter and exit her mind. They just did it faster.

Images of her beloved father flashed in front of her eyes. How much she loved him and the unbearable pain he must have felt at the hands of this alien monster. Even images of the alien child. Her father's mission, their trip to Chisil and what it had become, everything in fast forward. But she didn't let all of that distract her. *You can do this, Myra... you must do this.* She checked her aim for the final time, and as she was coming down, she pulled the trigger as hard as she could. The arrow bolted out like a rocket straight for the alien mother. It shattered her dome and penetrated deep inside of her. The mother let out a scream that was louder than any other she had in the past. The mother's dome exploded, and hundreds of tiny needle-thin wriggling worms shot up in the sky. A few of them landed on Myra's face and immediately pierced the sides of her forehead. Myra threw her bowgun away and pressed on her head as she dropped back on the ground. A dizzying sensation shot waves of pain into her face and head.

The alien mother stumbled as she tried to orient herself. Barry aimed the rifle that he had loaded from the back of the AUV and riddled the mother's body with pellet after pellet. As the mother stumbled, Barry's bullets drove her closer and closer to the sinkhole until she danced at the edge.

Barry took a deep breath and aimed the rifle at the alien mother's chest.

"Die, you motherfucking cunt!" Barry said as he pulled the trigger for one last time.

The bullet hit the mother straight in her chest. Her body jolted back, and with that, she stumbled into the darkness of the sinkhole that the plant bulb had created.

64

HOPE

"Myra, talk to me," Zeus said as he steered the RUV.

If it weren't for the RUV left behind by Artemis, Zeus didn't know how they would do it. As the lava flowed beneath the surface, toxic fumes escaped through any cracks and openings. Places that were already weakened had a chance to collapse under the pressure from underneath, providing gaping holes for the lava to further spread its fumes. If anything, they were glad the cone of the actual volcano hadn't started spewing things up in the air... at least not yet.

"Myra!" Barry said as he tried to keep her awake. He had already removed some of the needle worms that had struggled to enter her face and skull, at least the ones he could get a hold of. The rest were lodged somewhere deep under her skin, doing who knew what.

"I...I am O-," Myra replied as the pain and discomfort subsided for a brief moment.

"Don't worry, you're gonna be OK," Zeus said as he pressed his foot harder on the gas. He continued steering away from any rocks and boulders, as well as the newly created fume vents.

"Titan... where's he?" Myra asked half groggily.

Barry picked up the terrarium from the back and showed it to her. Myra saw Titan sitting quietly for a change, and a very faint smile appeared on her face. She knew she would have felt awful if they had left him behind. She took the terrarium from Barry and cradled it in her arms. It gave her comfort. Titan continued to sit quietly by the artificial pond inside.

"Almost there," Zeus said from the driver's seat. There was a feeling of euphoria in his tone. He knew they were almost there. More than anything, he was happy that he and Myra were still together, alive. It also didn't hurt that Barry was also with them. Zeus knew Myra would be OK once they find help. He was sure it was just a concussion and stress, nothing more. It couldn't be. He knew he would do anything in his power to make sure Myra made a full recovery. But for now, his number one goal was to take them where he was taking them.

65

HEATED

The alien mother limped her way into the now stuffy cave. The leg that she amputated when the lava had touched it a few minutes ago didn't slow down her stride. Even on threes, she was still fast. She had to be, if she were to reach her destination, in time. She tried not to turn her body as each and every twist brought immense pain with it. The arrow that Myra had shot down her skull was still embedded in her torso. She wondered how she had escaped death. Her luck was running out soon though, and the lights were fading fast. She hurried deeper into the cave system.

She reached a chamber so deep that the lava hadn't arrived there yet. Toxic fumes traveled faster, though. She stood at the edge of the large area and stared at hundreds of her own eggs. Layer after layer, they were everywhere, stacked on various levels. On the floor, on ledges, and some even hanging from vines, the mother had made sure every square inch was put to good use.

As she made her way in, she stumbled and fell hard. She stayed on the ground for several minutes. She felt her respiratory system shutting down. Was it the fumes? Whatever it was, it was working. As her eyes focused, she once again glanced at the hundreds of her own eggs. Somehow, that gave her energy. She mustered the courage and got up.

She grabbed one of the eggs from the clutch in front of her and cradled it in her arms. As she started making her way out, she noticed one egg that was slightly larger than others. She grabbed the new egg in her second arm and cradled that one, too. She tried to balance on one remaining limb while occasionally putting the hands with eggs still in them down for balance. She quickly decided to leave the smaller egg behind and rushed towards the exit, the bigger egg still cradled in her arm.

She sensed a rapid increase in temperature. Her respiratory system closing in tighter. She struggled as her limbs starting shaking. She wondered what was happening. Even with her enhanced capabilities of bodily function manipulation and knowledge, she was unable to figure out the reason. As her limbs shook more, the egg fell from her grip. It landed on top of a few other eggs but didn't break. She grabbed it again and raced towards the exit.

As she approached it, she noticed the red sea in front of her. With it came an intense rise in heat and toxic gases. She dropped the egg and ran back into the chamber. She moved around as she hunted for an exit, desperately. She heard the sizzle and pops as the advancing lava began incinerating her unborn babies one after another. Everything the lava touched, it destroyed.

She sat as far back into the corner as she could and just waited.

It took its own sweet time, but the lava did reach her. Inch by inch the 2000-degree liquid began vaporizing her from the feet up. She screamed and twitched, wailing in pain as she tried to escape, desperately. Her deafening cries echoed among her unborn children. As the lava melted her feet, she stumbled into the red sea, and her whole body dipped into the 2000-degree death. Her skin vaporized as the liquid penetrated every inch of her body.

Once again, there was silence in the chamber. No more screams. Only pops and cracks as the lava burned as many eggs as it could reach.

66

FAREWELL

" **W** hy the fuck did Leroy have to hide this thing here?" Barry asked as the low-hanging branches scraped against the plane's wings.

"Well, poachers need to hide, you know," Zeus replied as he steered the bush plane out of the jungle of overhanging branches.

A loud scraping sound startled Barry. His heartbeat raced. "Careful, Zeus!"

Myra stared out the window from the rear seat. The stinging pain was now only a lingering sensation. She wished it wouldn't return. For now, it was mild enough to let her be her usual self. Only occasionally did her attention go towards the things that might still be wriggling inside her skin, doing who knows what. But, this wasn't the time for her to focus on herself. Her attention was still external. Her attention was still on Chisil. All throughout the land that surrounded the volcano, micro vents spewed large quantities of fumes as the underground lava flowed. Like a high-pressure garden hose punctured at various points, the fumes jetted out, rising dozens of feet high. She wasn't sure what to think about. All sorts of emotions concocted and bubbled inside her. It didn't matter what Barry and Zeus were conversing about. This was a moment of solitude for her.

Myra remembered the moment when she had gone to complain about Frank to her father in his cabin on the *Polar Explorer*. How he had kissed her forehead. The touch of his hand. His eyes. Untold details flashed in front of her. She tried to remember more. But, only certain things came to her vividly, like the color of her father's eyes and how his touch had felt. The rest were not as clear, yet. Maybe if she spent more time pondering, more sensations would return. More memories would come back. She would have loved to remember everything. That's all she had left now: memories.

She barely felt it when the bush plane became airborne. Whatever Barry and Zeus were doing seemed to have been working. None of them were professional pilots, but their combined brains and past training in handling big machines and test planes at X-corp proved invaluable now.

"I hope that cunt died a slow painful death," Barry said as he stared down at Chisil from his window.

"I just hope she didn't survive!" Zeus said.

There was a long silence. "She didn't," said Myra from the back as she stared at Titan sitting quietly in his terrarium. She knew as calm as Titan may have been now, the alien mother couldn't have escaped the lethality of the arrow laced with his alkaloid poison.

Myra stared down as Chisil began shrinking under them. She noticed the dozens of small vents as well as the thick mass of plume shooting up high from the sinkhole. Chisil was burning. She was glad it was only part of it. The wildlife on the eastern edge was probably going to be just fine. She hoped the red river burned each and every trace of these invaders who had come, uninvited. The invaders who had taken her father away from her. In one moment she felt brave, and in another weak. The roller coaster of emotions played games with her heart and mind. The only constant among all were the vivid memories of her father. She just hoped he was still around, still around to tell her and Barry and Zeus whether they did well or not.

All her life, he had been there to guide her along every step. Now she was on her own. She realized she was an orphan once again. When her biological parents had abandoned her, they had robbed her of the chance of experiencing a healthy childhood. It was the end of her childhood when she was at the orphanage. And now, after having lost Eustace, it was once again her childhood's end. No matter how tall she had grown or how many years she had raked in, she would have still been a child in her father's eyes.

She would miss not being a child anymore. Not having that someone under whose wing you could hide anytime. Tears flowed down Myra's cheeks as more memories continued to flash in front of her.

Her headache returned. She closed her eyes gently and slipped into a thought.

Dad, I love you so much... I wish you were here... I miss you!

AFTERWORD

Thank you for reading my debut novel 'WAR MACHINES'!

It has taken me a full thirteen months to write and publish this book and I hope you enjoyed it. Although challenging, the journey to see this idea get developed into its current form has been extremely rewarding.

With the book now done, I plan to take this story further into different mediums such as games, and films.

You can let me know your thoughts about this book by leaving a review on the site you purchased this copy. Reviews really help the story reach its intended readers.

I would love to hear from you!

CREDITS

Produced By
URMI SHIKHA
PARTH PRATAP

Beta Reading
ARUN BALIGA

Editorial Assessment
ANDREW LOWE

Cover Design
eBookLaunch

ABOUT THE AUTHOR

Ayan Pratap is an author, director and game developer living in Los Angeles. He enjoys reading in science fiction and horror genres, and playing story driven video games. When not telling a story, he off-roads into the southern California deserts in search for new ideas, and animals to film.

His other hobbies include trap shooting, 3D art, and night nature exploration.

To join Ayan's mailing list for giveaways, promos, and early access to new releases, please visit:
https://www.ayanpratap.com/contact

a amazon.com/author/ayanpratap

BB bookbub.com/profile/ayan-pratap

🐦 twitter.com/ayanpratap

f facebook.com/AyanPratapTank

📷 instagram.com/ayan.pratap